# The Sorcery of Stories

## Emma Bradley

May our words match our honour

ISBN: 978-1-915909-13-8

# DEDICATION

For every reader who knows that stories are our legacy, our addiction and our salvation – you're welcome at the Word Court anytime.

# CHAPTER ONE
## TIRA

The Holly Queen of Faerie was due to arrive and the Lord of Words was nowhere to be seen. Tira Starhollow, the only natural child of the recently passed Lady of Words, raced through the court, her mind snagging on all the tasks still needing to be done. She scraped her endless sheet of muddy brown hair into a threadbare hairband as she ran, trying to breathe through the acidic nerves churning in her gut.

The main hall of the Word Court was deserted as she skidded to a halt on socked feet, casting a look around at the preparations for the queen's arrival. Everything had to be perfect, but she couldn't stem the bubbling pride as she surveyed the court.

The brisk high-mountain air whisked through a nearby open window and bit at her face, whistling quietly around the vast brownstone walls and pillars. The beams of the vaulted ceiling high above were painted in the court's colours of blue and silver that lightened the grey flagstones underfoot, and the enormous viewing balconies let in so much natural light that any darkness was chased away.

Tira eyed the various banners in the Word Court colours fluttering in the wind, and nodded with satisfaction before dashing off again.

"Where's the fire?" one of the nobles called out.

She rushed past him, her voice echoing over her

shoulder.

"The queen is coming, remember?"

"Orbs, better get a move on then!"

She noted that he didn't hang around or offer to help, but he had a point. While she was used to the piles of debate sheets strewn haphazardly on noticeboards and various book tables waiting to lure unsuspecting readers passing by, the queen deserved a proper royal welcome. She set off again at speed, trying to remember what needed doing the most.

A shadow appeared in front of her seconds before she slammed into a very solid person. She stumbled back and opened her mouth to apologise, but the words died on her tongue.

The man smirking down at her was one of her stepbrother Claudius's acquaintances. As the recently titled Lord of Words, Claudius Auren had surrounded their court with people that Tira didn't like the look of. Several were nobles who had supported the Forgotten and slunk away after the War of Queens, but after her mother's death they'd started reappearing.

The one in front of her made her insides crawl with revulsion. In his mid-twenties by the look of him, Lorens spent a ridiculous amount of time tossing his conker brown hair back and forth, and he had the kind of ageless Fae facial features that screamed 'I'm wearing a glamour'. But it was the fact that Lorens, despite having no known family name, was still so high up in her stepbrother's social chain that worried her most.

"Lady Tira," he said. "You shouldn't be running

through corridors."

The 'Lady' was more than likely being used to mock her since she'd abdicated her rule to Claus, but she was used to rising above the taunts.

"I have no idea where my brother is, Lorens," she said. "Maybe in his office. Excuse me."

He intercepted her attempt to dodge around him and planted himself back in front of her, grinning all the while.

"I do, I know exactly where your brother is. He's not what I'm here for."

Infuriating. He spoke in riddles more often than not, and he gave the impression that he was laughing at everyone with his artfully cocked eyebrows and the general arrogant swagger.

"Oh. Well, what are you still doing here then?"

Lorens inclined his head to flourish his hair and she choked down a snort. Usually during the late morning, the main hall would be full of courtiers debating issues and planning the day's events, but with the queen of Faerie about to arrive it wasn't a normal morning by any standards.

"I have my reasons," Lorens said with a sniff. "Your brother is merely a small part in a much bigger game, my lady."

Tira folded her arms. "Well, perhaps you should go play your games with him then."

He eyed her up and down, the gesture pointed and with no actual sign of intrigue in his eyes. She'd seen that look a lot growing up as a lady of the court. Self-centred nobles were only after one thing and it wasn't her mind; often it wasn't her looks either. Social standing was everything in Faerie and she had more than enough of that for people to want.

"I'd rather join you." Lorens whispered.

He leaned forward as if imparting secrets, his eyes ridiculously wide with fake earnestness. She fought the automatic sneer that threatened to leap onto her face.

"No thanks. I'm not interested."

"I'm sure I could pique your interest, lady. Everyone wants something."

*Eww.* She folded her arms and faced him down.

"I very much doubt you could offer me what I want, trust me on that. Besides, the queen is due any minute and we all have to pitch in. You can help if you want. There's still jobs in the kitchens to be done, or-"

"That would be my cue to make myself scarce then." He sighed loudly. "I don't want to waste time with those who pretend to consider themselves royalty."

"Then consider yourself dismissed."

He grinned. "From your service?"

"From my court for all I care." She hurried around him, leaving her parting shot lingering.

"Ah. But it's not your court, is it? Not anymore."

That stung. She held herself tall and continued walking purposefully, refusing to let him see that he'd hit a nerve. When she risked a look back, he was gone. She sagged and huffed in relief.

*Awful man. I hope he disappears and never comes back.*

She lifted a hand to sweep a strand of hair back from her face, wondering why he'd seemed so desperate to get out before the queen arrived.

*Almost as if he knows she'd recognise him, which makes him even more dangerous than I originally thought.*

Still, at least that meant he wouldn't be around when the queen arrived, but then neither was her brother. She assumed Claus was in his study but he could have been anywhere, shirking all responsibility for his court and leaving her to consider his guests.

"Orbs, and hardly anything is done yet!" she muttered, breaking into a run.

She still had to ensure the extra banners were fully up, although she could see people already setting to the task at the far end of the hall. She'd chosen that corner to place the collection of tables and chairs because it was nearest the main viewing deck that overlooked both the snow-capped mountains of their court and the lights of the town below at night.

She passed the court's chief aide, Marlon, and stumbled to a stop.

"Are they here yet?" he asked.

She twisted to face him and almost over-balanced to land on the stone floor.

"I don't think so, but I haven't seen Clau- my bro- *our Lord* yet either."

Marlon pulled a face, his black moustache twitching with disapproval when she mentioned her stepbrother's absence. Or possibly because she'd mentioned her stepbrother, she couldn't be sure. While her mother, the late Lady Eirenia, had intended Tira to take over the court as the next lady, her stepbrothers had insisted otherwise the moment her mother was laid to rest.

*You're sick, Tira, a weakling now.*

*You can't rule an entire court on your own.*

'On your own' soon disappeared until she had to admit they had a point. Her frequent headaches laid her up in bed sometimes for a day or two at a time. So she'd conceded her rule to Claus and carried her shame as modestly as she could among their court. She still managed their archives full of ancient documents and long-ago tomes, and she still held the weekly writers' circles and the debates which were mad and vicious and so much fun. But she needed to rest after them often, so her stepbrothers were right. The ruler of a court had to be strong and able to cope with any adversity whenever it came calling.

*Except our ruler isn't here to answer the call anyway. Not that the queen is visiting as an adversary. That I know of.*

"Relax." Marlon summoned a mug of *Beast Lite*, the perfect thing to settle her anxious stomach. "By all accounts the Holly Queen is kind and fair. She isn't so bothered with titles and propriety, only genuine goodness, which you have by the bucketload, my dear."

Tira rolled her eyes even though the small smile reached her lips all the same. Marlon had been fussing over her family since before she'd been born. He knew she'd been her mother's first choice, even if her stepbrothers had both forgotten it. She could tolerate their slips in behaviour, the increase in savage 'jokes' and explanations that they were both stressed. The suggestions that they could marry her off to some ancient lord to fund the court, even though they knew her emotions were definitely not focused on the male half of Faerie.

She also knew it was bullying, even without Marlon's disapproval of it. But what could she do other than protect the court her mother had fought so hard to improve? She was still lady of it in her own way, if only by keeping her stepbrothers as far from the actual running of it as possible.

She looked down at her dusty cargo trousers and ancient *Demon Babies* t-shirt with a grimace.

"I don't know about goodness, but I should have at least taken time to wear something appropriate."

"Um… hello."

A hesitant voice made her jump, her hands shaking a slosh of *Beast Lite* over the flagstone floor. She twisted and came face to face with Milo, chief aide to the queen, but thankfully he didn't have any members of actual royalty with him.

Large and broad-shouldered in a knitted navy cardigan much neater than her own, Milo managed to make himself look irrepressibly small somehow. It was the hesitant expression perhaps, the way he blinked at her like she might not remember who he was even though they'd met before. She had no idea of his familial name, but he had inspired a quiet sort of respect around the Word Court after a mere couple of visits. It wasn't so much his position in the Holly Court either, but because he seemed to know almost as much about the Word Court's literature collection as the scholars did.

"Oh, sorry Milo, you made me jump. Welcome back."

Tira let Marlon grab the cup from her, recognising his

under-the-breath grumble that she didn't drink any. She glanced around but other than another young man standing a few feet behind Milo, there was still no sign of the queen or any entourage.

"The queen offers her apologies," Milo said with a resigned huff. "Or she would if she didn't rely on me to assume she would and do it for her."

The man standing behind him smirked. He stood with his arms folded over his chest, the suggestion of muscles beneath the bulky cotton sweatshirt. He released his arms to sweep a hand over his short black hair before clearing his throat.

Milo's cheeks tinged pink. "Ah yeah, this is Ace."

Ace stepped forward until he stood at Milo's side, the amusement on his face suggesting he was well used to Milo forgetting him. Now that she had a name, Tira knew exactly who Ace was. Every short interaction she'd had with Milo about her court and his role in visiting them had featured the mysterious 'Ace' in some way.

"Bodyguard?" Tira asked, unable to stop herself smiling.

Ace grinned and held out his hand. "Boyfriend. Much more hassle for him apparently."

Milo huffed loudly but Tira had forgotten about the queen's imminent arrival and the continued absence of her stepbrother. She gave Ace her hand expecting a shake, but he bowed low and pretended to kiss it. Suitable respect for the lady of a court perhaps, but at least he was doing it to be polite rather than to charm her.

In taking her hand back, she eyed the rainbow bracelet

on Ace's wrist, identical to the one Milo had been wearing on his last visit. A quick check and she saw Milo was wearing his too. Claus would sneer but she thought it was adorable to have someone to wear matching bracelets with. But none of that would be an appropriate thing to say to people she barely knew.

"Welcome to the Court of Words," she said instead. "Our lord will hopefully be back in time for the queen's arrival, but he's been detained… somewhere."

No sense putting effort into word-tangling on his behalf. She couldn't openly defy Claus or embarrass him when he was around, not without making her own life awful, but she had to take tiny moments of rebellion whenever she could.

"We never have much hope at steering them," Milo muttered. "Demi's the same. She leaves me an orb message which literally says 'delayed, go to C of W, meet there'. Is she in danger? Do I need to send out any kind of statement to the other courts?"

"Well, we're here now," Ace placated.

Milo's face brightened immediately. "True. I want to show you all the archives."

"All of them?" Tira faked a gasp. "He'll be four hundred before you get through them all."

Ace lifted his head to stare around and Tira did the same. She was so used to the court that she often spent days running through it without remembering to stop and be in love with it. The brisk walks in the snow outside, the vistas tumbling down the sides of the mountain to the realm so far below them it needed flight to get down in a day. The towering halls, open to the chilly elements but lit with so many fires and reinforced with so much wood and insulation that it was like being encased in a furnace with a big breeze inside. Then the main hall was her favourite place with its doors that led onto the viewing balconies, the arcing brownstone pillars with strategic bookcases and reading nooks carved into them. It was home, and it was heaven.

"This is so cool," Ace said with a low whistle.

"Thanks." Tira beamed, pride in her court encompassing any lingering awkwardness.

"You grew up here?" he asked.

She nodded. "I did and I loved it. Still do. My childhood was spent on the mountains or venturing down into the town, which is much bigger and more entertaining than it looks."

"And you have two brothers?" Ace prompted.

Tira hesitated. "Stepbrothers yes, Claudius who is now Lord of Words and Lyle, who was recently sent to the Forever mountains." She glanced around to make sure the hall was still deserted. "He never did have much self-preservation beyond getting as far up the social chain as possible."

Ace nodded, quietly spinning around on the spot to take another look at the main hall. Tira did the same, pleased that the first of the queen's guests had admired it.

As a friend of the queen, if Ace was impressed then perhaps the queen might be too.

Tira loved the home her mother had built, even in spite of her stepbrothers. Lyle was now officially a traitor to the crowns and he'd never been particularly nice to her, but she made sure the court sent him things every month to ease his incarceration. She'd guessed that he would get himself into trouble eventually because although he was sneaky, he'd never been as manipulatively smart as Claus. But Claus had been nice enough to her when they were younger. Or he'd humoured her at least. Sort of.

"Never mind the archives." Ace strode toward the nearest window. "Do you have any skis?"

Tira frowned. "We have sledding boards if that's what you mean. There are often groups going down the mountain trails. I can ask them to set you up with a private tour if you like? There's a tavern partway down which is really popular."

His face lit up. "That would be awesome! Do you think Taz and Kainen would want to come as well?"

"Taz maybe." Milo sighed. "Not sure if Kainen's the outdoorsy type. But first we should see the archives. That *is* why we're here."

Tira smothered a laugh. Nobody who had any sense would believe that the queen and her entourage were simply there to tour the archives, even though Milo was stubbornly sticking to that excuse.

"Yes, helping us catalogue and collate info between the libraries," she said. "You know nobody's going to believe that. At best, they'll think the queen's court is snooping. At worst, they'll assume we're under investigation."

Milo's expression shuttered primly. "We're here to share our information, that's all."

"Sure, you stick to that. Is there anything specific you

need though?"

Milo glanced around. "There are a few texts I might have a non-royal interest in if there's time."

"A few thousand," Ace muttered cheerfully.

Milo shot him a look but Tira was on firmer ground there. She understood the desire to read as widely as possible.

"If you have a list I can give you access to the indices that will tell you where to look and what level of clearance you need." She hesitated, determined to make herself clear. "The court is my first priority but for what little it's worth, I support the queen. From all I've heard she's fair and kind, which Faerie definitely needs more of."

Milo's face relaxed slightly as if she'd given him some small reassurance, but she wanted to push her point home all the same.

"So, if I can be of any direct help to the queen's efforts, none of the usual court games, I'm available," she finished.

She might have said more but a door banged, the sound echoing across the wide hall and bouncing off the stone pillars as Claudius Auren, Lord of Words, hurried in. His cheeks were flushed and his floppy dark hair dishevelled, the cornflower blue shirt he wore over dark blue jeans not the ones he'd left in the night before.

"Please forgive my late arrival," he said, giving Milo his best unassuming smile. "I hope Tira has welcomed you adequately."

*Better than you have.*

She kept the retort in and nodded in what she hoped was a placatingly reassuring way.

Milo nodded. "Definitely. She's been a huge help already."

Claus gave her a lightning quick look, the darkness in his blue eyes suggesting he didn't trust her helpfulness unless it was directly in his favour or control. She never did see any remnant now of the stepbrother who'd been generally okay to her growing up.

"Has the queen gone to her quarters already?" he asked.

*Not yet, not that you bothered to go and check they'd been readied for her anyway as you should have done.*

The bitterness swelled and Tira fought to keep any sign of it off her face. Claus hadn't been trained for leadership like she had, but he'd sat in on many of their mother's lectures and lessons. Even he should have known to be present and do a final check before the queen's arrival.

"Oh, she's not here yet." Milo managed to hide his disapproval this time. "She had to divert because of some delay elsewhere."

Tira eyed her stepbrother's face but didn't see any look of surprise. Perhaps he saw in the queen the same arrogance at not arriving on time that he saw fit for himself.

"Tira's been keeping us company and explaining a little about the court," Ace added.

Claus gave her a dismissive look. "For all her ills, she has her uses. You look a bit peaky, Tira. Got another headache?"

She summoned a dredge of glamour to hide her burning cheeks, shaking her head as words failed her. He wasn't exactly the kindest brother but to belittle her in front of guests, important ones at that, seemed extra cruel somehow.

"There will be some others arriving any second now," Milo added. "Not sure if you've met the Eastwicks, but their reputation usually precedes them."

Ace nodded, his easy grin apparently long gone in Claus' presence, his shoulders more rigidly set.

"Or the distant bang of an explosion," he said.

Tira frowned. "They'd better not make any explosions anywhere near the archives. Some of the folios we have will crumble at the slightest sneeze."

"Tira." Claus' voice was laced with lethal warning. "The guests of the queen will do as they see fit. This place has been a tomb of random history for far too long as it is."

Tira slid her hand behind her back and clenched her fist tight. She wouldn't punch him because she would probably be on the worse end of some kind of mental manipulation or humiliation for even trying. She wouldn't show any sign he'd gotten to her and give him the satisfaction either.

"Oh don't worry, they will be on their best behaviour," Milo insisted. "Or I will have something to say about it."

Despite his reassurance, Tira couldn't avoid the realisation that she'd been trying to ignore for weeks now.

*I would have been a better lady sick than he is lord being healthy, at least for the wellbeing of the court.*

Her stomach plummeted as guilt swarmed. She flinched as Ace appeared beside her and gave her shoulder a gentle nudge with his arm.

"Milo is scary when he wants to be." He pretended to whisper. "Especially when there's literature of any kind involved. Your folios are safe with him around."

Milo huffed, something he seemed to do often, and Ace turned to give him a one-armed hug. That left Tira standing opposite everyone as three young women with mad hair colours materialised right behind them.

"Yeah, don't worry, we're the epitome of delicate operations."

Tira didn't even see which of the women spoke, but all three men jumped like scalded cats, including Claus which gave Tira some small measure of satisfaction.

"No need to introduce us." The girl with purple hair announced. "We know who we are. We've seen your lordship in passing too at the Flora Court. Who's this?"

Tira froze as a determined thumb was jabbed in her direction. She'd caught the dismissive tone of 'your lordship' as well, as if the girl didn't know if Claus was worth acknowledging yet, lord or not, and was reserving judgement.

*I like her already.*

"I'm Tira, daughter of the late Lady Eirenia," she offered.

Probably a hanging offence to refer to herself by relation to her mother instead of opting for 'stepsister to the Lord of Words', but in the face of these women who clearly weren't used to taking any disrespect from anyone, she found her sense of rebellion against her stepbrother spilling out.

"Well Tira, daughter of the late Lady Eirenia, I'm Beryl. That with the green hair is Cheryl, and Meryl is in blue."

"How come I get called 'that'?" green-haired Cheryl

grumbled.

"Because you were the one who insisted we realm-skip into the town and walk up, which was a ridiculous idea."

"I didn't know it would be that high up though, did I?"

Tira gawped in alarm. "You didn't climb all the way up did you?"

"Of course not." Beryl sniffed and wiped her sleeve over her face. "We walked for about twenty minutes, argued about how long it would actually take to climb a mountain this size, then skipped up here until we hit the court boundary, then invited ourselves in."

"We spent more time arguing than walking to be fair," Cheryl added.

As the two sisters started glaring at each other, Tira glanced at the third, silent as her sisters started bickering under their breaths. Even Claus seemed hesitant to intervene, which basically put the Eastwicks next to the fabled all-powerful deities from old human-tales in Tira's mind, but the third wasn't joining in with their banter.

*Beryl, Cheryl and silent Meryl,* Tira ran the names over in her mind. *I need to remember that.*

Then Meryl's head turned.

Tira gulped as Meryl's gaze fixed on her. Her blue hair was cut so that it fell around her ears and cheeks until it brushed her shoulders, and somehow the vividness of the colour made her brown eyes wide and deep. Unlike her sisters who showed hints of trained muscle in their arms, Meryl was curvier and her face softer somehow, more melancholy.

It was the sort of expression Tira recognised from

looking in the mirror some days, a distance from the liveliness of life from some kind of loss. That moment of smiling before remembering and guilt or grief slammed back in. Now here was a beautiful girl all but drowning in the same sea of loss that Tira still had to navigate after her mother's death.

Meryl snapped her gaze away, fixing instead on the group around them.

*She might be beautiful but she's clearly got too much stuff going on.*

Tira sighed and focused on her usual task of doing what her stepbrother kept forgetting.

"Fun as this is, shall I show you to your rooms?" she suggested. "When the queen arrives, we can reassemble. Or we can wait here with some chairs and drinks?"

Claus' expression darkened as the others turned to her with smiles and suggestions, all talking at once.

"I can see to our guests, Tira," he snapped. "It's my duty after all. You go rest or whatever."

He said it without looking at her but she caught the uneasy glances passing around the rest of the group. Given his sudden desire to play host now, she would probably pay at some point for stepping out of line.

# CHAPTER TWO
# REYAN

Receiving a fleeting royal visit wasn't what Reyan Roseglade had expected early on a random weekday morning. She wiped a hand over her face and wondered what fresh chaos could have warranted the queen to insist she'd be turning up all but unannounced.

Three months of relative quiet had passed since the last battle with the Forgotten. Reyan had done everything she could since then to pitch in with the effort against their enemy, running errands for the queen of Faerie whenever asked. It distracted her from the situation that waited for her every time she returned home to the Illusion Court.

The lines of her fake engagement with Kainen, lord of their court, had blurred so much that she had no idea if it was even pretence for him anymore. He showed no signs of interest in other courtiers. He welcomed her back from her errands each time with a hug or a kiss on the cheek in front of their people. But he made no attempt to speak to her about their engagement ruse, either to formalise it or cancel it, and she was too afraid to ask in case she got the answer she didn't want.

Now Demi and Taz, queen and king consort of Faerie, were due to arrive for an unplanned visit. In true inter-court style, Kainen had summoned their entire court to the main hall to welcome them, but they'd only had a few seconds to prepare.

The underground halls were dotted with skyholes, but it was evening in their realm so the illumination came from firelight flickering on the rocky walls and shimmering off the large pool of water in the centre of the main hall. Kainen had summoned a couple of extra banners in their court's colours of charcoal grey and silver hemmed with lilac, but beyond that they were lacking.

Reyan cast a look down at her ragged leggings and baggy shirt, hardly appropriate for welcoming royalty. She had no idea what Demi and Taz were visiting for, or why the announcement of it had to be so sudden, but it suggested that the recent quiet from the enemy camp was about to end.

*They could have at least given me time to change first.*

She considered glamouring her appearance but froze as Kainen hid a snicker beside her.

They shared a mental link to communicate through, but often when she wasn't concentrating her thoughts transmitted to him. Given the amused grin on his face, his dark eyes sparkling with wickedness, this was one of those times.

*Stop fussing.* His voice danced into her mind. *What this time, your hair? You look fine.*

She pulled a face at him, folded her arms across her middle and turned away from him. He didn't have to mock her, not about things he wasn't even supposed to be hearing. Especially when he was dressed in smart black trousers and a suit jacket that fit his lithe frame with no shirt on underneath, looking every inch a wicked young lord of the court that traded in illusions and trickery.

*Some gentleman,* she retorted, not quite able to take the moral high ground without sending something back.

*I'm not a gentleman, sweetheart. I'm a court lord, remember?*

And she was supposed to be their court's lady, or soon to be. Not that they'd discussed any element of how or when she'd be stepping down from that. Bad enough their relationship was a total fake, but now every time he smiled her insides fluttered. Her emotions were getting far too tangled where he was concerned, and she wasn't sure she relished the idea of him getting any further insights into her thoughts.

The air shivered in front of them, the space momentarily empty before Queen Demerara and King Consort Taz materialised. A hush fell over the crowd, the sounds of those gathered who were murmuring to themselves dribbling away.

The entire assembled court dropped to their knees, but Demi caught Reyan's eye before she could do the same.

"Don't you dare," she muttered before lifting her voice to the rest of the hall. "Rise and go about your business."

If Kainen had any issues with Demi ordering his court about he didn't show it. The awkward silence swilling through the hall remained, and it took Reyan a moment before she noticed the mouths of the crowd moving without sound.

Demi sighed, her black curls askew and her eyed ringed with shadows.

"I've dropped a bubble warding over us to shut out any

eavesdroppers," she announced. "I figured an impromptu appearance would also let the gossip mill know I'm still kicking as well. So, I need you to run a specific errand for me. There's someone currently at the Fauna Court refusing to leave it, but we need her to return to the Court of Words."

Kainen frowned. "And you think I'm the one to convince them?"

Reyan recognised the slight guardedness in his voice. No doubt Demi hoped he would use his compulsion gift on whoever they were meant to be luring out. Usually she would have some level of protectiveness firing through her at the thought of that, but she was too busy flushing as Kainen's arm slipped around her waist. A pretence for the court still watching them perhaps.

"Both of you," Demi said. "Once we get to the Court of Words I won't have much chance to chat, not about anything real. So, keep your eyes open when you get there."

"You don't trust Claus?" Kainen asked.

Demi frowned. "You do? I don't know him and he seems very rehearsed for every possible occasion. Milo has a fragile link with the Word Court already but we don't, not really."

"I wouldn't trust anyone." Kainen hesitated. "That sounds much more sinister than I intended. I started reading Reyan's books and now the mysteries are getting to me."

Demi broke into a broad grin, an unnerving one that drifted from Kainen to Reyan with dedicated intensity.

"Well then, you'll have a great time picking up Marinda Silverfern. The Fauna Court is expecting you."

Reyan gasped. *"The* Marinda Silverfern? Oh wow. I actually get to meet her?"

"That explains the 'both of you' bit then," Kainen said. "Reyan will fangirl so hard that Marinda runs to the Court of Words for a break."

"Hey!" Reyan glared at him and jabbed a savage elbow into his ribs. "Scared I'll put our court's good name into disrepute?"

He grinned. "Not sure about the 'good name', but it sounds simple enough. Pick up famed novelist of the bestselling *Carrie's Castle* series and skip her to the Word Court. I wonder if Tira's still there."

Demi frowned. "Tira?"

"Claus' stepsister," Taz said. "She's actually firstborn, the one her mother intended to rule the court, but by all accounts she's too sick for it. It's a shame, she was said to be one of the prettiest nobles in all of Faerie."

He stuck his tongue out at Demi and she rolled her eyes, not bothered by the taunt in the slightest. Reyan bit down a smile. No matter what happened in Faerie, Taz's devotion to his girlfriend was unshakeable, the one sure thing that everyone could have balanced their orb settings by.

Kainen nodded. "We were friends once, long time ago."

Reyan ignored the unexpected swirl of jealousy in the pit of her stomach.

*Stop it. He's not yours to be jealous over.*

She froze when she realised the thought might have

escaped, but Kainen showed no signs of having heard, no sudden frowns or looks her way.

Their relationship was all pretence for mutual benefit and she had to get that straight in her head. Although he'd shown signs of having feelings for her, being fond of her and seeing her as an amusing person to spend his time with, he was an actual court lord. She wasn't even from a titled family.

"Oh, one thing," Demi said, her tone suspiciously innocent. "Marinda is apparently really headstrong but she will do almost anything for her fans. Kind of why I'm sending you, Reyan, as she hasn't actually agreed to go to the Word Court yet."

Taz tipped his head back to inspect the ceiling with an equally innocent grin.

"She had a bit of a tiff with Claus a while back," he said. "Not sure why. When we asked her, she called him a vindictive brat and said she wouldn't be seen dea- um, yeah she's not too keen on him. Or going to his court."

Kainen sighed. "She was friends with Tira though, I remember that much. Never actually put the name to the person when people mentioned her books but now I think about it, definitely Marinda Silverfern."

"We'll do what we can," Reyan said firmly. "See you at the Word Court."

Demi took that as the directive it was. The noise of the court ricocheted back into being around them as she lifted the bubble warding. As Kainen clicked his fingers, Meri appeared before them as Demi and Taz vanished.

"A lightning quick visit then," Meri said, unimpressed.

"I'll cancel the preparations. And I suppose that means you're absconding to some random part of Faerie?"

Kainen nodded. "Only for a short while. You're in charge until we return and keep us updated."

Meri rolled her eyes and stormed off without waiting to be dismissed, muttering under her breath.

"She's mad at you," Reyan said with a grin.

Kainen laughed and caught her hand in his. "And yet I reckon if you'd told her, she would have been fine about it. I'm hurt."

Kainen summoned the trademark sparkling black smoke of his gift around them, but he made no move to realm-skip anywhere.

Reyan glanced up in time to catch his eye as the corner of his mouth lifted wider and his voice swirled into her mind with amused determination.

*What was that about being jealous? Are you developing some sort of secret crush on the king consort that I should be wary of?*

He was wordlessly refusing to realm-skip to the Fauna Court, holding them there until she answered him. Knowing Kainen he would wait all day if he decided to be petty.

*No!* She felt her cheeks heat. *As if I need that on top of everything else I have to deal with right now. Are we going or what?*

He stepped closer, one arm banding around her waist. She tensed. He'd pinned her several times in training over the last couple of days and held her hand to help her up. He'd even brushed off a cloud of dust from her legs with way more attention than was strictly necessary after she'd finally managed to pin him once. He often walked around his court with his arm around her waist or her shoulders, no doubt to enforce their pretence further to his courtiers so tongues wouldn't whisper. But those were all things she could explain away as necessary for the look of things, or him being his naturally flirtatious self. Even now they were still in front of their court, with many watchful eyes that would be fixed on them.

"I've cast a warding so nobody can see or hear us," he announced, dashing her reasoning to pieces. "We have a few minutes and I think we should have a chat about our situation."

Reyan gawped at him. "Here? Now? You're delaying a royal order you know."

"Yes, here in our court and now before you can run off to yet another random royal errand. Things have been quiet and calm for far too long and that worries me, so I want us to both know where we stand."

He sounded entirely serious but the subtle smile, the tiny crook in his bottom lip that perhaps nobody else had taken time to recognise, suggested he was more than likely toying with her.

"I know I'm a handful at times," he added. "But you and I are in this together, sweetheart. No escaping now."

She rolled her eyes even though her pulse was pounding, her mind racing too fast to process thoughts let alone transmit them to anyone else.

"What if I want to escape?"

He pouted. "Do you?"

Fae couldn't lie so he'd trapped her there. All she'd ever wanted to do growing up was escape. From her father's house to the Court of Illusions, where she'd served as sworn-in staff until Kainen chose her as his fake bride, she had dreamed of a life of her own. Kainen would let her go in a heartbeat if he thought she really wanted to leave. He'd given her the option before without caveats. But she'd been the one to suggest their arrangement continue.

"The situation is benefitting me right now," she said instead.

He grinned. "You're working for Demi. Even if you weren't going to be lady of our court, she'd still keep you on. But if it makes you feel better I'll make you a deal."

Knowing she was walking into a trap, she folded her arms, pinning them between her ribs and his as he held her close.

"What deal?" she asked.

"I'll let you escape if you give me the one thing you don't want to give."

She had no idea what that might be. The one thing she didn't want to give him right now was the truth about how she felt, and they seemed to be straying perilously close to him tricking her into admitting it. She didn't want to give up her freedom either, but she doubted even he'd be crass enough to taunt her with that when he'd gone to so much trouble securing it for her in the first place.

"And what's that?"

His brown eyes tinged with sparkles of black as he leaned closer, his nose an inch from hers. She stared back, breathless. Whatever it was, she wouldn't agree to it on principle. She would fight him right to the very end, simply because after so long being in service she finally had the ability to do so, and he knew it.

"A kiss."

"I-" her voice hitched. "Somehow I wasn't expecting that."

She hadn't had any time to expect anything, every part of her hypnotised by his closeness instead. She tried to race through whatever angle he was no doubt playing her with, but all she could work out was that he'd asked her to kiss him while knowing that taunting her about it would be the very thing to make her not do it.

Because of course he was trying to redeem himself in the eyes of Faerie and Demi and everyone else who now mattered. After being part of the Forgotten in the last war, he'd changed sides and fought for the Oak Queen in the end. Now he was determined that he and his court would side with Demi for the good of Faerie. Their fake engagement was part of that, part of his redeemed persona and he wouldn't want to lose it.

*Would he really string me along just to achieve that?*

"You left a lot of loopholes," she added, indignation and shame washing through her.

He frowned, pretending to think. "You know, I did. It doesn't clarify what you get to escape. Could just be training sessions with me, although I know they're the highlight of your day."

They were, but she'd been finding ways to moan about them to throw him off the idea that she was now somehow irrevocably infatuated with him.

"It doesn't clarify what kind of kiss either." She tried to take a step back but he clung on. "One peck on the cheek and I could be off into the sunset."

He made a show of presenting the side of his face right in front of hers, his cheek smooshed against her nose. She aimed a kick at his shin but he pre-empted it and widened his stance. Her foot swept in between his legs and she almost slid to the floor.

"Need to be quicker than that, sweetheart." He chuckled and tucked her back against his chest. "But yes, many, many loopholes. I could still kiss you after all."

"But you won't." She was almost sure about that.

"Not if you don't want me to."

*Don't ask. Don't ask. Don't ask.*

He grinned. "Don't ask what?"

In that moment, she hated the fact he'd tied their stupid brains together. But as much as it was a pain, she couldn't bear the thought of asking him to remove it.

"Never mind," she conceded. "Are we going?"

His amusement faded and he looked at her for countless seconds, really looked at her, his eyes slightly narrowed.

"Do not go into my mind," she warned.

He straightened up but didn't make any attempt to step back or release the arm around her waist.

"I wouldn't, not without permission, you know that."

"I know, but you're squinting at me."

His grin reappeared. "I was just astounded by your beauty."

"Oh shove off."

"Such eloquence!" He gasped ridiculously loudly even

though nobody else would hear it outside the warding. "It's a good thing we're bound for the Court of Words. Claus will want to steal you away from me when he hears your poetic talents. Do you know any limericks? Will I have to fight him?"

Reyan battled every single essence of her desire to laugh, determined not to give his ego any more ammunition.

"I'm not going to cause a scene here in case it breaks your warding, but when we get somewhere without people I am going to kick you so hard."

That only delighted him more, his grin widening.

"Did you say 'kick' or 'kiss'? Because I know which one I'd prefer."

"Realm-skip to the Fauna Court," she snapped. "Now."

He laughed, his arm tightening around her. "Anything you say my lady."

She would have said something back at him, but the swirling purple-grey wisp of the nether that surrounded the fabric of Faerie surrounded them, dissipating into zigzags of colourful movement and loud bangs as they arrived at the Fauna Court.

A rush of what looked like horses with ridged spines thundered past them, almost colliding with a tangle of people dashing the other way, gifts flying and sizzling everywhere.

Kainen pushed Reyan to the floor at the same time she threw up a protection warding over both of them, fighting her instinct to dissolve into the corners with her shadow-merging gift. It would get her out of harm's way, but not him.

"What the-"

Kainen rolled them sideways before she could finish the exclamation, his hand sliding beneath her head to protect it. She fought to get her own arms free from between them to do the same to him but they rolled into a wall first. Struggling to their feet, Kainen pulled her behind him so she had to peek around his shoulder.

"Forgotten," he shouted. "Recognise several."

Reyan's insides dropped. The enemy were taking full advantage of the recent calm period in typical Forgotten fashion, attacking without warning.

"Remember your training?" Kainen asked, his face a mask of fury.

She nodded, determination rising. "Yeah. Time to put it into practice."

Before she could find someone to attack, or at least defend against, a volley of metal spikes slammed into the wood above her head. She ducked as the top left edge of her protection zinged from the impact, pierced through by the spikes made from *metirin* iron.

She re-formed the warding around her, looking for a chance to be useful. Kainen stood in front of her with his arms held outward, swathes of glittering black smoke controlling multiple people to keep them from harming what looked like innocents caught in the battle. Several had wounded animals in their arms, dodging and weaving through the mayhem.

Kainen glanced over his shoulder, eyed the spikes above Reyan's head and faced forwards again. Sweat beaded on his brow from the effort of wielding his gift so hard away from the strength of his court, but it was the feral curl of his lip that worried her most. He'd once lost control of himself over worry for her, no doubt because his court got confused over how real their supposed relationship actually was, and that strengthened his loyalty toward her.

But he'd trained her well. She dodged someone running toward her and dissipated into the shadows, dredging up her transmutation gift. The earthen floor became a gloopy mass of mud, the man's feet slithering until he landed flat on his face.

Re-forming herself into flesh and bone again, she ran past Kainen and ignored his frantic command for her to come back. She wasn't sworn to his court anymore, only pretending to be lady of it, so he couldn't command her without using his gifts. She reinforced her warding moments before his attempt to compel her curled around her.

Unsure of what she was planning other than to create some safe way for those who couldn't fight to get through the battling masses, she looked around for something useful. The entire structure of the Fauna Court's reception hall was like a huge barn, tall wooden slat walls and roof with one side mostly open to the forests and fields beyond.

She spied a huge logpile outside and knew that what she was about to attempt would cost her big. Not necessarily in terms of gift use because she might not even be able to manage it. But either way, Kainen was going to be furious with her for even trying.

She dredged up the transmutation gift, thankful that she'd been practicing with it at any opportunity, her attention focused on the logs. If anyone shot *metirin* iron her way she was done for, but for now her warding kept out the attacks that buffeted her from all sides.

With her transmutation gift tingling through her limbs like a breath of icy air, she began to turn the woodpile to fragments. It took more effort than she'd ever used before; the wood was stubborn by nature, but chips and splinters soon swept through the shadows that leapt to carry them for her.

Her head ached with the effort but the shadows followed her vision, replacing the wood remnants in piles to cover the wide exit with only a door-sized sliver left free for people to escape through while keeping the enemy from escaping further into the court.

The ground met her knees with a thud and she had no idea when she'd closed her eyes. She wielded her gifts as one until she had to move the transmutation process from dismantling logs to reforming them in the exit.

With no ability to move freely, the battle would have less chance of spilling outside and crushing or injuring anyone who couldn't fight, or allow any of the enemy to escape easily. She could feel the shadows taking strength from the absence of light as their wall grew, but that didn't give her physical body any extra strength to wield her gift with.

*Reyan, stop.*

Kainen's voice echoed in her head as a sour taste wisped gently over her tongue, like licking a sour-pop. The command powered through any element of lingering independence, and she groggily realised she must have dropped her warding at some point if he could get into her head and compel her.

*Demi's here,* he added. *It's over.*

She tried to open her eyes but couldn't get her mind coordinated enough to communicate the message.

*Can you re-form? Can you speak?* He sounded frantic now.

She frowned. *Re-form?*

*Oh thank Faerie.* His voice echoed frantically in her mind. *You're still in shadow-form. I can see the outline of you and hear you, but I can't touch you. I swear, when you get your strength back I am going to yell at you so much. What were you thinking?*

Happiness bubbled up. He was worried about her. Of course he would be, but he sounded seriously worried, like he actually cared.

Locking that thought away for later, she clung to consciousness by focusing on their ability to mind-speak instead.

*This is what we were training me for though, wasn't it?* She shot back. *Stop moaning. Did it work? Did the wall help at all?*

"Okay, this is so weird watching you reappear. Can you hear me now?"

Her ears must have reformed because his voice was clear, and a dull thudding in her head suggested that part of her had materialised. She waited for her mouth to change from shadow to skin and bone, then smiled as wide as she could.

"I can hear you. You're very loud. Did my wall help?"

Hands brushed over her chilled arms, their warmth radiating through her shirt. She decided not to grumble as Kainen lifted her body against his and held her tight, his chin pressed on top of her head. The sweet scent of the *oia* berry shampoo he used and the more natural smell of him, all tangy grapes and woodsmoke, was all around her like a comforting blanket. She let her face drop into the crook of his neck.

"It helped." He huffed. "Several of them were trying to escape when Demi arrived and they got corralled by it. She's sending them all off to the Forever mountains now."

Reyan opened her eyes, getting a blur of pale skin for her trouble. She tried to lift her head and immediately wished she hadn't, so she settled her face against his shoulder instead to see the court around them.

"Good riddance. Are you skipping us to the Word Court now then?"

"We haven't succeeded in our mission yet," Kainen reminded her. "Are you able to stand up if I support you?"

"I think I can stand on my own if you help me up."

She started trying to wriggle free of him, but he clung on with far more strength than she could cope with.

"Let me rephrase that. Are you able to stand up so I can support you whether you like it or not? We're going to speak to Marinda and convince her to accompany us as planned to the Word Court. Then you and I are going to finish our little chat about priorities. Then I may consider yelling at you for pulling a stupid stunt like that."

Reyan grinned. "It's funny when you think you're telling me off."

His ragged sigh tumbled over her face, blowing wisps of her hair over her nose. She squeaked as he tipped forward, wriggled ungracefully a bit and managed to get them both onto their feet without letting go of her.

"Court lords shouldn't be caught manhandling people," she muttered.

"They can manhandle their lady however they orbing well like."

"I'm not-"

Her words became a muffle of outrage as he clamped a hand over her mouth, the other tight around her waist as Demi approached.

Demi gave his hold a disapproving look, but she didn't make any move to intervene.

"I won't keep you from whatever this is," she said. "I'm not sure how stable things are at the Fauna Court but I want to know what the Forgotten were invading for."

"Perhaps the Fauna Court made enemies of them?" Reyan suggested.

Demi grimaced. "I'm not so sure about that. Someone overheard one of the Forgotten muttering about wasted time in the court's old junk."

"Let me guess," Kainen said, his tone flat with resignation. "You need someone to also investigate the court's old junk, and you want us to do it."

Demi's lips twitched as she nodded. She glanced over her shoulder at the court still in disarray and lowered her voice.

"You can both get yourselves to safety easily enough which makes you better placed than others, and I can trust you."

Reyan took advantage of Kainen's momentary surprise, his eyes widening at the mention of trust.

"Has Lord Rydon agreed?" she asked.

A quick glance across the hall at the stoic frown on Lord Rydon's face suggested otherwise. He stood with his broad arms folded across his chest, a brown linen shirt open at the neck and the kind of thick trousers that had seen decades of work as opposed to a host of court revelries. His mossy green-brown skin was creased with age but although he was tall for a troll, his sharp grey eyes removed any suggestion of potential weakness.

Demi pulled a face. "I have to go and 'demand' that of him now. If you can still escort Marinda to the Court of Words, lay on the flattery, then come back here that'd be a huge help. But expect the worst."

"I always expect the worst," Kainen said with a snort.

Demi rolled her eyes. "Now you sound like Taz. Right, I'm going to get this over with."

Reyan watched her go until Kainen nudged her elbow with his and pointed to a woman striding toward them. A woman she recognised from the backs of book covers.

She fell still. Silent. Starstruck.

The woman in front of her looked exactly like the promo shots often featured on *The Faerie Net*, her black hair braided and her dark eyes piercing everyone around her.

"I'm told you're here for me." Marinda eyed them

warily. "Lady, Lord. What can I do for you? Public readings still have to go through my assistant regardless of rank. It's literally my only rule."

Reyan blinked back at her until Kainen squeezed her hip gently.

"We need to request your presence," he said. "But not for a reading. Reyan?"

She had no words. For someone who could backchat easily enough and had learned to roll with the punches of Kainen's incessant flirting and innuendoes, she was speechless in the face of the woman who had created the book world she was now addicted to.

"How does it work?" she asked.

Kainen stared at her like she'd grown three heads. Marinda frowned.

"What?"

"The stories. How do you come up with them? Do you already know how everything is going to end? Please tell me nothing's going to happen to Otto."

The words tumbled out before she could process them, let alone stop them. Kainen tensed beside her but Marinda was already smiling despite her weary sigh.

"Why is Otto the first one everyone worries about?" She rubbed a hand over her face. "I'm not in the habit of killing off the animals. That's going too far even for me, and I'd definitely never be invited back here if I did. Can you imagine the hate mail? Go on then, which book's your favourite?"

Reyan sagged, half with relief that her favourite character, an otter with the unreliable ability to alter time, was going to be okay and partly because she was so exhausted that it was only Kainen's strength holding her upright. She seemed to have enough strength for her mouth to keep burbling things though, strangely enough.

"*The Cursed Causeway*, definitely. I had no idea what was coming, and I'm usually pretty good at figuring out plot twists."

Marinda grinned. "All fans are, until they aren't. Keeps me on my toes. I was pretty pleased with that one though. Where is it you're expecting me to go exactly?"

She posed the question to Kainen, probably the more sensible choice considering he wasn't one step away from babbling more questions at her. Reyan took a deep breath and forced herself to calm down. All around her people were helping their friends with minor injuries and inspecting the state of her wall, and here she was fangirling.

"The Court of Words," Kainen said. "But-"

"No, absolutely not." Marinda's arms folded as she took a resolute step back.

"We were warned you'd say that, but-"

"Is that pile of excrement definitely now lord of it?"

Kainen's mouth started twitching while still half-open in protest. As he fought the smile, Reyan tried to focus on what Demi had asked them to do.

"If you mean Claus, yes." She hurried on before Marinda could shoot them down again. "I'm not sure what issues you have with him and that's between you two, but there are problems going on that affect the whole of Faerie and the queen wants you there."

Marinda glanced over her shoulder to where Demi was coordinating captured Fae whilst a troll with what looked like a crown of bones on his head whispered to her. Reyan had seen him once before at the Nether Court, Lord Rydon, but never spoken directly to him nor heard much about him either. He ruled the Fauna Court with stoic silence.

"Why didn't she ask directly?" Marinda huffed. "I appreciate I may not be royalty or any kind of noble, but-"

Reyan shook her head. "De- The queen doesn't care about that. If she's sent us to fetch you there'll be a reason. Trust me, she's as big a fan of *Carrie's Castle* as I am. She wouldn't miss this opportunity if it wasn't for a good reason. Maybe for your safety."

Marinda glanced around at the entrance hall, the hesitation a promising sign.

"There's minimal damage here," Kainen added smoothly. "I don't think anyone was seriously wounded, partially thanks to my lady's efforts, and I can see the queen is already dealing with Lord Rydon. I'm sure any goodbyes you need to make or promises you have to square off can be allowed."

Marinda eyed Lord Rydon until he looked her way. When he nodded once, she sighed heavily and faced them again.

"Right, you keep that self-absorbed alley-rat away from me, and I'll go. I mean it. I have three more books scheduled to release this year and I can't be doing promotional appearances by orb from the Forever mountains if I push him off a cliff."

"Of course." Kainen nodded. "Assuming you mean our

current Lord of Words, I wouldn't expect anything less. We can even have someone assigned to support you in keeping him away from you if you like."

Marinda no doubt caught the subtle reassurance in his eloquently frothy wording, but Reyan understood the reactions. Kainen had introduced Claus to her in passing once before, and Claus had been on fine Fae form, tormenting her about her low lineage and also whether Kainen was truly no longer part of the Forgotten flock. Demi had said earlier that she wasn't sure about him either. So they didn't trust him, not that Fae trusted anyone easily or often, but she hadn't heard any specific warning about him yet either.

"I'll fetch a few bits and have the rest of my things sent on." Marinda rubbed a hand over her mouth. "I have missed Tira though, bless her, and not kept in touch as I should have done."

She swept off without waiting for a reply and disappeared through one of the wooden archways still teaming with people. Reyan frowned after her, more absorbed in worries than taking notice of the animals now being ferried back through.

*We're definitely not friends with Claus then?* She had to ask.

Kainen turned her to face him, apparently not willing to let go of her while she was still struggling to stand unaided. She probably could have tried at least, but leaning on him was comfy and easy, and he wasn't exactly complaining about it either. She settled for bracing her arms against his chest and staring sleepily up at him.

*We're not friends with anyone, sweetheart. The other courts tolerate us as we do them. There might be a grudging respect there but I wouldn't exactly call it friendship.*

"That's really sad," she murmured. "Well, you might not be, but I am."

He smiled then, dregs of worry fading from his tired face. He hadn't been sleeping properly, rootling about at all hours in his study. He didn't know she knew, but she had a habit of asking their court's multiway door to give her what room he was in so that she could listen on the other side and check on him now and then. It felt bad to eavesdrop but apart from Meri, his second-in-command, he had nobody who actually cared enough to keep an eye on him. She couldn't exactly ask to take on some of the court responsibilities either, not when she wasn't actually going to be lady of it in the long run.

"That's true," he said. "You and Demi are on friendly terms at least, and you still speak to Odella at the Nether Court."

She nodded. "I even got a personal thank you from Lolly at the Revels and Flora Courts as well after we left them a few months back. It wasn't so much of a thank you as 'I'm so glad you've sent me this random exotic plant from the Illusion Court's realm because I've not had one of these before', but the thought was there."

"You're the new face of our court, sweetheart, and nobody would argue against it."

*Except I'm not though, am I?* She sent the thought into his mind. *It's all a fake. What happens when we have to go back to reality eventually?*

She could see over his shoulder that Marinda was already on her way back to them, stopping enroute to say goodbye to people. Whether she'd summoned the bag now hanging across her back or had asked someone to run and fetch it, Reyan had no idea, but now the thought of going to the Word Court instead of home made her irritable. She almost missed the amused smirk on Kainen's face before it gave way to his pretend serious face, all furrow-browed and quirked mouth.

"That's what I need to talk to you about."

She froze. She'd prepared for this, steeled herself to be ready for the day where he said their ruse was at an end and she wouldn't get to see him any longer. Or she might see him here and there in passing, but never as closely as she did now. Preparing hadn't done a single droplet of good because it still hurt. Playing it cool hadn't ever been her strong point, but she couldn't let him know how deeply upset the mere thought of it made her.

"After you're done yelling at me," she bluffed.

"Exactly." He leaned closer even though he didn't need to as his next words whispered into her mind. *I've got every reason to yell at you for pulling a stunt like that. Once we finally stop this ridiculous fake nonsense, you can't go putting yourself in danger like that.*

Reyan blinked at him. Reassessed what she thought she'd heard. He stared down at her, entirely serious this time by the hard look on his face.

"I- what?"

Before she could get him to clarify, Marinda appeared

beside them.

"Are we going then?" she demanded. "Remember, you're to keep him away from me or I won't be responsible for the horrible things that happen to him. Writers are excessively creative about all sorts of endings."

Kainen kept one arm welded around Reyan's waist as he held out his hand to Marinda like a gentleman, as if he was someone who hadn't just thrown a disgustingly stinky *Kimptaberry* bomb all over the clean and orderly assessment Reyan had of their arrangement.

*This isn't over,* she warned him as Marinda took his hand. *If you're wanting to end the engagement ruse then we need to discuss how.*

Glittering black smoke wraithed around their fingers and flickered in his eyes as he looked right at her, right through to the very soul of her.

*No, sweetheart, it's definitely far, far from over.*

# CHAPTER THREE
## MERYL

Tira Starhollow was a completely unexpected disaster. She stood around smiling nervously at Milo and Ace, checking out everyone else with furtive glances from her enormous green eyes.

Meryl slid her hand into the pocket of her sweatshirt and clenched her fist tight. She'd chosen her best clothes, the soft wool sweatshirt in a similar dusky and deep blue to the Word Court's banners and also her hair, which desperately needed cutting. She had her nicest fitting jeans on too.

Matching colours was the kind of effort she would have made for any unknown court, especially one she considered to be the most intriguing.

Unlike her sisters. Beryl and Cheryl had insisted on outlandish colours that matched their hair, Beryl in a bright purple jumpsuit and Cheryl rocking green flares with a matching shirt. Hutch and Harvey had instantly glamoured themselves to match and Meryl was taking great comfort in hiding behind four pillars of brightly matching colour.

"What do you think?" Beryl shoved her elbow. "I couldn't imagine haunting a place like this for long."

"Shh!" Cheryl hissed.

Beryl rolled her eyes but Meryl sank into the familiar routine. Her sisters were determined to jolly her along, insufferably so, but even they in all their exuberance knew when to let her brood in silence. Luckily, this was one of those times.

*After Petra's... now that she's gone, I got the peace from them I've always secretly craved and it's like a desolate cavern of loneliness.*

She was getting used to that feeling. It was a different kind of alone to becoming the third wheel the moment Hutch and Harvey took a dedicated interest in her sisters. But now that she'd experienced a brief, bittersweet dip into that sensation of having a special someone, having them torn away had soured all elements of dealing with other people.

She risked another look at Tira, a lady by birth who looked nothing like a lady in a ragged t-shirt, faded jeans and her brown hair scraped into a lumpy ponytail. A row of silver hoops lined the top of one ear and the hint of a tattoo peeked out from under the neck of her t-shirt. Despite the unladylike appearance, Tira Starhollow was breathtakingly beautiful in a delicate sort of way, wide eyed and graceful.

It completely and utterly sucked.

Tira's gaze lifted and Meryl flinched as it fixed on her. She almost tore a muscle in her neck by turning her head so quickly, staring with rigid determination through the nearest window instead.

*What is wrong with me?*

She breathed in deep and slow to calm the sudden pounding of her pulse. It didn't help.

"Mer?" Cheryl's face appeared inches from hers. "Are you okay with your own room?"

Meryl frowned. "I- what?"

"Your own room. We have two apparently, so two of us will have to share."

A room to herself. She couldn't quite imagine such a luxury because they shared at Arcanium and on the rare occasions they went home to see family.

"I can take the single," she said far too quickly.

Cheryl grinned. "Don't sound too distraught. Fine, but if Beryl steals my boots again and I throw her out of the window, it's your fault. Or I'll make her go stay in Hutch and Harvey's room instead."

The ghost of a smile flickered at the corners of Meryl's mouth but she had to force it the rest of the way, an automatic reaction she'd learned would keep her sisters from hounding her about her feelings.

"You wouldn't dare." Beryl huffed. "But we can also use that as an excuse to not be where we're supposed to be."

Cheryl snorted. "You would make an awful spy. You know your voice is basically bouncing off the stone, right?"

Harvey slung his arm around Beryl's shoulders, grinning right in her face.

"It's true, it is," he agreed. "It's a beautiful voice, strong and throaty- *OW.*"

He spluttered from the elbow flung into his middle but Meryl knew he could handle her sister. He was the only one who could get Beryl to soften in any possible way, not that it showed often.

"Well, either way Demi's given us our orders," Cheryl murmured.

Beryl scoffed. "Before absconding to some other part of Faerie. 'Keep your eyes out' she says, but that's it. Keep our eyes out for what?"

"The Forgotten, obviously," Cheryl muttered.

Meryl froze, tension knotting further into the core of her body. Even the mention of the group that had taken Petra from them sent irrepressible fury needling over her skin. She clenched her fist tighter inside her pocket, her palm smarting and starting to go numb as her nails dug even harder.

"So, what's there to do in this place?" Hutch asked.

Claus Auren, the current Lord of Words, rolled his eyes. He looked nothing like his sister, his hair dark and straight where hers was like a wavy blanket of dark caramel. But where he seemed to be exasperated by the mere sight of them, Tira's eyes brightened at the mention of the court.

She hesitated, casting a quick glance at her brother.

"It depends what your interests are," she said. "For those who like peace and quiet, we have the archives and reading rooms. For anyone who wants something livelier we hold regular debates and talks most evenings on a variety of subjects. Or if you're more active, we have sledding on the mountain and bike trails."

Hutch and Harvey high-fived each other at the mention of sledding and bike trails, and Meryl knew her sisters would be attending every possible debate that gave them a chance to argue with someone.

"You can see some of the trails from the window over there," Tira pointed to the nearest open archway leading outside. "Just let us- *me* know what you want to do and I can have it organised for you."

Her voice grew stronger the more she talked about the court and Meryl had a vague, hazy recollection of conversation drifting around in her mind, something about Tira originally being intended to be Lady of Words instead of her brother.

Meryl rubbed a hand over her forehead. Normally, she would have liked the sound of going to talks or taking a sled down the mountainside, but she hadn't had much inclination for anything, not since Petra.

"We'll definitely want to see *everything*," Beryl insisted.

Tira laughed and something that had been permanently tight in Meryl's gut since her grief settled, then gave an unnerving spasm.

"You'd be best sticking with Milo then," Tira said wickedly. "He's going to explore every single folio and scrap of paper ever recorded at the Word Court."

Milo smiled shyly at being teased, a sure sign that Tira had his respect which wasn't as easy to earn as some might believe. Beryl stared at Tira in horror at the mere thought of having to tour a bunch of old books.

"Don't ruin it!" Harvey hissed. "I promise she doesn't speak for all of us."

Beryl growled at him and Meryl felt the unfamiliar urge to laugh welling up, but a stab of guilt swiped it away again.

*Petra's been gone a couple of months and I'm laughing like nothing happened.*

She pressed her free hand to her chest and rubbed to

ease the pressure threatening to choke her.

"Would anyone like a drink while we wait for the queen?" Tira asked, amusement still lifting her lips.

Claus clicked his fingers before anyone could answer, a loud, showy sound echoing through the air.

A door swung open and the hasty tapping of shoes on stone grew louder as a young woman hurried toward them. She bobbed a curtsey to Tira first, then grimaced and turned to bow low to Claus.

A flicker of venom flared in his eyes, his mouth twisting at the insult, but he seemed to remember he had guests and smiled again.

"We'll take a table of refreshments. Immediately."

Meryl raised her eyebrows at the curt directive. Despite the established hierarchy of courts she'd spent the past year with Demi, who always said please far too often with a lot of grimacing despite being a queen. Before that, she'd grown up on the fringes of the Flora Court where most people were at least kind and fair despite being more formal.

"Fancies himself, that one," Cheryl muttered.

Harvey nodded. "Only been a lord for all of a couple of months and thinks he's untouchable."

"Be a shame if something were to go wrong," Beryl added.

"Something small of course."

"Of course." Beryl grinned. "Harvey's the epitome of small-*oi*!"

She struggled as Harvey pinned her in a bear-hug until her cheeks were red.

Again Meryl fought the urge to smile. She took another glance at Tira, the last one she promised herself, before she forced all unwelcome thoughts of 'what if' aside.

She was here for one thing, and no matter how pretty or inconveniently placed Tira Starhollow was, nothing would stop her getting revenge on the Forgotten for killing the girl she'd been in love with.

# CHAPTER FOUR
## TIRA

The conversation was drying out fast. Claus didn't seem too inclined to talk to anyone beyond a few vague pleasantries about the court, as though they were too beneath him to focus on. He had at least summoned refreshments from the kitchen, but only after she'd suggested it for the second time. Tira had also noticed the bratty look Clary, one of the younger court members, had shot at his back as she stalked off.

The Eastwick sisters and Ace were too busy peering out of the windows to notice, taking bets on how long it would take to fall down the side of the mountain to the bottom. That left Tira with the job of making small talk even though Claus gave her irritated looks when she did. Luckily, Milo could have gone on for a decade about books and eventually all she had to do was nod and agree or throw in the odd bit of information.

The air shivered halfway through Milo's devoted moratorium on the fabled indexes of the Book of Faerie.

"Finally," Claus muttered before pasting on a smile. "Welcome, my queen, to the Court of- oh. What are you doing here? And with such a noble entourage too?"

Tira gawped to see Lady Reyan and Lord Kainen of the Illusion Court standing in front of them. Their gazes roved around the main hall before settling on her stepbrother, but Tira focused wholly on the woman standing beside them.

A flutter of happiness filled her chest at the sight of Marinda. As an old friend of hers and her mother's before that, Marinda had been away from court for far too long. Whispers suggested that Marinda and Claus had a falling out. Others said they were scorned lovers in a fight. None of them had seen the real fight or witnessed Marinda's fury when Tira finally agreed to step down from the role of lady.

But manners dictated that lords and ladies be dealt with first and old friends second. Something her brother seemed to have forgotten as he stood sneering at Marinda.

*I'll just do everything then, shall I?*

She fixed a smile on her face.

"Welcome Lord, Lady. We have rooms for you if you need them," she said with a bob of her head. "You're both most welcome."

Lord Kainen shook his head. "Thank you, we have other places to be but it's nice to see you again. You may not remember me but we have met before."

"I do remember, at the summer revel four years ago. You were named Lord of the Feast."

"And you won the thorn-dart competition," he said with a grin.

She still had the winning thorn-dart on her bedside table, a memory of an easier time. But nobody needed to know that.

"It's good to meet you again then," she said. "And you, Lady."

Reyan smiled. "Please drop the lady stuff. From what I hear, you were almost one yourself and I almost wasn't, so we're even."

Tira saw the lightning quick look of disgust on her stepbrother's face before it sank back into a vacant smile. Even without that tiny victory Reyan had given her over him, she guessed they could easily become good friends.

An exceedingly dramatic throat cleared itself a moment later.

"Well this is all very touching, but I haven't seen you in almost a year."

Tira's face threatened to split wide as Marinda dodged around the others and pulled her into a tight hug. No admonishments, no awkwardness. Just possessive, familial comfort as though she'd never been away. She hugged Marinda back just as fiercely.

Over Marinda's shoulder, Tira noticed Milo and Reyan exchange a look, both of them eying Marinda with the tell-tale sign of starstruck admiration. Marinda showed no signs of letting her go, probably so she didn't have to be forced to acknowledge Claus as lord of the court. Tuning in her hearing gift, Tira picked up the frantic whispers from the group by the window and peeked their way.

"What do you mean, who is she?" Beryl hissed. "That's Marinda Silverfern."

"Ohhh… that explains why Milo's staring at her like a cherry-glazed doughnut," Ace said.

"A what?"

"You know, the round pastry things from the human world? They have the jam inside and the icing on them?"

"Right. I don't go up to the human world. Scary place."

"So, that's the woman who wrote the *Carrie's Castle*

books they're all so obsessed with?" Cheryl asked.

Ace nodded. "Yep."

"And we're going to have to hear about it for days because Milo's finally met her?"

"Yep."

Tira stifled a grin. Throughout the whole conversation, Meryl stood a few steps apart from their group with her gaze fixed outside. The wind ruffled her blue hair back from her face, outlining the distant sadness there. Tira wondered who she must be mourning with a look like that, but then Marinda finally let her go and she had to draw her attention away.

All heads turned when Claus pointedly cleared his throat, mimicking Marinda's noise without anywhere near as much effectiveness.

Marinda stiffened and let Tira go with a final squeeze that puffed the remaining breath out of her.

"You're still welcome in our halls, Marinda," Claus said, cold amusement playing on his lips. "Don't worry."

Marinda rotated around until she stood beside Tira, her eyes narrowed. Then she gave Lord Kainen an expectant look, folding her arms across her chest.

"Oh, yeah, she's not speaking to you," Kainen explained.

Reyan looked like she was trying to hide a smile, and she managed it much better than the rest. Claus never once dropped his amusement, but Tira recognised the slight stiffening of his shoulders. It was a serious insult not to greet someone hosting you, and an outright offense to disrespect a lord or lady of a court like that. But Marinda refused to budge, stubborn as ever.

Before Tira could think of some way to smooth the situation, one which unfortunately didn't involve shoving her brother onto a sled-board and off the nearest cliff, a shiver rippled through the air.

Tira stared for a long moment as the Holly Queen of Faerie and her king consort appeared. Remembering her manners just in time, Tira dropped to her knees with her head bowed.

"No need to kneel," the queen said with a weary sigh. "We've just come from an attack on the Fauna Court, so we all need to be prepared. Milo, can you update the other courts and tell them to be on alert?"

Milo nodded as the queen surveyed the hall. Tira risked lifting her head and bit her lip as the royal gaze took in the main hall. More decorations should have been put up to celebrate the arrival. The entire court should have been summoned to welcome her. Marlon had the kitchens prepared with food and drink but perhaps the queen would expect a much more lavish welcome. Claus hadn't thought of it and she technically didn't have to.

*But I should have done anyway. Mother would have.*

"Only one person I don't recognise." The queen gave Claus a pointed look.

He frowned. "One pers- Oh. Of course. This is my stepsister, Tira Starhollow."

Tira rose to her feet like her mother had shown her, firm posture and ready legs. She bowed her head and shoulders low before finally meeting the young queen's gaze.

"We're honoured to have you visit us," she said. "I can

arrange a tour of our archives if you like? Or the kitchens are waiting if you're hungry or thirsty, and of course your rooms are ready too."

The queen tilted her head to one side, the almost imperceptible narrowing of her vivid blue eyes giving Tira jitters. Despite the crown of silver and holly tangled in her black curls, the queen was dressed in jeans and a *Demon Babies* hoodie that had seen better days.

"Call me Demi at my request," she said. "A tour would be great if you're able to keep moving past things. Otherwise take Milo instead because he'll take an age."

Tira smiled. "I know the archives well enough not to need to stop unless you wish me to. Also, I'll ask someone to set up sledding on the mountain for those that want adrenalin over literature."

Demi glanced over her shoulder in time to see the king consort's eyes light up.

"Fair enough." She shrugged. "I'll take the tour now then. Yes, Milo, I know there's more paperwork that needs doing. But anyone who wants to throw themselves down a mountain on a bit of wood can do."

Two of the Eastwick sisters cheered at that, Milo looking scandalised at the noise and Ace laughing beside him. The king consort hurried over to see the mountainside for himself, leaving Tira with only her brother, the queen, Kainen and Reyan to deal with. And Marinda, who was rolling her teeth over her lips in a decidedly contemplative manner.

"I haven't had a chance to pay the appropriate homage yet, you'll have to forgive me," Marinda said.

All eyes turned to her, but Marinda wasn't looking at the queen. Tira could only assume they knew each other already as Marinda only had eyes for Claus now.

Claus lifted his head, unsure and wary in an instant. He knew Marinda almost as well as Tira did in terms of how spirited she was, and formality wasn't in any way one of her strong points. He stood a little straighter though as she left Tira's side and walked toward him. A slight curl of victory reached on his lips as Marinda sank down onto one knee.

"My queen, forgive me."

It took every single part of Tira's resolve not to burst into laughter. Claus froze, realising not only that he'd assumed too early in his arrogance, but that everyone around him had seen Marinda prove it.

Demi smiled, waving a lazy hand in Marinda's direction.

"Don't bother, I'm a huge fan of your work and I'm not so much with the titles where I can avoid it. Although, it's taken all my resolve not to ask for an advance copy of the next book. The cliffhanger was pure evil."

"No spoilers!" Reyan clamped her hands over her ears. "Not a single one. Wait until I'm not here."

Demi nodded. "No spoilers, don't worry. The tour first then, and we will have to all get together, the lords and ladies at least, to discuss what we need to do next."

Tira wondered if she would ever be in a privileged enough position to call the queen by her first name. She wasn't sure she'd have the bravery to risk it. But with Claus souring behind his fake smile and no sign he was going to offer to lead the tour, she would have to assume he was going to be as useless at actual court protocol now as he had been since taking the title.

She noticed Marlon skulking innocently with a duster in the far corner. His role was at least four levels above doing the dusting and she grinned as she waved him over.

"Marlon, can you arrange for a sled-boarding tour for our guests please? And have the kitchens ready for everyone returning, but I'm sure you've more than done that already."

Marlon nodded after a startlingly low bow in the queen's general direction.

"Of course. Anya's been under Niko's feet all morning so she'll be happy to take people outside. If anyone who wants to join the sledding group can follow me please."

Tira bit her lip as Ace, the two Eastwick sisters and the king consort hurried after Marlon. Claus should have spoken up before now, but he was sending her cold glances and taking no initiative to intervene.

*Is he expecting me to parent him into it? I'm not speaking for him, that'd only make things look worse.*

"Reyan and I have other errands to run," Kainen announced. "We'll keep you updated. Nice to see you again, Tira. You're always welcome at our court anytime."

Reyan nodded her agreement at that, her hand curled in his like the most natural thing in the world. As they faded away, realm-skipping to whatever errand they had next, Tira caught a flash of amusement on Kainen's face and the instant morphing to irritation on Reyan's, as if she was about to tell him off for something.

That left her with Milo, the queen, Claus, and Meryl, who hadn't followed her sisters outside. She gave Claus an expectant look but he was focused on the queen. Even though the royal face was a mask of confidence, Tira noticed the subtle tension of the queen's shoulders, and a repeated twitch of her hand in her pocket.

*She's nervous. Or uneasy. I'm not having that, not in my court.*

"We'll start the tour with the basic communal areas, assuming no objections?" She waited for her brother to bite, but he merely gave her a 'really?' look. "Not the most interesting but at least then you'll know where to find things, although you can always ask. Anyone at court will be happy to help. Then we can dip down into the archives. Let me know if you want to stop at any time though, or see anything specific."

A loud crash overrode the last of her words, closely followed by yips of excitement from a nearby open window. Demi grinned, her shoulders relaxing slightly.

"That'll be our lot. Lead on then." She glanced at Claus. "Are you coming with us?"

He shrugged. "If you prefer, of course, but my sister knows the court well enough by now."

Hot prickles rippled over Tira's skin. It was bordering on dismissive; he didn't even bother to veil his disinterest in showing off his court, or placating the queen with it.

Demi raised her eyebrows for a moment before shrugging.

"Fair enough. No need to join us then if Tira's better placed to hold court."

Tira froze as Demi's gaze dropped to her next, but it was softened and accompanied by a hesitant smile.

The snub was unmistakeable, a queen wielding an insult back to a court lord with lethal grace. A reminder that even though Claus had been named Lord of Words, she could undo the title just as easily.

*She might have heard that I was meant to be lady originally, if not from Milo then from Faerie gossip.*

Made bolder by that, Tira stood straighter and set off toward the inner halls.

"The court is set over many levels to keep the best of the sunlight streaming in for the court itself," she explained, heading for the kitchens first. "But the archives are inside the mountain itself to keep the collections protected from the elements. Milo, please feel free to jump in at any point. You know this place probably as well as I do now, at least in theory."

Milo smiled shyly. "Definitely not there yet. But you've got to show me the origin records, especially the folios in the old script."

"Of course. We'll do the tour now then I'll have one of the scribes kit you up to inspect them, or I can grab someone as we pass if you want to get started right away?"

They slowed down to open the doors to the inner halls, and Milo's face twisted with ruefulness.

"Oh, no, after the tour's fine…"

"Go on." Demi laughed. "You don't need to trail around after me. I promise I will sign whatever you leave on my desk, *and* I'll even read it properly. Go have some fun. Everyone else is."

Milo's round face lit up, his cheeks tinging even pinker than they were from the brisk mountain air. Tira heaved the door open and waved everyone through.

"Kitchens and the main reception hall are on the left here. Staff quarters down the stairs on the left. Unless you need someone, you can just orb in and ask for what you want, they're all really nice here. On the right we've got a couple of smaller reception rooms."

Tira gave them a quick look into the kitchens, pleased when several of the staff nearby stopped to smile and wave, then bow or kneel when they noticed the queen gawking in at them.

"Is it just the origin stuff you're interested in, Milo?" she asked innocently as they carried on toward the archives.

He hesitated, then glanced at Demi. She nodded.

"Mainly," he admitted. "Anything useful to the flow of origins or the prime realm. We're also hunting keys of some kind, or ways of entry."

As they came to the archive doors, Tira stopped outside with a frown.

"A lot of that stuff will be in the old language most likely. We have some translation books I can dig up for you if you like? It'll be heavy going though. There's a lot of disagreement among scholars about origin of the linguistics and pronunciation crossovers."

Milo's face was almost transcendent with delight.

"Absolutely! Anything you have will be helpful. I've been told I'm not allowed to take copies." He gave Demi a disgusted look.

"I didn't say you couldn't," she said mildly. "Only that you should ask permission first. The Word Court might not want you scurrying down all their secrets."

The big brown eyes were on her expectantly, and Tira knew it wasn't her place to give permission or deny it. Considering her stepbrother's strange, dismissive behaviour before, he might even decide to be difficult and say no on principle. But it wouldn't be worth taking the hit if she agreed against his wishes without asking first.

"You'd need to ask my brother about the copies, I'm afraid. But if there's anything you need, information or certain access, I can go pretty much anywhere everyone else can't." She glanced around for listening ears, just in case. "If this were my court, you'd have free rein to see and copy what you like. I don't think knowledge should be gatekept."

Milo nodded. "I'll ask him officially. If not, you'll have to, Demi."

Seeing someone at the other end of the hall, Tira lifted her head and raised her arm.

"Simone!" She waved. "Can you do an inspection visit for us please?"

Simone changed direction and headed toward them. A few metres away she clocked who the guests actually were and dropped to her knees with an ungraceful thud. How the woman could be so delicate with crumbling pages but have no idea for her own spatial awareness, Tira couldn't fathom.

"Of course. What specifically?"

"Simone is one of the chief archivists at court," she

explained. "Anything we don't have written down she probably has in her head. This is Milo. He needs anything on the origins, flow of origins, prime realm, history about the fabric of Faerie or the nether, fables or legends, anything we've got."

Simone's eyebrows lifted but she didn't hesitate to rise to her feet with a curious nod.

"Then we need level three passes," she said. "Probably level four. You'll approve I take it?"

Tira nodded. "Yeah. I doubt anyone will question you though. Anything the queen or her guests need is approved until specifically specified otherwise. Wherever you can assume safely, assume it's okay."

"Got it." Simone grinned. "Okay Milo, nice to meet you. I've heard a lot about you in passing but I was away for your last few visits. I have questions."

Milo looked somewhat startled at the abrupt mention of questions, but when Simone led them through the doors and into the archives, he followed her toward the lifts on the right hand wall without a word.

Tira faced Demi and Meryl and waved to the wide, spiralling staircase running down the left wall.

"We can walk down a way then get the lift back up. Each level is accessible from the stairs."

"It's a bit like the Arcanium library," Demi said as they started downward. "Except we have a round chamber that goes down a long way and the stacks are all inside that with little corridors off of them."

"It's a bit like that here with the corridors, but this is the only way in or out. We won't see the whole thing unless you want to, as it's all much the same. But we'll do the inspection room and a couple of the stacks so you can get an idea."

"It's strange." Meryl's voice floated quietly from behind them. "Every court has so much literature on the past, so many old books and folios. We search all of them for things we need which takes up so much time, but everywhere we go people in every court are clinging onto them like lifelines."

Tira frowned. "Words matter. The past matters. It's how we learn. Granted, there are still so many problems going on, different expectations of how things should work. But without keeping records, we'd only have fiction and hearsay."

"Fiction can be important too," Demi added.

"Definitely, we need it to dream and escape and practice what we don't yet know ourselves, kind of like a test run for life a bit. Stories can sometimes have more fundamental truth about life in them than factual books too. But the old histories, even if they are fiction and fable, they all have grains of various reality in them. They're guidelines for future Fae. The rest is down to us."

She pushed open the first door more forcefully than she intended, wincing and leaping to catch the handle before it swung into the wall.

"Oops. So these are our inspection centres. Each level has its own at the beginning so we don't have to risk bringing the documents out of the controlled conditions any more than we have to."

She stood aside to let Demi and Meryl peer in at the

long corridor with glass-protected inspection rooms on either side. A couple of the archivists sat at the long tables pouring over various manuscripts with sterile tweezers, magnifiers and treating solutions handy, but it was otherwise quiet.

"We can have a walk through to the actual archives as well," she added. "Many of the books on this level are still handleable."

Demi straightened up with a determined gleam lighting in her eyes.

"I didn't realise it was this thorough. We have nothing like this at Arcanium. At least, not that I've ever seen. Impressive. Be careful Milo doesn't 'liberate' anything. I've remembered something I have to do now, there's always paperwork, but you two go on."

Meryl's eyes widened as Demi shuffled backwards to the stairs.

"I can see you back-" she began.

"No need, have a good look around. I can remember the way back up."

Tira frowned. "But you don't know where your room is!"

Demi grinned, a swipe of Fae wickedness sharpening her pale face.

"I'm sure your brother can show me. I need to have a few words with him anyway, and I'm sure I'll find him easily enough. If not, I can ask, right?"

"Of course, anyone here will be happy to-"

"Great, have fun!"

She strode up the stairs without hesitating or looking

back. Tira stood with Meryl, watching the queen until she was through the doors at the top and out of sight.

*Okay, this is awkward.* She gave Meryl a hesitant smile.

"We don't have to see all of it if you don't want," she gabbled. "Or any of it. I know it's not everyone's thing. I'll probably have to go through it all again with Milo at some point anyway."

Meryl managed the tiniest flicker of a smile at that, a simple upward twitch of her lips that softened her sad brown eyes. She swept a blue strand of hair behind her ear and sighed.

"Maybe one level. She did say to have a good look."

Tira nodded. "Make sure we're not up to anything unsavoury. I'll be honest, I thought it would be Milo sent in with all the questions, but he's been really tight-lipped about everything so far."

She held out her hand to indicate Meryl should go in front of her and shut the hall door behind them. The clinical lights overhead painted everything in a stark hue, but Meryl's hair remained as bright and blue as ever, the only thing about her that didn't seem faded.

"He's very protective of her really," Meryl said. "She did him a huge favour once and he's never quite let it go. That's why he takes the whole court thing so seriously, so she doesn't have to."

Tira hadn't ever heard that piece of information before and her view of Milo improved even further.

Meryl didn't venture any more conversation beyond occasional nods and hums of agreement as they moved past the inspection rooms and into the cool firelit shadows of the stacks. She seemed distracted, her glances vacant and her occasional responses slightly delayed. But Tira wondered if perhaps Demi had hoped the distraction would be as much for Meryl's benefit as for the information she might gather along the way.

# CHAPTER FIVE
## REYAN

The signs of the battle were already fading when Kainen skipped them back to the Fauna Court. Reyan sagged against him, the combination of using her gift so strongly before and the rush of skipping back and forth making her want to sleep for a week. She didn't even have any real energy to properly argue when he teasingly suggested taking her home to bed.

Her wall stood strong still, blocking most of the Fauna Court's entranceway, but people were already working to bring it down with axes. Kainen's arm stiffened around her waist and he stood taller, drawing her attention to Lord Rydon striding toward them. Despite his status as lord, he was covered in as much dust and grime as the rest of his court, his broad, mossy green arms scratched and his clothing singed in places.

"Lord Kainen." Lord Rydon nodded to him, then to Reyan. "The queen explained you would be gracing us with your presence a while. I have a room set up for you in the cabins outside."

Kainen returned the nod curtly. "Your hospitality is appreciated. I don't think you've been personally introduced to the lady of my court yet. Lady Reyan meet Lord Rydon of the Fauna Court."

As lady of his court Reyan knew she should incline her head, but given the dismissive look Lord Rydon was giving her, she bowed her shoulders. Kainen's arm drew her up again sharply but Lord Rydon sniffed in recognition.

"You'll forgive me, my lord, but we obey the laws and traditions of Faerie here. As far as I'm aware, she is not lady yet."

Kainen's smile widened, instant hostility dancing dark in his eyes.

"Be that as it may, she is lady of my court and you will treat her as such."

Lord Rydon glanced over his shoulder as something dropped with a loud bang, then shook his head.

"If the queen had titled her to rule alongside you, then maybe. Or if you'd married her she would be lady until you chose to divorce. But I've heard of no marriage and had no statement from either queen to confirm it."

Kainen's fingers warmed against Reyan's hip, but she recognised a stubborn man when she saw one. She was more than used to it after dealing with Kainen for months now, and the nobles at court long before that. Both of them looked her way when she laughed.

"My family lineage might not have much to recommend it, but I do what I can in service to my queen and my court," she said. "I'll leave you to your *lordly* discussions."

Leaving the mocking inflection lingering on the last words, she tried to step away but Kainen clung on. Lord Rydon watched them, no doubt with some variation of 'it's nothing personal' bubbling on his lips.

"You have scribes and handlers who are used to all of Faerie's animals, yes my lord?" she asked.

He nodded. "We do and we're proud of it. Why?"

Reyan dug into the depths of her energy and called out silently through the shadows.

"I have something I'd like their opinion on, if you'll permit it."

She held out her arm as the sensation of shadow crawled up her leg, slithering over Kainen's hand and curling around her arm. Lord Rydon's eyes widened as Betty took form, the solid length of her shadow-snake body wrapping around Reyan's shoulders.

"You keep a shadow-snake as a… *pet*?" he asked, the word dirt on his tongue.

"No, she comes and goes as she sees fit. She at least sees some kind of merit in staying close to me though, lady or not. Do you have anyone who might have some more information on her, or perhaps some old records, anything I could be doing to make sure she's safe or comfortable?"

She waited, hoping that appealing to the nature of his court rather than his title might soften him toward them. While Kainen could draw on his family line and his natural title, that clearly that wouldn't work for her here. But Lord Rydon was lord of a court that specialised in animal care and she had an animal she was determined to care for.

"You'd be wise to not take anything as it seems," Lord Rydon said, his tone gruff and quiet. "Had all sorts around lately asking questions and from what I hear, things aren't safe in any court or corner lately. You'd be best off sending your creature back to the safety of your own court."

Reyan stared at him, eyes wide. That was a not-so-veiled warning if ever she'd heard one. Tilting Betty into her palm and cupping her fingers, she waited until Betty had squished her shadow into the small space, then slipped the sleepy shadow-snake into the pocket of her jeans.

"I'm afraid I'm very busy." Lord Rydon raised his voice loud enough to be heard. "The queen's request is taxing as it is without us having to host guests. If you insist on spending time chatting, I'll have my daughter Cerys come and speak to you about the creatures we care for."

Reyan nodded. "Thank you, that's very kind of you. I'd be honoured to meet your daughter and learn more about the Fauna Court."

The tension of Kainen's arm around her waist suggested he wouldn't be letting her out of his sight any time soon, but he let her carry the conversation.

"We often get forgotten because we're more absorbed with the animals in our care," Lord Rydon admitted. "The wider schemes of Faerie and Fae tend to leave us to our own devices, at least until recently. But we also collect a lot of sense about people that the loftiness of Words and the wooden headedness of Flora doesn't take into account. I'll have someone show you to your cabin for now."

Reyan nodded but Kainen's pinched smile suggested he wasn't happy about it.

*I don't want you left alone,* he insisted.

She frowned. *I doubt anything's going to happen to me here. We do what we need to do, and what is that exactly?*

He didn't answer, eying Lord Rydon instead.

"We'll take your offer of the cabin for now then, with our thanks," he said.

Lord Rydon called over someone to take them and Reyan let Kainen cling to her as they followed past her wall and out into the Fauna Court. Sunshine beamed down on them, the smell of earth and freshness mingling with the more overwhelming scent of animals. Trees clustered all around the patchwork of fields, and a body of water sparkled like silver in between them.

"Infuriating Fae," Kainen grumbled.

Mindful of the woman striding several paces ahead of them, Reyan dropped her voice low.

"He has a point though. I'm not lady yet and we both know why that really is."

He rolled his eyes. "Yes, because we haven't had a spare minute to discuss it yet. But not here. At least, not right now. I have to go and enter into some ridiculous verbal sparring match to request their help with something that I'm not even fully aware of yet, because nobody told us what we're actually here for."

Reyan smiled. Worry about her position seemed far away suddenly as they crossed a wooden bridge over a large pond with leaping golden fish and the calming trickle of a small waterfall nearby. They had to discuss their situation eventually, and she had no guarantee being a true lady was possible even if that was what Kainen truly wanted. She also had no idea if he even wanted that, or her, but she had time to rest first and get herself prepared to face it.

"Well, you're good at that, talking about stuff without any idea of what's going on," she teased.

Kainen's expression froze, then a wicked grin spread across his face.

"A backhanded compliment? For me? You must be

feverish."

She tried to elbow him but he dodged and grabbed her hand in his, bringing it to his lips. Her insides somersaulted as he kissed it, her cheeks burning as they approached a hexagonal wooden cabin under the shade of the trees.

"This is beautiful," she said.

He huffed. "Isolated. Both a good thing and a worrying thing."

"I won't ask why."

"Please do. I'm very impressed with my answer."

She laughed. "You're impressed with yourself in general."

Lady or not, he let her go ahead of him into the cabin and didn't deign to answer her. She rotated around the circular room, noting the high ceiling and the abundance of windows letting in the sunlight. A large bed sat opposite the door with a small area in the middle full of cushions to sit on. Pale cream furnishings lined with dark red echoed the Fauna Court colours, and Reyan guessed Kainen was marking out potential exits and entrances as he gave it a grim nod.

"I'll bring refreshments, Lord," the woman said, bowing as she closed the door behind her.

Kainen finished inspecting the room and thudded down onto the pile of cushions. When he held his hand out to her, Reyan hesitated so long that he frowned.

"I won't yell at you if you don't want," he said. "Even though I should."

Reyan took his hand, squeaking when he pulled her down beside him. She was so used to his arm around her now that she barely even questioned it, but sitting budged up beside him seemed overly intimate now that nobody else was around to see. When she straightened and tried to tug her hand free, he held on.

"Do you have any idea why we're here?" she asked.

He sighed, letting his head fall back. "I have some idea. Demi thinks-" He switched to mind-speak. *Demi thinks there are answers here. She isn't sure where, or how we can find them, but all we know is the location of the skipway to the prime realm in the human world. There's meant to be keys to get through, but nobody has any idea what these keys are or where to find them.*

Reyan let that sink in. The Forgotten wanted to get into the prime realm, either to find a way to dominate it and then use the resources to take over Faerie, or to utilise whoever was on the other side as a fighting force. Demi was adamant they stop the Forgotten from succeeding, a sentiment she wholeheartedly agreed with.

*Why doesn't she just have the Forgotten watched?* She asked. *Or the location?*

Kainen started playing with her hand, running his fingertips over the lengths of her fingers. She shivered, her mind straying away from outside perils and back to inside ones.

"I'm sure she has that covered already," he murmured. "But last time I spoke to Milo, he said that Ace is adamant it's a big place. Too much ground to keep covered when we don't know what exactly we're looking for. They'll be searching for information at the Word Court but we're clearly here for something as well."

Reyan nodded, her eyes lidded with exhaustion. "Okay. Fauna isn't just animals though, it's people too, right? So maybe there's some answers in the history of people."

"Not just a pretty face are you." He chuckled. "Alright, sweetheart. I'll play lord for the nobles and you play spy among the people, deal?"

She nodded. "Alright. Can I have a nap first?"

"Of course. I'll have Meri send some of our things over in a bit. Do you need a pillow?"

"No, you're pillowy enough."

She had no desire to fight or fret as he tightened the arm around her waist and wrapped the other across her shoulders, hauling her onto his chest. He might be taking comfort from her or perhaps he really cared as his fingers stroked through her hair, but in that moment living out her favourite daydream was enough.

A loud knock startled her awake before she could do much of anything, Kainen's cursing echoing above her head.

"We've barely been here two minutes," he muttered. "*What?*"

The door opened and Reyan sat up, embarrassed. To all the world she and Kainen were madly in love, but even now she found pretending excruciating. Much easier to be in private and believe her own pretence than have to actually perform it for others.

The door swung open and Reyan scrambled to her feet before Kainen could do anything mad like cling on to her.

"Lord Rydon said you want to speak to me about animals?"

The young woman standing in the doorway eyed the situation and swiped a hand through her hip-length red hair. Tall for a troll and lithe with signs of muscle on her mossy-brown arms, Cerys looked like she had no trouble wrangling errant animals or people if they gave her any trouble. Reyan half expected to see some signs of claw scars after hearing the kinds of fearsome creatures the Fauna Court offered sanctuary for, but she couldn't see any and didn't want to be caught staring.

"Hi, you must be Cerys," Reyan said, her cheeks burning.

*Wow, she's tall for a troll.* Kainen's voice strolled lazily into her mind.

Reyan kept a smile on her face but Cerys had no such intentions, flicking a withering look at Kainen instead.

"Let me guess," she said. "You've not seen a troll this tall before?"

Kainen chuckled as he got to his feet and slid his arm around Reyan's waist.

"Apologies, I'm intrigued by your diadem of feathers," he said smoothly. "The intricacy is breathtaking. Is that a Revel Court specialty?"

"No." She frowned at him, then at Reyan. "You must be Reyan. I hear you have questions for me?"

Reyan tensed. "Nothing so demanding, but I was speaking to your father about shadow-snakes, and he suggested you might have the be the best person to speak to."

Cerys raised her brow in surprise. "You have a shadow-snake? They're unbelievably rare. Where did you find it?"

"Oh I'm asking academically." She word-tangled quickly past any mention of Betty. "I'm a shadow-weaver and I overheard someone mention them a while back. I figured if they're actually out there, I might be able to find some."

No lies as such, as she had overheard Blossom mention them once before, and finding more would be amazing.

Kainen's arm tightened around her.

*Your word-tangling is improving, sweetheart, but less telling people about what you are please. We don't need other courts hunting to recruit you. Or steal you.*

Reyan fought the urge to grin. *I'd love to see them try.*

Cerys leaned back against the doorframe, the door staying open beside her. Reyan wanted to suggest they sit but it seemed a bit forward to take charge in someone else's court and the only available seating was the floor of cushions. She couldn't trust Kainen wouldn't try and wrap himself around her again, company or no company. A smile broke across her face before she could stop it.

"Shadow-snakes are thought to be a myth by most," Cerys said. "By many accounts, they're not bound by the nether and can move between realms of Faerie when in shadow form. They can grow extremely large and apparently can't change their size once grown, although if in shadow form they should be able to shift into any dark space available."

"You do know a lot about them by the sound of it," Reyan said.

Cerys shrugged. "It's the Fauna Court's responsibility to know these things. There are various accounts, brief mentions, but as I say, they're thought to be a myth by most."

"Well, that's really helpful," she said, ignoring the not-so-deceptively vague way Cerys had worded everything.

"Their fangs are incredibly valuable," Cerys continued. "They were hunted for them. I think there are some histories in a pile of dusty old junk here, might be something in that, but I have much better things to do than sort through stuff that has no bearing on my court's present."

"What kind of histories?" Kainen asked.

"Old texts about the history of the court, some tapestries, and a bunch of random paintings that came from some other court a long while ago."

Lord Rydon appeared beside her and gave her a sideways glance, wariness on his face.

*He's wondering how much she's told us,* Kainen suggested.

Reyan would have agreed but Cerys strode past her father without another word or any farewell.

"She seems… spirited," Kainen offered.

Lord Rydon frowned deeper. "No point flapping around with propriety. The queen has issued me with a request and time is never on her side it seems. We keep some old histories here that she wishes you to have access to. I'll escort you."

Reyan lifted a foot to follow him out but Kainen stayed put, his hand tightening on her hip to hold her in place.

"Right now?" he demanded. "I'll remind you that Reyan singlehandedly turned the tide of this morning's attack to help your court. She needs time to recover.”

Lord Rydon’s expression soured but he caught Reyan’s eye roll and might have twitched his lips ever so slightly in her direction.

“We rarely have time for rest, so I’d advise that it has to be right now, yes. *If* you can deign to follow the royal orders in a timely fashion.”

Reyan smothered a giggle. Lord Rydon seemed desperate to get rid of them, but she was desperate to get home so she didn’t care.

Kainen grabbed her hand the moment they started walking but as they set off through the idyllic woodland, dodging around a carpet of blue and yellow flowers, Lord Rydon appeared on her other side.

“You’re not born to nobility,” he announced.

Reyan shook her head. “Nope. Not by a long shot. My family line is old but no longer noble by any means. I did my fair share of work growing up if that’s what you’re getting at.”

He shrugged. “It’s not my place to judge, but I know the queen has anti-traditionalist leanings.”

“She sees Fae as people not resources, that’s all. It might be fine for nobility to pick and judge who prospers and who serves, but when you aren’t in the Faerie elite life isn’t always sunny.”

“True enough. It is the way of things though. The dealings of the noble world are underhanded and dark, not a place for normal Fae-folk. Best off out of it, making a peaceful life without the troubles that leading brings.”

Reyan clung to Kainen’s hand as the woodland

darkened around them, the trees towering and closing in to block out the sunlight above. The shadows flocked to her, whispering of old air and rarely disturbed secrets.

"It's only the way of things because those who benefit choose to keep it that way," she argued. "Lead the people or make use of them, it's a choice."

Lord Rydon chuckled then, a hoarse rolling sound that echoed through the dense air.

"Well spoken, but it's not the way of the realms that we all live in."

Surprised that Kainen was being so passively silent, Reyan frowned.

"It will be one day. The queen won't stop fighting until things are more equal for people that are sick of being squashed and sat on by nobles."

"We'll see." Lord Rydon stopped and pointed through the trees. "At the end of the path is a route into the underground cavern we keep our histories in. Search all you like and take a rest after if you must, but I'd advise you to move on after that. No need to bother yourself with returning for farewells either."

Kainen nodded, no sign of disappointment or even surprise written on his face.

"I'm sure the queen will be most grateful to you for conceding to allow us some measure of support."

Lord Rydon scoffed under his breath and turned away, striding toward the main hub of his court without another word or a single look back.

"He doesn't want to lodge an allegiance," Reyan murmured.

Kainen shrugged. "Or he already has and is playing nice to keep the fight from his door. I don't want you out of my sight while we're here, got it?"

Amused, Reyan dropped his hand before he could cling on and took a couple of quick steps toward the hill rising up ahead.

"Is that an order, court lord?" she taunted.

Kainen's eyes sparked with mischief and he shot forward, his arms winding around her middle.

"Yes."

"You can't order me about now," she said, laughter bursting out in breathless huffs as she pretended to struggle. "I'm not sworn to your court any longer."

"No, you're lady of it now. You can do as you like, whatever *he* says." He flicked his head backwards to where Lord Rydon had already disappeared.

"If you say so. Come on, the quicker we get through whatever's in there, the quicker we can get home. Or get to the Word Court, do whatever needs doing there, then go home."

He let her go but she didn't fight as he slipped his hand around hers and pulled her flush against his side.

"Is that *our* home you're speaking of now?" he teased. "Are you claiming us at long last?"

She pulled a face. "That's the home that has my bed in it where I can get some sleep without you constantly hanging on the end of me."

She held their hands up between them but squeezed ever so slightly tighter to reassure him.

"Ouch sweetheart, that actually hurts. Alright then.

Time to sort through some hideously boring old stuff. I'll see if Meri can send us some food and drink to keep us going a while. I won't ask Lord Rydon to lower himself to actually being hospitable toward us."

"You do take me to the most glamorous places."

He laughed, a wistful smile crossing his face.

"Only the best for you."

# CHAPTER SIX
## MERYL

Demi might be queen of Faerie, but she was also a royal pain in the behind. The moment the three of them walked into the archive to start the tour, Demi had fled and left her alone with Tira.

Meryl tried her best to look interested in the bright lights of the viewing rooms for the ancient books and the rambling library floor beyond that, but each time Tira spoke or smiled, she had that awful fluttering in her gut.

Now wasn't the time to develop a crush on someone. Not after Petra had been gone so short a time and her death unavenged. Especially not considering Tira was born to a court, a lady in her own right by birth, part of the nobility and therefore way above Meryl's station socially.

*Orbs, not that I'm even considering- stop it!*

Meryl thought of Lolly and Tyren, apparently working well together to move the Revel Court to a distant part of the Flora Court's realm. Cheryl and Lolly were in constant contact, as were Lolly and Milo, but Meryl had stopped answering orb calls. Everyone knew if they wanted something from the Eastwicks, it was Beryl or Cheryl that would answer now.

Meryl wiped a hand over her face, utterly exhausted. She couldn't remember a time when she wasn't drained and weary from having to wake up, to pretend like she was okay. To balance the fine line between being respectfully sad but also not dramatically grief-stricken.

She stumbled to a halt as Tira led her back to the main stairs of the archives and swung to face her.

"I'm sorry." Tira grimaced. "I know most people aren't that bothered about seeing the archives. There isn't much variation beyond what I've already shown you anyway, so I'll take you to your room now."

Meryl blinked in surprise. She wanted to say something 'normal', anything that would show she wasn't a complete wreck incapable of social interaction, but all she had was the ability to nod.

Tira gazed back at her for a moment longer, searching her face for something. Then she smiled awkwardly and started up the stairs back toward the main centre of the court.

Meryl followed, her insides tumbling with uneasiness. She had no idea what to say but the urge to say something stuck, flicking in her head like a broken orb-message.

"It's beautiful here."

There, she'd managed to not only say something, but something polite too.

Tira slowed her pace and glanced back, her smile growing.

"I've always thought so. This far up it's snowy all year, but you don't have to go down that far to get to fields and rivers in the summer. I actually think- Sorry, I don't mean to harp on."

Meryl frowned. "I don't mind. I live with my sisters day in and day out, so your enthusiasm is better than their constant whining."

A stab of uneasiness came at the thought of being disloyal to her sisters, something she'd never have worried about before. Nothing made sense anymore, like walking a tightrope or a rope bridge with no way of seeing if the next step was still in front of you.

"They are certainly lively," Tira admitted. "But it must be nice to have family who actually care about you around. Well, anyway, as I said to the queen, if there's anything in my power to grant, she has my full support. My stepbrother however… I'm sure you can draw your own conclusions."

Meryl managed a short, sharp chuckling sound.

"Oh, we will, don't worry. We know how to manage difficult people and courts by now."

Tira stopped at the top of the stairs, eyes wide with alarm.

"I hope that's not a threat."

Meryl grimaced. "Not really. I think Demi's hoping to get information while we're here, but she'll probably ask you herself. I only meant that my sisters and I grew up close to the Flora Court so we know how to play the game."

Tira pushed open the door and walked down the hall past what smelled like the kitchens. The delicious richness, like thick gravy or some kind of meaty soup, filled Meryl's nose. She slowed in surprise as her stomach growled. She'd lost almost all her appetite, nibbling on whatever was put in front of her at her sisters' insistence for weeks, until she knew she had to be sensible and eat what she could manage. But with that smell circling around her, she felt almost dizzy from wanting some of it.

Tira slowed to a halt and gave her a hesitant smile.

"Sorry, I just need to check on things in here, it'll only take a minute."

Meryl nodded and closed her eyes momentarily as Tira swung the kitchen door open and the irresistible scent wrapped around them.

*I can't ask what it is, because even without knowing her she'll insist on feeding me.*

Meryl pushed aside the uncomfortable urge to smile at that thought. She stepped into the kitchen, eying the enormous fires, the vast counters full of produce and the various sharp implements hanging from various nooks.

A subtle chill brushed in from a nearby door, along with a familiar tinkling sound, so faint she could have imagined it. She started toward the door, peering around the frame.

"Hello," she murmured.

Three adolescent frost cats lifted their silvery heads, the ice on their fur tinkling.

Averting her gaze and rounding her shoulders, Meryl dropped into a crouch. She offered the back of her hand and the smallest one gave it a cursory sniff before yowling quietly. The remaining two stopped puffing up their icy fur, glowing green eyes returning to where they rootled in the snow.

Frost cats as a rule weren't tameable but they understood mutual respect, something Fae saw as a battlefield at the best of times.

"Oh." Tira appeared in the doorway. "They don't usually let people get close."

Meryl noted that the frost cats didn't bat an eyelid at

Tira, another tick in her favour.

"We have a couple at Arcanium that I made friends with, kind of," Meryl admitted.

"They don't usually do 'friends', do they?"

Meryl's lips lifted. "Not easily. I learned their body language enough to show I'm not a threat. I like animals. They aren't all show and no substance like people."

"I get that." Tira laughed, leaning against the doorframe. "Fae are extremely showy as a rule, none more so than nobles at court. I try to steer away from the political chaos, although I do like arguing with people in the debating room."

Meryl glanced up as a pale green butterfly fluttered past her face, then landed right between the frost cat's ears. The cat shook its head with a hiss and tried rolling over in the snow to paw at it.

Another butterfly arrived, then another.

Meryl watched as a fourth one passed the cats and dipped over her head, coming to rest on Tira's outstretched finger.

"It's not something I easily admit," Tira said. "But I get the feeling you can be trusted with a secret. I can communicate with them, but I've had to hide it from my stepbrothers over the years. They used to enjoy squishing bugs in front of me."

She pulled a face and Meryl inhaled sharply at the thought.

"You have two stepbrothers, right?"

Tira nodded. "Lyle is currently languishing in the Forever mountains as a traitor. While Claus is lord of all he surveys. Neither are my favourite people."

Meryl clambered to her feet, freezing when one of the butterflies landed on her shoulder.

"But your mother was Lady of Words," she confirmed.

"She was. She married their father to help progress the court financially but he was old and rich and harmless. He wanted a restful place for his final days, but his sons wanted power."

Another butterfly began to flutter around the frost cats' heads and two of them rolled, batting up with their paws like kittens.

Meryl couldn't help the chuckle that rasped out.

"Anyway, I can show you your room now," Tira suggested.

Meryl nodded. She would find an excuse to come back and sit out here a while, close to the warmth of the kitchen and the brisk chill of the mountains.

She followed Tira out of the kitchen and back to the main hall with a remnant of calmness filling her head, an echo of *before*. Pushing the natural urge to dwell aside, she soaked in the chilly air, so deliciously crisp and fresh.

It seemed like a nice place to be. A couple of people shouted things to Tira, jokes and affectionate taunts about seeing her around the debating table later, and Tira happily called the odd remark back to them.

*Why isn't she lady of the court now?* Meryl wondered. *She's clearly well liked and Claus definitely isn't.*

Unsure whether she should ask, she followed Tira along another wide hallway of stone decked in long deep blue rugs. The windows on the left side of the hall were open wide and hanging blue banners fluttered in a brisk breeze.

Tira stopped at a door at the other end of the hall and pushed it open, standing aside with a hopeful smile on her face.

"This one should be yours," she said. "Assuming that's your bag on the bed anyway."

Meryl walked past her, flinching when a waft of what she assumed was Tira's sugary sweet perfume swirled around her head. It was so different to the sweet but tangy orange scent Petra had used.

The comparison twisted in her chest and she pressed her hand to the pain, searching her frantic brain for anything she could say to get the thoughts out of her head.

"I'm in here on my own," she murmured.

She heard Tira's soft inhale but couldn't bring herself to turn around, hovering on the brink of tears. She was five days tear-free; she couldn't succumb to them now, not here of all places.

"Oh, orbs, I'm so sorry," Tira said. "Were you expecting to be sharing with your sisters? Of course you would be, I'm sorry. We're not trying to isolate you or separate you or anything. It must have been a mix-up somewhere. I'll have it fixed-"

"Don't."

Meryl curled her toes inside her shoes and clenched her gut into a tight knot, forcing herself to be calm. The way Petra had taught her.

She turned around to find Tira wide-eyed and sliding a forefinger back and forth over the studs and rings in her ear.

"Don't," she repeated.

Tira frowned. "No?"

"Solitude is great. I forgot. I'm not used to it."

"Oh." Tira hesitated a moment before smiling gently. "Well, if you change your mind just ask and we'll make amendments. Someone will send you some details for the evening's events, but your sisters are next door anyway."

Her smile, so hopeful, lifted one corner of Meryl's mouth before she could process the action and the words tumbled out of her mouth.

"Sure you couldn't put them somewhere else? Like further down the mountain?"

Tira snorted a surprised laugh.

"Hey!"

Beryl's indignant voice made both of them jump. A moment later, she and Cheryl clustered around Tira in the doorway with absolutely no thought for the fact she was a lady and therefore probably wasn't used to them crowding her.

"That was mean." Beryl sniffed. "But you made an *actual joke* so I'll let you off. This place isn't too bad is it? No offense or anything, your ladyship. Not my style, but it's nice."

Cheryl rolled her eyes. "This is where you apologise and keep your mouth shut a while."

"Rude," Beryl muttered.

"No point keeping your mouth shut here," Tira said. "They'll think there's all sorts of things wrong with you if you don't join in the debates. You're more than welcome to join in by the way. It's not a court only thing. I can only imagine how different an FDP's viewpoint on things would be to the nobles we tend to get around here."

"All nobles, is it?" Cheryl asked.

Tira nodded. "Mostly. We have non-nobles too but most are staff in some form or another. But they're more than welcome to voice their opinions. There are no hierarchies inside the debate room."

"I do like debating things," Beryl said.

Meryl chuckled. "You like hearing yourself talk more like. What?"

She froze when she saw her sisters staring at her in amazement. Then she realised it was the first time they'd heard her laugh since…

The panicked feeling started to rise again but Tira took a step back and cleared her throat.

"Well, you'll be sent information to your rooms about times of things," she said. "If there's anything you need in terms of help, ask me or ask for Marlon. If there's anything you need in terms of permissions, I might have to refer you to my stepbrother, so best assume you've got the queen's permission if you haven't got his."

Beryl grinned. "We're good at circumventing rules, don't worry."

"I can absolutely believe it." Tira laughed, her eyes shining with delight. "How about you stay away from the archives and we'll get on fine."

She spared a fleeting smile for Meryl, one that made awful flutters take flight, but Meryl clamped down on them immediately.

Cheryl popped her head around the doorframe, no doubt

watching to make sure Tira left before shutting the door.

"You laughed," she announced.

Meryl scowled. "So? Banned now, is it?"

"No, but it's good to see you processing things. We should take a walk though, do what Demi asked us to."

Meryl eyed the bed in the centre of the room, far too plush and inviting to be healthy with all its many pillows. There was an actual fireplace in the far wall too, already blazing. The mixture of roaring heat and crisp air from the open window was the perfect balance of extreme temperatures.

But her plan for revenge overrode any hope for her own comfort. If the Word Court was being frequented by Forgotten sympathisers as Demi believed, they would need to be on their guard.

"Come on then." She sighed. "I passed the kitchen on the way up here and it smelled fantastic."

"Well that's good," Cheryl added, leading the way out of the room and down the hall. "You've been looking a bit peaky so a proper meal will do you some good."

"Well, I know *I'll* need a proper dinner if I'm going to be debating people all evening," Beryl said.

Meryl groaned but gave her sister an affectionate shove with her shoulder.

"They have no idea what's about to happen to them. It is beautiful here though."

Beryl and Cheryl nodded as they walked into the main hall and looked around at the crowds gathered. Several groups seemed to be in debate already, and one cluster in the far corner were having a full-on argument that sounded like it had something to do with Fae politics.

"Hey, isn't that-" Beryl hesitated, craning her neck to see better. "It is, look!"

Meryl followed the line of Beryl's finger and her Fae connection bubbled awake inside her. It fired through her limbs, burning over her skin like molten metal.

She recognised the man walking through the crowd with none other than the Lord of Words himself, deep in hushed conversation. His previously short brown hair was longer now, long enough to reach his jaw which could only mean it was part of a glamour after a mere few months. With the deceptively ageless face and an overwhelming air of swaggering arrogance, Lorens clearly felt he was untouchable.

"Okay, calming it down," Cheryl muttered. "Demi let him go so we can't attack yet. We have to watch and wait. You good, Mer?"

Her words filtered through and Meryl fought every urge she had to run at him and start tearing into him with her fingers. If she got deep enough, she could make any trace elements of metal in his blood dance and *burn*.

"*Meryl.*"

Beryl's voice was laced with warning, the seriousness something so unusual that it punctured a small hole in the rage.

Meryl breathed in deeply, fixing her focus onto the frosty air and the chill flushing her cheeks. She trusted Demi's judgement on when to strike. She could wait, for now.

*Besides, I don't want to cause Tira extra stress by*

*tearing her stepbrother's guests to pieces.*

"I'm fine." She paused to unclench her jaw. "I'm fine. We have to tell Demi."

Cheryl shoved her arm through Meryl's and clamped down tight.

"Guessing she already knows, but yeah, we should. If he's here, that's a bad sign."

"Or a sign we're in the right place," Beryl added. "There must be something worth finding here if he's lurking about."

She jumped with a feral hiss as Harvey swooped up behind her and planted a disgustingly wet kiss on her cheek.

"What are you whispering so prettily about?" he asked.

Cheryl pointed and Harvey's jovial expression faded to a scowl.

"Maybe Demi will let us blast him to the Forever mountains with all his traitor friends," he suggested. "He's obviously here for the same reason we are."

Meryl sighed. "We know the location, but Demi keeps muttering about these keys."

Harvey's grin reappeared.

"Yeah, I don't think Beryl suggesting we check the pile of keys in the Ogle was quite what she meant though."

"Well, why couldn't it be an actual key?" Beryl retorted, her arms folding across her chest as she glowered back at him.

"More likely to be something linked to Faerie or the nether, some kind of complex magic system," Cheryl said.

"Too complex for us no doubt."

"Speak for yourself."

Beryl grinned. "I generally do."

Meryl conceded to a small smile as Cheryl linked arms with her and started walking.

"Come on. Maybe Beryl will batter him with her wits tonight. First time for everything."

"HEY!"

# CHAPTER SEVEN
# TIRA

Tira rubbed at her forehead as she slumped over one of the desks in the archives a day after the queen's arrival. The sledders had returned for lunch then disappeared again for a second go, rolling in after dark with rosy cheeks and big smiles. Even the queen seemed happy enough with her day at the court when she joined them.

She remembered the previous evening with a smile. Experiencing the Eastwick sisters, Beryl and Cheryl at least, at the debate table was an absolute delight. They merrily out-argued anyone they came up against, including some of the staunch professionals at court. Tira grinned as she remembered a couple of the nobles flouncing out of the debating room after losing their arguments, their noses firmly in the air.

She'd even managed to dodge Claus. He hadn't bothered coming to her room to hound her at any rate, so she considered that a win although the worry of it had left her with the subtle hint of a headache needling at one side of her head.

She sighed and glanced around at the assembled group. Marinda and Milo had corralled her along with them right after breakfast, marching down to the level two archives. Milo then spent the morning leafing carefully through huge ancient texts while Marinda huffed continually over her writing pad.

That would have been bearable enough, nice even, but the ominous presence sitting at a nearby table soured the atmosphere.

From the odd furtive glance, Tira could tell Claus wasn't actually reading the book in his hands, more like watching them over it. Whether he wanted to while away hours by enacting some kind of silent revenge on Marinda for snubbing them or he didn't trust Milo as part of the queen's court, Tira couldn't tell.

"I can't write in my room," Marinda muttered. "You know I can't. But tell me why we have to sit here with him."

Tira didn't dare look up at her stepbrother again, hoping he couldn't hear them. He hadn't turned a single page in a long time and kept smirking at them over the top of it. She had diplomatically suggested moving to another level, but Marinda refused to give him the satisfaction of being chased out.

"He's probably trying to unsettle you after you didn't show respect yesterday," Tira whispered.

Marinda pulled a face. "Disgusting oaf. I'm going to push a shelving unit onto him."

Given that the woman was prone to dramatics, Tira guessed she meant it in sentiment but wasn't actually going to do it. She hoped not at least.

*Although it would solve an awful lot of problems.*

"Make sure there aren't any books on it first," Milo murmured, not looking up once.

Marinda scowled. "Wouldn't be all that heavy then."

"Well, take the books off and fill it with rocks instead.

Plenty of those around."

*My brother isn't very popular it seems.*

Tira turned her attention back to the lists she was supposed to be reviewing. They weren't her lists to review of course, but Claus wouldn't bother with them and the court still needed to function.

The door to the main stairs opened and Tira's heartrate picked up when she saw the flash of blue heading toward them. Meryl had her hair tied back but the short spiky tail of it trailed over the shoulder of her white t-shirt, and a host of colourful bracelets on her right arm tinkled as they brushed against her light blue jeans.

Tira gulped and sat up straighter, glancing down to check her own black jeans and fitted blue shirt were somewhat respectable.

Meryl caught her eye and smiled a little before eying Marinda and Milo, then glancing over at Claus.

"Demi asked me to check in," she explained, keeping her voice slightly hushed. "I'm not sure why, or what for, but here I am."

Tira pulled a chair around for her as both Marinda and Milo grunted a greeting.

"Nothing to report," she replied. "These two are in their own bookish worlds and I'm doing boring stuff."

Meryl slid into the chair with a quiet groan.

"I could do with some peace for a while. My sisters are bored stiff already which means they're arguing. Ace is trying to find things for them and Taz to do. FDPs are supposed to be ready for anything but one whiff of boredom and they're rioting like toddlers."

Tira stared back at her. "What's it like being an FDP? It must be so cool. Have you had many adventures?"

Apparently the wrong thing to say. Meryl's expression froze seconds before shuttering, her gaze snapping to the table.

"Sorry, I didn't mean to pry." Tira bit her lip. "It's none of my business. Do you want me to find you a book, or something to write on? We have orb readers too if that's better?"

Meryl shook her head, inhaling sharply. "No thanks, I'm fine."

Tira slid off her seat and grabbed the nearest book at random. She didn't need to do anything with it but taking it back to its shelf beat sitting in the awkwardness she'd just created. As she walked away, the not-so-subtle whispers echoed behind her.

"That was slightly rude," Marinda said.

"Leave her be," Milo added. "She's dealing with some stuff at the moment."

Memories of Meryl's obvious sadness filled Tira's head, along with a huge dose of guilt hitting right in the gut. She shouldn't have pried. It had to be something bad; she missed her mother and sometimes the grief overwhelmed her, but she never grouched away from an excuse to talk about her.

She carried on down the aisles before she could overhear anymore and slid the book back into place. The queen visiting had caused some stir among the rest of the court before the evening meal, but she'd managed to placate them by suggesting the merits and pitfalls of hierarchical rule as a topic for the debate. By the time she fled to make sure the queen and her friends would be well taken care of overnight, the entire court was in good-natured, albeit loud, uproar.

"Hello, Lady. How glad I am to see you."

Tira held in the deep groan fighting to break free. She turned and flinched to find Lorens not only far too close to her, his breath almost hitting her face, but also blocking her way out.

She held her ground despite the urge to step back.

"Hello. My brother is in the main section, you can't have missed him."

Even as the words came out, she realised she hadn't seen Lorens come in.

*Which means he was lurking in here already all this time. But why?*

"I didn't," he said. "He'll keep. I have things I want to ask you."

Tira frowned. "My brother has the authority to grant anything you need. It'd be more than I'm worth to go against him, so you can't be ignorant enough to suggest that."

Lorens grinned and lifted a hand as if to settle it on her cheek. She batted it away and took that necessary step back, anger firing like an explosion. He only smiled wider.

"Spirited as always, my lady. Never mind. What I really need right now is archive access."

Tira guessed if she shouted loud enough, Milo and the others would come running. But she'd keep that as a last resort.

"Again, my brother has authority. Since you're such good friends, you should ask him."

"Ah, I did. He was very accommodating on the permission, but not so much the information."

"He didn't know, you mean." Tira scoffed.

"Well, when you put it that way it makes him sound very remiss. But your archivists also seem stubbornly determined not to do things without your say so, even when I have his. They have errands to run elsewhere, or important documents ready to crumble at the slightest delay."

Tira stilled, a strain of fierce pride searing through her chest. It wasn't just Marlon who showed her continuing loyalty, but most of the court too. She lifted her head and stood tall like a court lady should, calm in the depths of her domain.

"What are you after then?" she asked, tone steady like her mother had taught her.

"If you were to give me a total inventory, that would be enough."

She shook her head. "There's an inventory in the main entrance. Other than that, either I or the archivists can locate what you need."

Irritation flashed across his face, so fleeting she'd have assumed she imagined it had she not trusted her instincts. She folded her arms tighter.

"I can't tell you what I need unless I know I can trust you."

"Then you're out of luck. Excuse me."

He blocked her path as she'd expected him to. The

indolent smirk was back, but frustration curled its tight talons around his muscles, his movements less fluid than before.

"I have many powerful friends," he insisted. "And I could be a great asset and consort to this court, especially if you wanted your brother set aside. When the time comes, you could have everything you ever wanted, if only you'd agree to concede on this one tiny thing."

Tira stared at him, her mind ferreting over the words.

"I'm sorry, I think my brain just skipped a realm. Consort? Are you saying you'll somehow de-title my brother and marry me if I give you a total inventory of the archives?"

Lorens nodded. "To start with. Your brother can have some other position, a court of his own if he wishes. The Court of Words would be yours if you were mine."

Wild words, but he couldn't lie. Tira hugged herself tighter as her skin rippled with revulsion. Catching the look on her face, Lorens laughed.

"It would be a marriage of convenience. I have no interest in young women who barely have any experience with the more natural ways of life. But your court may have the information I need."

Tira took a shuffling step back. If she had to, she could climb over the lower stacks at the far end of the row and run. She could shout for the others.

*He can't lie. If he's saying he has powerful enough friends to put my brother in a new court and give me this one, he means it.*

His danger factor shot even higher with that realisation,

but Tira clung onto her elbows with pinching fingers, forcing herself to stay strong. Claus wrecking her court was one thing, but Lorens and whoever his friends were getting even a fingernail into it was unthinkable.

"How is this in any way a deal to suit me?" she bluffed. "I'd rather marry a rock, court or no court."

Lorens shrugged. "Well then, remember that I can easily convince dear Claus to force the issue if need be. He wouldn't care in the slightest, as long as your marriage benefited him."

Tira took a deep breath and twisted, summoning her connection as she took a step to run.

Before she could dredge up a protection warding, punishing fingers curled tight around her wrist. She kicked out, her heel connecting with his kneecap as she opened her mouth to scream.

But it wasn't her voice that blasted through the air.

"Get that rancid excuse for a man away from me right this second, or I swear-"

Lorens lifted his head as the sound shattered through the silence, the distraction a mixed blessing. Tira tore her arm free of him and dodged, pushing enough of her protection around her that the sheer panicked force of it shoved him to one side.

She ran as fast as her feet could tumble, careening around the edge of the row and dashing toward the relative safety of the group.

Which didn't look in any way safe at all.

Claus stood in front of Marinda, who was holding a huge book in both hands and trying to take swipes at him while Meryl held her back with surprising strength. Milo dodged back and forth, his face a picture of horror as he tried to rescue the book. Tira glanced over her shoulder to make sure Lorens hadn't followed her, but she kept the warding going strong all the same as she faced the now more pressing issue in front of her.

"That's enough," she called out.

She had no hope of her stepbrother listening to her, and Marinda probably wouldn't back down either, but Milo and Meryl might consider it. Milo slowed with his eyes fixed on the book. After a tense pause, Marinda handed it back.

Tira sagged with relief. "There, now we all need to-orbs alive, put the chair down!"

Milo bounded away from the scuffle with the book clutched against his chest, cradling it like a newborn kitten. Marinda held the wooden chair aloft with abject fury in her eyes while Claus leaned closer, wordlessly goading her to swing and attack a court lord.

Tira had no idea which one she should try and sort out first, but then Meryl started laughing. She wiped a hand over her face with her other arm still anchored firm around Marinda's waist, and even Milo stopped checking the book to give her a worried look.

"I'm letting go now," she said. "If you batter him with a chair, you'll get into trouble. Think of your books. What would the fans say?"

Marinda scowled. "They'd agree it was warranted."

"Maybe you can write me into a book," Claus crowed. "The dashing hero role would suit me."

Marinda placed the chair down and smiled sweetly, venom swarming from every part of her.

"I have several times already. You die a lot. Painfully. You're not the villain though, they have brains. Ingenuity. No, you're more like the one everyone laughs at and nobody remembers or misses when they're gone."

Tira pressed a hand to her forehead as the headache intensified. She would need to rest through the afternoon and sleep well overnight if she had any hope of avoiding being ill. She'd managed a whole two weeks of being mostly pain-free which was a good stint, especially during her period, but apparently that peace wasn't to last any longer.

Kneading her fingertips into her temple, she prepared herself for Claus's wrath. His face twisted with ire and his hand raised in preparation.

"No." Tira stormed between them. "Not here. Take it outside. You are here as a guest, Marinda, and Claus you may see this as a dump full of old relics, but it's supposed to be your dump so have a bit of respect for our heritage if nothing else. Out, both of you."

Claus turned a look of pure fury on her and she wound her protection warding tighter. She couldn't strengthen it as well when she was sick, but assuming she made it out of the archives alive, she could rest after.

"Tira's right," Meryl said, her tone soothing. "I'm sure you have much more important things to do, Lord, than slum around with us. Marinda, perhaps you need a break if you've been writing so hard you're resorting to violence. The queen wants everyone to group together soon anyway, so we probably need to start putting these books away."

Milo checked the time on his orb and gasped in alarm. "It's way past time, I had no idea. I'll tidy these."

Claus glowered at Tira as Milo started fussing around them. She held the gaze, knowing she should back down, show some sign of subservience or apology. But with Meryl watching, she couldn't stomach the thought of being so meek and subservient.

"Remember who and what you are, Tira," he spat. "I'm the lord of this court for a reason. You're family, but there's nothing to say family have to stay or be kept."

He turned on his heel before Marinda could react, so by the time she sent a feral growl and a pencil flying after him he was already gone.

"I hate him so much," Marinda insisted.

In that moment, Tira knew she did too. But she rubbed her forehead and managed a weary smile at Meryl who stood watching her carefully.

"Families, huh? Sorry you had to see that. I'll help Milo with the books."

Marinda gathered her writing things and set off after Claus.

*Even if she does catch up with him and do something awful, I can't manage that right now.*

The familiar acidic burn was sloshing inside her stomach, a sure sign that she was on the tipping point of overdoing it. She'd have to ask Marlon for a tincture later.

"That's nothing," Meryl said, gathering a couple of the newer looking books. "My sisters and I are close, but our mum and her sisters are awful when they argue. Gift fights over the smallest thing. Dinner, who drives, where we go, who brought who what present eleven years ago, everything."

Milo had disappeared into the stacks already but Tira trusted him to restack the books correctly. She stayed beside Meryl as they moved at a slower pace with an armful of books each and started down the aisles in silence.

She wanted to ask questions, anything to dispel the awkwardness, but wasn't sure what she was okay discussing.

A sparkle caught the light and she noticed a bracelet on Meryl's wrist then, identical to the ones she'd seen Ace and Milo wearing.

"Is that…" She wasn't sure how to ask. "I noticed Milo and Ace wearing those, but I've not seen anything like them here and we usually have a lot of sellers passing through."

Meryl eyed the bracelet then shrugged.

"Demi gave them to us a while back. Someone at the Nether Court makes them I think."

Tira managed a weak smile. "Not magic then. There are so many fables about magic jewellery. We could probably have someone write an entire tome on the histories of magic jewels."

"No, not magic sadly."

The silence swallowed them immediately after and Tira pushed one of the books back in place before hurrying on, acutely aware of the woman having to walk almost arm against arm with her.

"Borders and origins of Faerie." Meryl read one of the

spines she was carrying aloud. "That's a big subject."

Tira nodded, relieved. "We don't know as much as we probably should about the origins. I've done some reading on it, not much but we've had a few old texts come through that needed refurbishing and it's hard to refurbish something without reading it at the same time."

Meryl nodded and held out a couple of books when Tira got rid of the last of hers.

"My sister has a gift where she can read anything once and remember it," Meryl said. "Demi gave it to her. I tend to get distracted and my mind wanders off before I can remember things though."

Tira nodded encouragingly. "I think a lot of people don't retain information unless it interests them. I was the same with lessons."

"I can't imagine lady lessons were much fun, learning when to bow and when to curtsey."

"How to flirt, when to shout and when to simper."

Meryl stared. "Really?"

"Oh yeah. Like card games, apparently where you place your cards or fan can highlight certain assets." She wrinkled her nose at the thought. "The flirting is apparently a huge part of it."

Tira batted her eyelashes violently until Meryl chuckled, the sound sending a warm flush over her skin. Dropping her gaze to the remaining books, she set off again down the aisle.

"It's a lot of manipulation in truth, the way of the Fae, but I'm glad the queen is a bit more genuine about things, or she seems it."

"She is." Meryl nodded. "Here, give me that one."

She stopped Tira from climbing up the unit to reach the top shelf by grabbing it and reaching right over her. Tira stood frozen between her and the bookcase, the subtle scent of something sharp yet sweet folding around her moments before Meryl stepped back.

"Demi has stuff she needs to find and fast," she said. "Any help the Word Court can give us is great."

Tira blinked up at her, bewildered by how flustered she was, her cheeks hot and her insides fluttering in a way that had nothing to do with her normal poorly symptoms.

"We're happy to help. Well, most of us. I am anyway. I hope my stepbrother isn't causing too much trouble though."

Meryl smiled, the sadness still swimming in her eyes. They had no books left. The only way to go was back up to the court, but Tira couldn't get her feet to start moving.

"I'm sure Demi can more than handle anyone who causes her trouble. Not everyone is so invincible though."

The spell broke. Tira nodded and turned toward the exit. Beautiful girl or not, Meryl was clearly mourning someone who meant a lot to her, and Tira would likely never see her again after everyone left with the queen anyway.

"Well, invincible or not, if there's anything I can do without much power behind me, it's up for grabs," she said. "But Milo will probably find it if it's here anyway."

Meryl nodded. "True. Access is appreciated though. If we don't find how to access the prime realm, the Forgotten will likely get there first and then we're all in trouble."

"The Forgotten, are they truly back then?" Tira's

insides chilled at the thought. "I've heard loads of rumours, I've heard about scuffles at other courts, but nothing true."

Meryl nodded. "They are. You know Belladonna Elverhill at all?"

"In passing. She was a friend to my stepbrothers more than me, they were very much in her social group when they were younger. I showed her the appropriate respect but I don't think she ever really liked me much."

"You're probably too honest for her liking."

Tira snorted. "Maybe. But yeah, she's ruthless, heartless and devoid of anything good from what I remember. If she's leading the Blood Court or whatever the rumours are calling it now, I can understand why the queen is worried."

Meryl wiped a hand over her face, the skin paled in the harsh light of the inspection room corridor.

"And up against a short timeframe too considering we're all looking for the same thing. If we don't figure out what these *atan* keys or whatever they're called are-"

She froze in the doorway to the central hall and the stairs, her mouth dropping open.

*She wasn't meant to tell me that*. Tira gasped, but it wasn't Meryl's mistake that had rattled her.

"Did you say *atan* keys?"

Meryl shook her head. Then she grimaced and nodded, twisting back and forth to see if they were alone. She looked so distraught that Tira raised a hand to reassure her, but stopped shy of touching her arm before pulling back.

"I won't tell anyone, don't worry," she promised. "But I know that term. I can't remember where from, but it's in my head somewhere. My mother used to mention it when we walked past her favourite painting actually, but I can't remember why."

She took a step toward the exit, halting in alarm when she noticed the intent clear on Meryl's face.

"I would very much like to see that painting."

# CHAPTER EIGHT
# MERYL

Meryl drew her protection warding tight around her as Tira led them deep into the depths of the archives. The brownstone walls lit by firelight became an endless, chilly labyrinth as they walked side-by-side, but Meryl knew her protection wouldn't be obvious unless Tira tried to touch her. It was as much protection from her own unexpected feelings as for safety.

Not that she had any concerns about Tira doing anything awful to her, but after seeing Lorens talking to Claus like they were great friends, she couldn't trust anyone.

"It's not much further," Tira said. "I'm not sure why you want to see it, but I suppose this is one of those top secret 'don't ask' things far above the likes of me."

Meryl smiled, she couldn't help it. Even when they were marching through her domain, Tira was a strange blend of politely hesitant and unfailingly sarcastic.

"Definitely top secret. I'm sure though if you were to ask Demi, she'd tell you."

Tira turned them down another corridor, this one lined with portraits and clustered with piles of books and scrolls. The court seemed to be lighting their way as they moved but the halls behind them stayed lit as though marking their way back out. A subtle scent of age filled the air, but a quick check of the nearest shelf showed no dust, even the most distant parts of the court still managed and cared for.

"Do you know your way through all the halls here?" she asked.

Tira nodded. "Most. There's a couple of times I've been turned around but I have a sort of map in my head. My mother… she insisted."

"You were meant to take over the court from her," Meryl prompted gently.

"I was originally, but Claus took over when it was clear I wasn't well enough to manage a court."

A shard of bitterness swelled in her voice, but Meryl noticed the dark patches under Tira's eyes and the way she seemed to be struggling to keep pace. Meryl fought the natural instinct to insist they abandon seeing the painting. The tremor of guilt at being so demanding added to all the unshed guilt already roiling around inside her. She couldn't shake that all-encompassing assumption that if she'd been better, stronger, more present, perhaps Petra wouldn't have died.

"Here we are."

Tira stopped in front of an enormous painting covering most of the wall. She pressed her hand to the gold-painted frame and leaned against it with flushed cheeks.

Meryl forced her gaze away from the girl beside her and focused on the oiled canvas.

It showed a dark, vaulted hall of what looked like brown stone. The scene filled the entire canvas but it was the four pillars that dominated, as well as a large forest scene painted at the back of the hall.

"It's a painting within a painting," Tira explained. "This

one was my mother's favourite. The artist apparently painted four identical copies but we only know the whereabouts of this one. Mother used to insist that you always had to look beyond what you could see, what things were. Windows as exits, that sort of thing."

Still encased in her layer of protection, Meryl sensed the thrum of familiar energy calling to her gift. It rippled in waves, tugging at her to play with it. Her gift had gone unused for months now, spiking out in moments of uncontrollable anger. But what use was it if she couldn't use it to save the people she loved? She'd all but rejected it since.

Despite that, it wanted to tell her something now. She frowned, reaching her hand out to touch the bottom of the frame.

"Why did it need so much metal to hang it?" she asked. "I've seen big paintings like this before, we have them all over Arcanium, and it's never this much."

Meryl started feeling around the edge of the frame as Tira wiped a hand over her forehead.

"I don't know. Some of these- hey, what are you doing?!"

Tira reached out as Meryl gave the frame a sturdy pull, but she let out a yelp as her fingers glanced off Meryl's protection warding.

Her eyes widened with something similar to betrayal, and Meryl grimaced to see it, her heart sinking.

"There's a lock mechanism here," she said.

Tira pulled her hands into her chest, a frown now furrowing between her eyebrows.

"Oh."

That was all the response Meryl was going to get and clearly she'd hurt Tira's feelings by having a protection up around her. It was FDP rule number one, something she often forgot way more than she should, but she was finding it hard to focus around Tira, which was dangerous for many reasons.

"I have a metal gift," she explained. "There's a lock here."

"Wait… A lock? Windows as exits…"

Meryl nodded. "Or paintings as secret doorways. I guess I should ask permission to open it?"

Tira shrugged, her face a mask of indifference now that realisation about the painting had faded.

"Would there be any point? I'm sure you could simply call the queen here to override it."

*Ouch.* Meryl grimaced at the sharp tone. *Definitely hurt her feelings.*

Instead of arguing, or succumbing to the scarily desperate urge to apologise, Meryl focused her gift around the mechanism, weakening the metal of the ancient lock so that the hefty catch could pop free.

She hauled on the edge of the frame but it didn't budge until Tira grabbed the bottom to help. The painting swung outward, both of them stumbling back to an awful creaking from the hinges as a waft of stale air swamped them.

"Whoa." Tira's exclamation puffed out as a tiny breath. "This was here all this time."

She peered through the now open gap, wrinkling her nose at the mass of dust and cobwebs decorating the bare stone walls.

"You didn't have any idea?" Meryl asked.

Tira shook her head. "No, mother never said a word, I promise I knew nothing about this."

"It sounds like she was leaving you clues within stories."

Tira sighed. "And I never guessed. What an idiot."

"Hey, don't say that. You wouldn't have known."

Tira shrugged again and stared through the gap into the small square space beyond.

Not empty.

Leaning against the two walls either side of the gap were two enormous paintings. Both featured the same scene as the painting in the hall, the vaulted ceiling, the four pillars and the forest image in the middle as art on the painting's back wall.

"I should get Demi," Meryl said.

Tira nodded. "Yeah, you should. I'll wait outside and shunt the original closed, but nobody we'd need to worry about would venture this far down anyway."

"No need." Meryl pulled her orb out. "Demi? Can you find where I am? We've got something to show you."

She half-expected a weary confirmation that Demi would join them in a minute, but a mere handful of seconds later Demi popped into being beside them.

Tira jumped but Meryl was used to the queen of Faerie randomly appearing wherever she saw fit. Demi smoothed a hand over her hair, curly black strands escaping everywhere and tilted her head in query.

"What's- oh. Oh, brilliant!"

Demi shuffled past them into the secret room and eyed one painting, then the second.

"These look like something Milo found mention of in one of the ancient books upstairs," she said. "You see here, this pillar has a marking on it. And this one has a different marking on a different pillar. I wish I hadn't nagged him about those verb tables for the old language now."

Meryl had noticed the different markings, but before she could explain about the third painting outside, Tira was pointing to the base of each frame.

"There's a painting outside too with the same scene," she explained. "We knew there were four but nobody told me we had two more of them." She frowned and rubbed her forehead. "And look, the titles are different too."

She hunched over with a pained grunt and tapped her fingertip on the brass plaque at the base of the frame.

"This one is 'light', and that one is 'shadow'," Demi murmured. "And the wording is interesting, same as in her diary. Hmm. Show me the one outside?"

Tira led the way but Meryl saw the way she seemed to be using brief touches on the wall to steady herself. Whatever illness had led to Claus taking over the court, it was making an appearance now. Worry gripped her insides, panic beading heat over her face.

"And this one is called 'death' with the same strange wording," Demi said. "Some of the wording of the old language looks familiar too. This is perfect."

Tira nodded. "I would assume the titles are relevant. There's a fourth out there somewhere, but if we're talking light and shadow, then death should probably be accompanied-”

“By life,” Demi finished. “The four no doubt somehow correspond to the symbols on the four pillars too, one in each painting on a different pillar.”

Tira managed a weak smile. “If you need to take them please do. You should probably ask my brother, but if you don’t get time to… well, I can hardly refuse a queen now, can I?”

Demi grinned. “No, probably best not to. I’ll have someone come and get these somehow. Not sure how exactly we’ll move these, translocation maybe, but we’ll figure it out. We may need to remove the one from the wall as well.”

“Of course.” Tira nodded, a shy smile creeping over her face. “I know nobody usually ventures down this far, but I’ll ask Marlon to see if we can’t glamour the gap or move a tapestry from somewhere.”

Together they closed the painting over the hidden room, Demi and Tira holding it firm while Meryl reformed the lock enough to hold.

Meryl settled her gift still zinging inside her bones and eyed the others with a frown. If Tira was needed again Demi would summon her, but she was looking worse with every passing minute, increasingly pale and pained.

Demi gave Tira a pertinent once over before Meryl could think up some excuse to get them back up to the main hub of the court, her gaze narrowing with realisation.

“Right, important you two go and be seen doing whatever you need to be doing,” she commanded. “I’ll wait here and call Taz for back-up.”

Meryl snorted. "He'll be delighted."

Demi chuckled and waved them away. Meryl wanted to offer Tira some help as they started walking back toward the main part of the court, but she didn't want to make the awkwardness still hanging between them any worse. As they kept going in silence though and Tira's face grew paler, the urge got too hard to ignore.

"Are you okay?" Meryl pressed a gentle hand to Tira's shoulder. "Should I call someone?"

Tira flinched and eyed Meryl's hand like it might suck her into another realm or turn her bones to jelly. The memory of how hurt she'd looked when bumping up against the protection warding earlier flickered in Meryl's mind.

Tira shook her head and winced, walking on without waiting.

"I have headaches," she explained. "I just need to rest. I'll have a think about, you know, what I remembered earlier, the word you mentioned, and see if I can remember more, but it won't come while I'm like this I'm afraid."

Meryl's fingers firmed around her shoulder as they reached the archive's main stairs. No need for protection now, she was too worried about having dragged the poor girl into what appeared to be a full-blown migraine.

"No of course not. Come on. Where's your room? Do you need me to get you anything?"

Tira ambled up the stairs before Meryl could suggest they take one of the lifts, so she rushed ahead to open the door to the kitchen hall.

"I'll pick something up from the kitchen," Tira said.

"You can go find your sisters if you want. I know where I'm going."

Meryl frowned. "No, I'll see you back to your room."

Tira raised her eyebrows at that but didn't argue, pushing open the door to the kitchen instead.

Meryl followed her through and the overwhelming waft of something delicious wrapped around her. Cold still wafted in from the wide windows and the open back door, but also the comforting blasts of heat from the fireplaces on the far right-hand wall. She eyed the gigantic cooking pots hung over the fires and the slightest sound of bubbling had her stomach growling in answer. Meryl glanced at Tira, drinking in the way her shoulders lowered with relief and the pinched look lessened around her eyes slightly.

Tira turned to a man bent over a plate on a counter beside one of the vast sinks and her lips lifted.

"Have you finally chased Niko away?" she asked, lifting her voice to be heard.

The man straightened up, his twinkling eyes fixing on both of them as he smoothed his brown moustache.

"Would I be in any state to be eating food if I had?" he countered with a wide smile.

He hesitated, the smile freezing, then his face descended into weary realisation.

"You've overdone it again." He raised a hand as Tira opened her mouth to argue. "Go to bed, I'll bring your tincture with some lunch and a cool cloth, no protests. The rest of the queen's entourage have been taken on a trip to the town. His lordship realm-skipped somewhere else a few minutes ago with no word about when he might return.

If anyone needs anything, I'm prepared."

Tira nodded as he bustled toward her and clicked his fingers with a sharp snap to summon a cup. She accepted it with a muttered thanks when he pressed into her hands but didn't drink any. Meryl looked longingly at the kitchen again as Tira left the room with her head bowed, but all she could do was follow her back through the main hall to the court apartment wing.

"Is your room okay?" Tira asked.

Meryl nodded. "It's lovely. Better than I'm used to. Arcanium accommodates everyone as it needs to but I share with my sisters there, and here I have my own room. Although I did hear Beryl threatening to hang Cheryl out of the window and drop her on her head last night."

Tira smiled but it was a weak effort, her face scrunched with pain. Meryl reached out to help her open the door she stopped in front of, but Tira turned the handle and slipped into the gloom beyond, keeping the door almost closed as she peered through the tiny gap.

"If you could please tell Demi anything I missed," she murmured, keeping her voice low. "I'll try to remember what I can as well."

Meryl nodded. "Rest for now. If anything exciting happens, I'll slip a note under your door."

Tira smiled and this time it reached her eyes.

"I'll hold you to that. Thanks."

She shut the door and Meryl stood staring at it for a while after. Tasks ran through her mind, darting round and round. She should go back down to Demi, but Demi would summon her if needed. She should go and find her sisters, but they were out sledding or in town or whatever the man in the kitchen had said.

No, what she *wanted* to do was knock on Tira's door and ask if she needed company or just someone to sit in silence with her while she rested.

Petra had never needed any taking care of, not by anyone. She liked people and tolerated them in equal measure.

Meryl sighed and stepped away from the door.

*Tira isn't Petra, and Petra is... gone.* She'd forced herself to say it once a day.

Despite Petra not wanting to be tied down in any kind of formal relationship, they'd formed a companionship of understanding instead and Meryl had been content with that. Being the only one was enough, even if it had no spoken promise of forever.

But Tira wasn't Petra. She was her own person with her own problems. Her own charms.

Meryl wiped a hand over her face and set off toward the kitchens. If she was going to do something utterly insane, like start thinking of potential futures, she should try and make friends and the best place for that would be the kitchens.

Retracing her steps, she walked back into the heavenly smelling kitchen and looked around with envy. Arcanium had the canteen and the Braunees who ran it were amazing at cooking, but it was an organised sort of chaos.

Here there were herbs growing near windowsills and pans hanging from arches and that deliciously rich smell from the pots over the fire that made her feel like she'd evaporate if she didn't try some soon.

"Anything I can help you with?"

Meryl turned her head to find the man who'd fussed over Tira bearing down on her. She recognised his expression too; he was someone who made a living being polite and helpful, but he also recognised that she'd recently been in the vicinity of someone he would protect to the bitter end. Until he knew exactly what harm or help she intended toward Tira, he would be watching her.

Oddly nervous, she smiled and folded her arms in pre-emptive defence.

"I'm..." she hesitated then went for the truth. "Honestly? I'm starving and whatever that is over there is stopping me from thinking straight."

The man blinked at her in confusion for a moment, then laughter rang out through the room.

"Oh, help yourself by all means. Tira likes a joke but Niko won't mind, especially not for guests of the queen. I think there are some fresh rolls left over from lunch too. I'm betting any *percats* Tira didn't bother to eat anything?"

He didn't wait for an answer, whooshing off to flick a bowl up from a nearby pile and summoning one of the hanging ladles as he passed it.

Meryl followed him, feeling like a puppy following its mother. There was a definite air of brisk caretaker about him and it was frighteningly easy to succumb to being fussed over.

"She worries herself sick," he grumbled. "She rushes about and worries, then forgets to eat or rest and she wonders why she gets worn down."

Meryl sat obediently on the chair he pointed her to, complete with little table at one end of the room. He brought over a huge bowl of what looked like cured meat in thick red-brown gravy and crispy root vegetables glistening with some kind of salt or herb coating.

"Tuck in," he insisted.

So she did, listening all the while as he explained about Lady Eirenia raising Tira to run the court, and how no matter what he or the others said, Claus managed to wear Tira into abdicating the role to him.

"He sounds like a total pain," Meryl muttered.

"I couldn't possibly comment."

Which said all it needed to for Fae who couldn't lie. Meryl couldn't help wondering whether Tira had wanted the leadership of the court, or merely thought she was supposed to take it.

"Orbs, I've been distracting you," she said. "What about Tira's tincture and things?"

The man stopped fussing around at the counter, a curious little smile playing on his lips.

"I can translocate within the court boundaries to serve as needed, so she already has everything she needs. She'll sleep a while, then I'll find an excuse to go in and make her eat something. It's like a little game that we play, how inventive can I be at forcing her to look after herself."

His rosy cheeks bunched as he smiled. So astonished at how delighted he was in the sneakiness of caring for Tira, Meryl started laughing.

"I bet she sees through every single one."

He nodded. "She does, but someone has to care for her

now her mother's gone. She feels the loss so deeply but pretends to be fine."

Meryl's insides plummeted and she pressed her hands to the table. She hadn't pretended to be fine at all in the last three months. Her sisters had borne the brunt of her silences and her sullen tempers with dogged determination, but Tira had lost someone she'd known and loved all her life.

"Don't try to quantify it."

She flinched as he appeared in front of her to collect her empty bowl.

"Don't try to compare snow with grass," he insisted. "Whoever you've lost, you don't have to match your grief with hers. Those we've lost never leave us as long as we remember them, but we can't stop living either. Waste of time."

All the rage that usually surfaced when someone tried to parent her through her grief seemed to struggle, sputtering to take hold and flare bright. She sagged with her elbows on the table.

"I don't know how to 'be' after it," she admitted.

He shrugged. "You don't try to 'be' anything. You take each moment as it comes. You cry when the tears come, laugh when something makes you smile. You live on. Now, I need to get some errands run or Tira will never agree to rest ever again."

He bustled off but Meryl called after him as he grabbed a ridiculous amount of wicker baskets over one arm.

"I don't know your name."

He reached the kitchen door before looking back with a

soft smile.

"Marlon."

She nodded in recognition. "I'm Meryl."

"Nice to meet you, Meryl. I have a feeling we're going to be very good friends."

He left the kitchen but she sat there a while longer, soaking in the peace and the blissful smells.

Something had punctured a hole in the ballooning grief that had been taking over every part of her. Whether it was worry for Tira or Marlon's attentiveness, she didn't know, but she couldn't even dredge up the usual crunch of guilt at feeling lighter than she had in months.

*Perhaps this is safest, what I needed. It can't happen either way. Tira's still a lady of a noble family even if she's not Lady of the Word Court.*

Hoping for any kind of relationship would be improper and extremely unlikely. But letting herself daydream just a little? Maybe that was taking a first step like Marlon had suggested. And deep down she knew, as she'd always known, that Petra of all people would have been happy for her if she moved on.

# CHAPTER NINE
# REYAN

Reyan sifted through the last pile of papers in her dusty corner of the Fauna Court's woodland cavern, her eyes blurring over the faded text. They had firelight and a dim glow of daylight coming in from the entrance, but she'd found nothing so far that would help them. She wasn't even sure what exactly they were looking for, just that there was an entrance somewhere to the Prime Realm and they were meant to find some kind of keys to get through to it.

She wiped a hand over her face with a ragged sigh. They'd only been at the Fauna Court for one night and already she was dying to leave, and not just because the previous night had consisted of sharing an enormous pile of cushions with Kainen. Despite them having shared a bed on occasions before out of necessity, their unfinished conversation lingered. After going to sleep with half of Faerie's worth of bedding between them and still waking up with her head on his shoulder, she was irritable and about to riot.

"I'm beginning to think we were sent here for nothing," Kainen grumbled.

He stood in the middle pawing through a collection of old paintings, not giving them the care and delicacy they probably needed.

Reyan dropped the sheaf of yellowing papers in her hands with a sigh and moved onto the nearest pile of dusty old books. If they were quick, they could call the job done and return home instead of staying at the Fauna Court for another night.

"This one's weird," Kainen muttered. "It has the old language on it too, look."

Reyan lifted her weary head in time to see him sweep a bit of old fabric aside, coughing against the huge cloud of grit and dust that plumed around him. The painting behind it was the size of a wall, the gold-painted frame chipped and faded.

"You didn't think to check that first?" she asked.

He frowned. "Well, neither did you."

"It was on your side."

"We were taking sides?"

She didn't get a chance to retort as he attempted to haul the huge frame away from the wall, sending other smaller works of art resting against it clattering to the floor. The painting almost reached the roof of the cavern, towering over him. He flinched as it wobbled and Reyan panicked.

"Careful!"

She hurried over to brace her hands against the frame on the opposite side to him.

"Worried about me, sweetheart?" He grinned.

She rolled her eyes. "You don't want to be damaging it. Imagine the cost of restoring something this old."

"Worry about restoring me, I cost less."

"Barely." She hid her smile badly.

"I can't tell if that's a compliment or not. Help me

shuffle it back against the wall."

Together they heaved the painting with tiny little shoves closer to the wall near the entrance. Reyan stared at the scene with a frown.

A large portion in the centre of the canvas was taken up with another painting, vivid lines clearer than the rest depicting a pasture full of golden grass dotted with bright pink flowers. Outside of the scene was a room of brown stone, pillars forming an avenue leading to the painting.

"A step to the beginning." She read the title inscribed on the bottom of the frame, reaching down to run her fingers through the dust. "*Ata- -nanya maladora- Eidyn.* Some of the letters have been worn clean away."

Kainen frowned. "Isn't that what you called your beastie at the Nether Court?"

"*Maladorac*, that's what they called the void in my vision when I faced it. I don't recognise the other words though."

"You said that you saw a woman and a place you didn't recognise as well, and we know the *Maladorac* was ancient."

She nodded. "I have wondered sometimes if I somehow saw the prime realm, but there's no guarantee it was anything to do with that."

Kainen reached into his pocket and pulled out his orb. "Milo."

A moment later, Milo's face popped up. "Hello. Is it urgent?"

"Maybe." Kainen frowned. "We found a painting of a painting and it has wording on it, partially worn off but one of the words is similar to what Reyan found under the Nether Court, and Demi said you're working on deciphering the old language?"

The pearlescent grey vision of Milo's face bobbed a nod. "What is it? And give me the spelling to be safe."

As Kainen spelled the letters out, Reyan peered closer at the painting. She could see figures morphed into the pillars of the wider painting now, each one holding out their hands toward it. A shiver of realisation went through her as she saw the shapes on their palms.

Milo's face disappeared before she could say anything, but she reached out and tugged on Kainen's sleeve.

"Look. See here, that swirl is darker than the others. Could it be representing shadow?"

Kainen squinted with his nose all but pressed against the canvas.

"It could be. And look here, this one is a leaf. And here, a flame- no, a spark of some kind. Ah, and that one looks like a spirit rising from a body. Creepy."

"This might not mean anything though," she reminded him. "It could just be a random painting."

He held one hand against the frame while staring at her, his face shrouded with doubt.

"Might be, but Demi had some reason to think we'd find something here, and how many ancient fables and books have you seen the *Maladorac* mentioned in?"

Reyan eyed the size of the frame doubtfully. "Do you think they'd notice if we took it with us?"

"Who cares?" Kainen grinned. "I'll take it home now and we'll go tell Lord Rydon we're done. Then we can collect it and take it to Demi at the Word Court."

"You're going to steal it? How on earth are you going to get something that big through the nether?"

He blew her a kiss. "Borrow, sweetheart. And I'm technically going to skip and summon it from the power of the court, much less hassle. Wait here a second and don't you dare move a muscle."

Reyan had no time to protest as he vanished, realm-skipping back to their court. Before she even had a chance to brace the frame in case it fell on her, it vanished.

"Don't move a muscle," she muttered to herself. "He's getting awfully demanding."

She shuffled slightly to the left just to be belligerent, and in seconds he was back beside her.

"Come on." He held out his hand. "I know Rydon said not to bother with goodbyes but we might as well play the bigger part. I'm sure he'll be absolutely distraught to see us go."

Reyan rolled her eyes and took his hand. "Be nice. If we're really good, Demi might let us stay home for a few days before everything inevitably kicks off again."

Kainen grinned and set off at a blistering pace through the waning daylight outside. Reyan had to almost jog to keep up with him, wondering if it was the idea of going home that kept him moving. He stormed past their cabin until they found someone on the bridge feeding the fish, the same woman who'd shown them to their cabin earlier.

"Bet she's been told to keep an eye on us when we return," Kainen muttered, pasting on a charming smile. "Hello, we're looking for your lord."

The woman nodded, not looking up. "Lord Rydon is in the far fields right now. If you wait in your cabin, I'll let him know you're looking for him."

Kainen eyed Reyan and she shrugged. A short rest before going home wouldn't hurt, and it would be rude to leave without at least thanking Lord Rydon for putting up with their presence when he clearly didn't want them there. Even if he'd told them not to.

The moment they were back inside the cabin, Reyan sank onto the cushions, but Kainen walked around closing all the windows. Only once he was sure there was no way in other than the door did he sit beside her.

"Well, while we're waiting, we should have that chat," Kainen suggested.

Reyan held in a groan, her insides clenching tight at the thought.

"Go on then."

He raised one eyebrow. "You don't sound too thrilled."

"Well, be fair. This whole thing has always been pretence, we both know it. Even Demi knows it. It was always meant to end sometime."

"Perhaps in the beginning, but the court has claimed you."

"Only because you started this. The courtiers haven't and you know it."

He grabbed her hand, his face descending into an irritable scowl.

"They'll soon learn and if not I'll banish them."

Her heart swelled, emotion clogging her throat. In that moment she knew he meant every word of it too.

"You can't go around banishing everyone who doesn't like the thought of a nobody marrying a lord," she said gently. "It's not even a real engagement."

He nodded. "I can. Being able to banish people is the one good thing about being titled. I know that probably makes me a bad person, but don't I deserve to be happy too? At least, maybe now I do. I don't know. The court recognises you as its lady. If I died right now, you would take over."

"Don't." She shuddered. "Nothing's going to happen to you so that's irrelevant. But Lord Rydon's right, even if you chose me for real and made me lady, you could get bored of me, get rid of me, and I'd have no claim to any of it. I don't have the luxury of being born to it like you do."

He said nothing for a long while, his hand stubbornly fixed around hers and his fingers jittering over her skin. Black smoke flickered around his fingertips and sent a zinging warmth right up her arm. Even though he was what she wanted, she was fighting him when he was offering it, not even sure what she needed to hear from him.

"So, you're rejecting me?" he asked.

She froze. "What do you mean?"

"You're happy to play lady of the court until you have to actually do it, and you're happy to entertain me until I want you for real."

"I don't-"

"I'm sick of pretending. I'm tired of worrying that one day I'll be waiting at home and you just won't come back. You talk about me getting bored of you, but I'm the one that's been waiting patiently for you to wake up and realise."

Pain radiated from his voice, his gaze resolutely fixed on the floor in front of them.

"I have to pretend because it's not real," she said. "How can it be anything else?"

"What was it you said to Rydon before? Nobles and folk, it's a choice. Well, this one is yours."

She pulled her hand away. "No, it's ours. This is the point. It's easy for you to choose because if you change your mind, you don't lose anything. You're still born to be a lord with all the power of a court. If you change your mind, I go back to having nothing. I'm used to that, but stop making it sound like this should be so easy for me. It's not. I have no desire to be 'kept' if I can be discarded as easily."

"I get that, I do." He huffed and raised his eyes to the ceiling before looking back at her, as if sucking in whatever residue of hope he still had. "But you're here arguing with me, you're not saying no. What is it you want? A guarantee? You've got it. I'll swear to it if I have to, anything you want is yours, whether you choose me or not. I promised you that before and it still stands. You'd never have to worry about anything ever again, even if you don't want to be our lady or be mine. So, I'll ask you again, what if I decide I want to keep you?"

"It's not a game, Kainen! I'm not some prize to be won or 'kept'."

"I never said you were." He twisted to face her, his nose bumping hers and his breath wisping over her lips. "If it was a game, I would do whatever it took to win. But as it's not, what is your choice, my lady? I think I've made it very clear I want you. For real. Forever. Not just for the court, but for me. I will give you anything you ask for. So, what is it *you* want?"

She stared back at him, her blood pounding in her ears.

"I…" The words got stuck.

She'd waited so long to hear those words, dreamed of them in every possible scenario and worked out exactly how she'd respond.

Now, nothing.

A flash of hurt wiped over Kainen's face moments before the emotion swirling in his dark eyes shuttered. He dropped her hand and stood up.

"I need… I'll be back in a minute," he muttered.

She opened her mouth to stop him, already fighting against the squishy cushions to get to her feet, but he realm-skipped away and left her in thundering silence and regret. She dug into her pocket with a frantic hand, finding the smooth orb she rarely used.

"Kainen?" She held it up in front of her.

No answer. Before she could shout, demand he answer her, a sharp knock on the door drew her attention. One step away from crying, she folded the orb in her fist. She would get rid of whoever it was and realm-skip home to find him. No doubt he'd gone to sulk in his study until Lord Rydon came to find them.

"Come in," she called out.

Breathing sharply against the burn in her eyes, she watched as the woman from the bridge came in with a tray.

"Tea," she said.

Reyan nodded. She took the cup the woman rather forcefully handed to her with a mumbled thank you.

Kainen would be back for her once he'd finished sulking.

*Won't he?*

"Good for what ails you," the woman insisted.

"Does it ward against an arrogant arse of a court lord?" Reyan asked, aware that right now the one probably in the wrong was her.

"Ah, it'll do that and more. Lord Rydon's on his way back and he's very proud of the produce here."

Not wanting to insult their host any further by rejecting his tea, Reyan sipped the warm liquid. It tasted like honey and something faintly sour like lemons. With a shrug she drained the entire cup and placed it on the tray.

"Thanks. I need to orb someone before Lord Rydon gets here," she added.

The woman clicked her fingers and vanished the tray and tea things before moving toward the door again.

"Oh, you won't need to do that."

Reyan tensed as the woman shut the door and turned to face her. The features that Reyan hadn't even bothered to take notice of shivered. The brown hair lengthened and turned darkly gold, the face narrowing and the body growing taller until a smart grey pantsuit covered the elegant woman in front of her.

Fear raced alongside recognition. Reyan's gut churned as she gathered her weary strength and wound a protection warding tight around her.

"Don't bother calling for Kainen either," Belladonna

said with a sickening grin. "I've warded against any unwelcome intruders. I thought I'd have to wait a lot longer to get you alone, but off he flits just like that. So convenient. Don't worry about fighting me either. That tea has bound your gifts until we see fit to release them."

Reyan tried to dissolve into the shadow, the panic punching through her in waves when a familiar rigidity pierced her muscles, like before when she'd been sworn to Kainen's court and her shadow-merging gift had been bound. She tried to realm-skip home with the gift Demi had given her a while back, or summon some essence of her transmutation power even, but nothing answered.

As she sagged in distress, Belladonna tutted mockingly.

"My sister will be here any moment. We have great plans for your gift, you see."

Reyan stared down at her hands, willing them to become part of the shadows with all her might.

"Oh, you won't be disappearing on me." Belladonna stalked closer. "That little brew I gave you has turned you into nothing more than a *human*."

Reyan ignored the disgust on Belladonna's face as panic raced through her.

Thoughts of calling out for Kainen filled her head but even with her blood pounding in her ears, she couldn't risk bringing him into danger. The shadows strained, trying to get through her skin, to soothe her.

*I can still feel them.* She raised her hand.

Belladonna stumbled as she hit the protection warding, her eyes widening. With her mind screaming that she was on a one-way ticket to an early grave, Reyan forced a haughty sneer over her lips.

"Did you forget that all Fae can still ward themselves, gifts or not?" she asked, risking a disapproving sigh. "Apparently royal bloodlines are so arrogant that they can't remember the basics."

Belladonna arced out a hand against the warding and the slam sent Reyan back against the wall. She gritted her teeth as something solid and sharp pushed into her thigh, but she held the warding as strong as she could.

*She's probably so confident that she's not bothered to lock the door.*

With Belladonna seething at the edge of the warding, Reyan took a couple of shuffling steps to the side.

"I'm sorry to disappoint you, but you missed Kainen," she said.

Belladonna scoffed, tracking each movement Reyan made like an eagle waiting to pounce on a mouse.

"What do I need with a self-absorbed traitor? His time will come, and I'll make it hurt. No, it's you we need. You're coming to the human world with us, won't that be fun?"

Reyan's insides curdled with fear. She kept shuffling, not once daring to look at the door and give Belladonna any idea of what she was aiming for.

"No thanks." She forced her voice to stay strong. "I'm not helping you, going with you or any of that."

She wanted to say Kainen would pull the entire world down to find her, human or otherwise, but after their argument doubt crept its insidious claws into her head as Belladonna laughed.

"Oh, you don't have a choice. But I prefer doing this the hard way, so much more *personal.*"

Reyan inched toward the door, achingly almost within reach. She didn't have much hope that she could outrun Belladonna, but if Lord Rydon was-

*He's probably in on it. If he had Belladonna in his court, he'd report her to Demi straight away if he was loyal.*

But she had to at least give it a shot. Kainen was expecting Lord Rydon to return for them, so he'd have to reappear sometime soon. If she could evade Belladonna until then, escape into the forest maybe, Kainen could skip them both home.

*Unless he's so mad at me, he's not coming back. He took the painting home already.*

The thought that he was too busy currying favour with Demi for previous reasons made her feel sick, but she kept moving toward the door.

"No quippy comebacks?" Belladonna sighed happily. "What a shame."

Reyan reached behind her for the handle. Her fingers brushed it as Belladonna clicked her fingers and a sparking blast shoved Reyan sideways. She crashed onto her side, her mind fixed with frantic intent on her warding.

Lifting her head and scrambling on uneven limbs to stand again, she eyed Belladonna's tiny frown. Even with all of her bountiful power and royal blood, she wasn't getting through Reyan's protection.

"So, the whole thing is real then," Belladonna muttered. "And I thought Kainen was just toying with you for kicks.

No matter. Court lady or nobody, you're coming with me. I can fill the court with a hundred better nobles when I'm queen."

Reyan ignored the Belladonna-specific parts about better nobles and becoming queen, focusing on the one truth she could still cling to.

"Kainen chose me to stand beside him because I actually have a heart, unlike so many of your fancy nobles."

Belladonna snorted. "Who cares? I thought you were his consort, essentially a powerless figurehead, but the court itself has chosen you now, with or without hi- why am I explaining myself to you?"

Reyan froze.

*What? The court itself has claimed me? Everything he said... I thought he was just assuming it, making pretty words to keep me happy.*

Beneath the unrelenting pulse of fear ricocheting through her system, a small ember of pride that she'd been nursing burst into fireworks.

The court had claimed her. Not because of Kainen or by Demi's command, but the court itself, made of the fabric of Faerie and the nether. Even the Fae inside it, like Meri and possibly even some of the courtiers who had quietly embraced the new ways of Faerie, those were her people. Her court.

Straightening up, she levelled her chin and stared Belladonna down. She still had no gifts to fight with but she could protect herself and, thanks to Kainen, she could defend herself well enough in physical combat.

"Faerie recognises me as a court lady over you as an outcast princess then," she said. "You can't pierce my warding and I can't attack you without gifts. But I will get them back. I will get more. I will do whatever it takes to defend my court from scum like you."

Belladonna's eyes sparked with delight and Reyan let her hand drift slowly across a side table to grab something to defend herself with.

"Brilliant. Breaking you will be so much fun. I've been desperate for it since Petra was taken from me before I could really get going."

Memories roared, visions filling her mind of Petra half-dead at Belladonna's hand, then entirely dead while those who loved her were stuck in mourning, filled with rage they couldn't exorcise.

Reyan grabbed a sturdy metal bowl and took aim. The bowl sailed through the air and struck Belladonna on the chest. She stumbled back several paces, arms and legs flailing until she tumbled into the mound of cushions in the centre of the room. She rose like an irate monster from a pillow swamp and the air crackled with fury.

Tensing, Reyan made a bid for the door.

"I wouldn't."

A soft click brought Reyan's feet to a halt, her hand welded to the door handle. She looked over her shoulder at the crossbow Belladonna had levelled at her.

"I'm a great shot and this is a *metirin* iron arrow. Even if I don't hit you, your protection will be gone, and you're no use to me dead."

Reyan inhaled a sharp breath. The warmth of the Fauna

Court outside and the soft sounds of nature were entirely at odds with the situation she was in, but she left the door open as she turned around.

"Why me then?" she demanded.

*If I'm going down, maybe I can get some information this way first.* She couldn't stop her limbs shaking but she could be brave for her court. And for Kainen. *At least he's safe somewhere else.*

She folded her arms, letting the muscular tension feed into her warding, holding her strong.

"That's my business," Belladonna said.

"Mine too considering it involves me, probably leading me to my death knowing you."

"We'll see. Your family line is old, I know that much. The Illusion Court has claimed you. We'll see how long your uses hold."

Reyan couldn't choke back the incredulous laughter.

"Are you bargaining with me?"

Belladonna sniffed. "I don't bargain. I'm giving you a chance to be useful to me. If you prove your uses go beyond the immediate then who knows. You're not entirely dim, so you'll know that you have your court and its members to consider. Every single crushable one of them."

So absorbed in her own grandeur, Belladonna didn't notice nor sense the shadows taking form behind her. Reyan's heart cried out but she kept the words in her mind, forcing her lips to quiver instead, to pretend she was thinking over Belladonna's warning.

*Shall I eat her?* Betty hissed softly. *I might not be able to manage it before she kills us, but I could definitely take a large bite.*

Relief burbled into hysteria and Reyan fought the urge to grin. She didn't want to risk Betty getting hurt if she took her solid form, but she could play along with Belladonna for the sake of her court. For now.

*No, go to Kainen. Find him and tell him that Belladonna has taken me. She's contained my gifts too. I'm not sure where they're taking me-*

Betty dissipated into shadow the second the air shivered, as though she'd sensed someone realm-skipping and knew to keep herself hidden. Blossom materialised in the centre of the room and eyed Reyan with something akin to disgust flitting over her face. Then she fixed a hopeful smile for Belladonna.

"Everyone's assembled at the meeting point. Are we going straight to the human world and the prime realm now?"

Belladonna froze for a single moment before glancing at her, but it was enough to make Blossom flinch away until Belladonna's eyes narrowed.

"Yes. She's your responsibility until she's needed." She nodded in Reyan's direction. "If she fights or tries to run, shoot her in the arm, or the leg."

Blossom took the crossbow tossed her way and muttered something until it vanished. Reyan held her warding around her.

"I have no intention of getting spiked by a *metirin* arrow," she said. "If you want to avoid attention, I'll keep my warding going."

Belladonna laughed. "If you want to pretend you have any power, why not. You have no gifts left and we can decimate your court any time we choose. I can appreciate the nobility of wanting your dignity though. Something so many have forgotten."

She flicked a disparaging glance Blossom's way but Reyan couldn't bring herself to feel sorry for her new captor.

Betty would go to Kainen for her, and he had the painting. She had to hope he'd taken it to Demi and they would know the time to strike was now.

"After you then," Blossom spat.

Reyan glanced to the door. "Parading through the Fauna Court? At least that marks their loyalties for all to see I suppose. Anywhere in particular, or are we going to do a couple of laps first?"

Blossom scowled, her large eyes barely shrinking beneath her lined brow, but Belladonna laughed.

"To their main hall. We will realm-skip to a point where we can enter the human world. Perhaps there will be some fun to chase on the way through."

Reyan didn't want to even consider what Belladonna might consider fun when it came to humans, but she refused to dignify that with a reaction.

She strode out of the hut and toward the main swell of the Fauna Court, almost daring the others to fall behind.

*Belladonna has a grudging respect for arrogance, or it keeps her interest at least. If I can keep her from killing me, I might just make it.*

The thought didn't give her any relief but she powered

on past the furtive glances from people they passed until she spied Lord Rydon up ahead. His face betrayed no emotion, but she realised that she was apparently Lady of the Illusion Court by right now, which made her equal to him in status and better than him by miles in loyalty to the queen.

Belladonna stalked into the main hall, hollering to a cluster of Fae gathered in the centre. Reyan gave Lord Rydon her best dismissive look as he approached, keeping a fair distance with Blossom beside them.

"I did warn you that it was better to be folk than noble," he said.

Reyan nodded. "You did but I have my court to consider. It claimed me by my own right apparently. At least I'm not selling it out, or myself, to a bunch of traitors."

Blossom hissed under her breath but Reyan didn't catch the words.

"I have my own court to consider," Lord Rydon muttered. Then, "Lady."

A tiny concession of sorts, one she would treasure for her own pride because beyond that it didn't give her anything useful. Even Cerys, Lord Rydon's daughter, gave her a subtle nod of recognition.

"You might be protecting your court now," she said, keeping her tone conversational. "But eventually the evil will come for them all and there will be no choices then. It's only a matter of time."

Thoughts of Betty flitting through the shadow to find Kainen kept her strong, but she had no idea if Betty could even communicate with him. His gifts were of smoke and darkness, but he'd never shown any sign of understanding Betty's hissing before.

Her heart sank as Belladonna beckoned to her and Blossom.

Much like Lord Rydon had made a choice for the benefit of his court out of fear of the Forgotten, she'd refused to make a choice about Kainen because of fear too. Fear that he'd get bored of her, or that she'd be the one to end up hurt and unwanted.

But the court had claimed her on its own, and how Kainen felt had never had anything to do with the court at all. She stepped up beside Belladonna, realising she would have to reach through her protection to realm-skip with them. As everyone joined hands, she forced herself to reach through her warding and take the equally unwilling grip of Blossom's fingers.

As the nether leapt up around them, she sent every essence of her being into her ability to mind-speak through the link she had with him.

*I'm sorry. If you get this, I accept your offer. You, the court, all of it. I'm yours.*

# CHAPTER TEN
# TIRA

Tira opened her eyes to the familiar sight of the canopy above her bed, the drapes in the deep blue piped with silver that formed the Word Court colours. Mornings that involved waking up pain free were a blessing, but it seemed one of her migraine attacks had been narrowly averted this time.

A knocking sounded at her door, gentle but insistent.

"I'm awake," she called out.

Given the light streaming in through the windows already, she'd slept late, but Marlon usually left her to rest as long as he could before finding some excuse to come in and fuss over her. She sat up as the door swung open to reveal not the bustling middle-aged man she was expecting, but a young woman with blue hair and a hesitant expression.

Tira stared at Meryl for countless seconds before Meryl's eyes widened at the absolute chaos of the room.

"It's not usually-" She couldn't finish that without lying. "I've been meaning to- I should-"

Meryl chuckled, still in the doorway with both hands wrapped around a big mug.

"Don't worry, Beryl's side of our room at home is worse, and at least this is what looks like art stuff and not piles of underpants and leftover mugs growing civilisations.”

She peered at one of the nearest piles doubtfully while Tira frantically scanned the perimeter for anything salvageable.

“Marlon asked me to bring this up for you,” Meryl added, holding up a mug as evidence.

“He did? Why? Has something happened?”

“Not that I know of, but I went to the kitchen to see how you were this morning and he asked me to bring it in, so here I am. Is anything going to jump out at me if I bring it over?”

Her tone was light enough that Tira knew she was teasing, but she covered her face with her hands and groaned as Meryl approached.

She took the mug of *Beast Lite*, the perfect brew to settle her still slightly uneasy stomach, and gulped it down with her cheeks still burning.

“I’m mortified,” she mumbled afterwards. “But I am feeling okay this morning. I tried to wrack my brains over the thing we discussed yesterday too, the *atan* part, but nothing’s surfacing yet.”

“That’s okay. I shouldn’t have said anything in the first place to trigger it to be fair, but I guess it’s good I did. Demi’s had the paintings moved and nobody’s told anyone anything so the secret is safe.”

Tira shrugged. “As long as it helps. I can’t even remember where I’ve heard *atan* before or think of any texts with it mentioned. Sad thing is, with a hearing gift it might have even been a snatch of conversation that I wasn’t meant to hear and I’ll never get the information back."

She tensed as Meryl sat on the edge of her bed.

"You have a hearing gift?"

"Yeah, it comes in handy now and then but I try not to listen on purpose. Not to anything that might be private anyway. Everyone here knows not to whisper secrets around me, although I wouldn't tell unless someone was in danger or something. But they tend to give me a wide berth with the whispers all the same."

Meryl chuckled. "Sometimes I'd be glad of something like that."

"Do you have any? Gifts I mean? I'm guessing you must do being an FDP, and you managed to open the painting yesterday."

"Yeah, although mine's elemental. I can wield metal."

Tira blinked, her mind rushing through the potential possibilities. "Wow that sounds brilliant. So you can bend spoons and warp locks and things."

"I can now but it was hard to learn. I kind of struggled a lot with it growing up, I didn't seem to 'get it' as quick as everyone else did." Meryl's face shadowed, her gaze drifting down to her hands in her lap. "It was only when I found someone to help me I started understanding how I could make it work."

"Is it someone special?" Tira asked, keeping her voice soft.

Meryl nodded, her eyes misting over. "She was. I think her mother came from your court actually, or lived here when she was young. Then they moved to the Flora Court, until she came to Arcanium. Until…"

Realisation dawned and the words frothed out before Tira could stop herself.

"Oh orbs, you're talking about Petra, aren't you? I didn't know her well, only in passing when her mother visited, but she was really nice. I'm so sorry."

Meryl wiped a hand over her face, her breath tumbling out in a ragged sigh.

"We were good friends, really close. She was the one person who seemed to understand somehow." She hesitated, inhaling sharply before the words tumbled out in a long rush. "Funny how you go through most of your life without someone then one day they're there and it's like they always have been. Then they're gone and you can't go back to not expecting to see them or talk to them. It's like being in a haze of rage, you feel bad for laughing or smiling or-"

"Or living when they don't get to anymore."

Meryl nodded. "Exactly. Rationality tends to take a long jump off a cliff somehow."

"We have a lot of cliffs here, and when the debates get raging not much rationality either. You'd fit in fine."

Meryl huffed a laugh and wiped at her eyes. Tira bit her lip, pity and reminiscence swooping through her chest.

"Sorry, I didn't mean to upset you," she said. "I just kind of know how it feels after my mother died, in a way at least. But I'm glad you came up here if it helps to talk, even if you did have to see my disaster of a room to do it."

Meryl managed a tiny smile. "I was also meant to tell you that Demi wants a word with you. No rush, nothing urgent. If you want to shower or whatever first that's fine."

"Are you hinting I smell?" Tira raised her eyebrows, tilting her head to have what she hoped was a discreet sniff as Meryl stood up.

"Definitely not, just reassuring. Milo's in the archives already but I think Demi's avoiding him because he keeps muttering 'paperwork' under his breath, so I'd try her rooms first."

Tira grinned at the thought, pleased when Meryl gave her another smile before weaving her way to the door. She didn't turn back to say goodbye or anything, but Tira sat staring at the door for a few minutes after it closed behind her.

*She and Petra definitely had something 'other' I reckon.* She swung her legs out of bed and grabbed a towel from the nearby cupboard. *Shame because she's so pretty and seems really nice, but perhaps we can at least be friends.*

The thought revolved around her head while she washed and ferreted through her wardrobe for fresh clothes. Dark green jeans and a button down black shirt would be a better fit for entertaining royalty while still looking casually smart than the dusty combats and holey t-shirt she'd been wearing when they arrived. Scraping her hair back and twisting it into a bun, she walked through the corridors toward the reception hall. She might be summoned by the queen, but Meryl had insisted it wasn't urgent and her stomach was being summoned by the kitchens.

A few clusters of people occupied the reception hall which wasn't unusual, meeting to discuss plans or exchange ideas. Tira slowed her pace as she walked through them with a frown.

She recognised some of them as regular court members, people who nodded or smiled at her as she passed. But she recognised some others too sequestered in the furthest corner. Most she could remember by name, and she knew that they hadn't been at court for a while now. Either her mother had asked them to leave, or their loyalties had not been with the queens when the Forgotten fell and they had to leave society in disgrace.

Several of them glanced her way, but there were no nods or signs of greeting this time, and all the smiles were mocking.

*They shouldn't be here.*

She wondered if she had enough about her to move them on or at least demand to know what they were doing there. She almost let out a sigh of relief when her brother appeared, marching through the hall with a determined stride. But he was smiling back at them, stopping in front of them and greeting them like old friends.

*Because they are old friends of his. And clearly still friends despite their beliefs and allegiances siding against the queens. I have to tell Demi this. They can't be trusted so something bad is definitely going on.*

Worry filled her head, a dizzying urge to run and panic squeezing the air out of her. Forcing herself to keep walking, to pretend she wasn't unnerved at seeing them, she made it to the inner hall and hurried along to the kitchens.

Swinging the door open, she tumbled inside hoping Niko would feed her fast. Then Marlon might be able to tell her where to find the queen without walking through the main hall again.

She blinked in surprise when a pair of bright blue eyes stared back at her.

"Oh, there you are." Demi stood frozen by the counter with a pastry halfway to her lips. "Your cook said I could."

Tira nodded and closed the door behind her.

"There are people outside," she said, looking around and lowering her voice. "People who shouldn't be here. Old friends of my brother's that have been 'forgotten', if you get my meaning."

Demi finished off the pastry and brushed her hands on her jeans.

"Good to know, thanks. Is there anyone here you truly trust?"

"Marlon, definitely. He's been here longer than I have and he was devoted to my mother and me. Not too keen on my brother though."

She glanced around again, convinced someone was going to come railing at her for speaking ill of their lord, even though most of the regulars at court couldn't stand him.

"I've cast a blanket warding so nobody will be able to hear us, don't worry," Demi said. "I wasn't sure if I was going mad but people seem to be watching me more than usual here, and that's saying something these days. There were a couple of people in odd places too, like my room."

Tira froze. "People have been in your room? Who?"

"Could have just been cleaning staff." Demi shrugged. "But stuff's definitely been moved in random places. Can you make sure that Marlon is the only one officially allowed to 'serve' me so I can filter out who is in there that shouldn't be?"

Tira grimaced. "I will definitely tell him that, but you should probably make that request to the lord of the court."

"Of course." Demi laughed. "I will do for the look of it, but I want someone *you* trust, even if I have to ask him for it for appearances. I get the feeling that allegiances are shifting, which means we're running out of time."

Tira nodded, warring between being honest which might drop Meryl in it and saying nothing to keep the peace. She didn't have any actual information on the whole *atan* keys thing, but if Demi knew that she knew, she might tell her more that could jog something else.

"Oh, I almost forgot to give you one of these," Demi added.

She reached into her pocket and pulled out a small, glimmering circle of colour and silver.

Tira stared at the bracelet hanging from Demi's fingers, identical to the ones she'd seen Ace, Milo and Meryl wearing. Now that she looked, she could see the hint of one lurking underneath the cuff of Demi's sleeve.

"Thank you." She took it and pushed it onto her wrist.

Demi smiled. "If you wear it, we'll know you're you. No telling anyone else mind."

Tira nodded, about to promise she would never tell and also never take it off, but a noise reached her before she could.

She tensed as something clattered nearby, a subtle echo that sounded like claws on tile. She eyed the ground nearby but couldn't see any movement. The frost cats sometimes came to the kitchen door to beg scraps if they were desperate but that wasn't often, and they never ventured inside.

Shaking her head at her skittishness, she focused on the issue waiting for them outside in the main hall.

"What do we do about my brother's new friends?" she asked. "Or not new exactly, but they've returned. It might impact on what you're looking for if they start hanging around the archives."

Demi plucked another pastry from the tray and twiddled it between her fingers.

"We don't do anything, not yet. Let them think they have the upper hand. Meryl mentioned she let something slip to you last night."

"She did, something about *atan* keys. The word is familiar but I can't remember where from. I've been trying, but my mother filled my head with so many stories that held lessons and opportunities for debate I've tangled most of them now."

Demi chuckled. "That's okay. You've already given us way more than we had before. The paintings have given us a huge step forward."

"Well, that's something." Tira hesitated.

She wanted to ask more but she didn't feel like she could demand answers of a queen, even one so apparently casual as Demi.

"Have you heard of the Wachala?" Demi asked.

Tira nodded. "Most Fae have I guess in younger years. It's more a scare story to get kids to behave. Does that one have some specific meaning too then?"

"Um, not exactly. I accidentally sent Reyan to meet her without realising who she was."

Tira's jaw dropped. "She's *real*?"

"Very real according to Reyan. She mentioned about stories and images, and also hinted we might find what we need here. Then we find the paintings."

"Wow. I thought she was a myth to be honest."

Demi groaned. "I didn't even know of her until after I sent Reyan in. You have no idea how irate Kainen was."

"I can imagine." Tira shuddered. "He was always polite enough to me, but I know he used to run in a very elite crowd at one time. Where do we start looking for the fourth painting though? I don't know if we can expect Meryl to check every single painting in our archives for hidey-holes."

"No, probably not." Demi grabbed a pastry from the counter and inspected it. "Lord Rydon of the Fauna Court admitted he has a lot of old junk left over from a previous war long ago, and that some of them were paintings or old accounts, so I've sent Reyan there to check."

Swiping a stray strand of hair back from her face, Tira tried to shove her hands in her pockets but the jeans were too fashionable and stiff to be functional. The surreal realisation that she was in the kitchen of her court chatting with a queen like they were friends made her smile.

Before she could think of some way to keep the conversation going, she heard the strange clacking noise again.

"Did you hear that?" she asked. "I swear there's this

skittering claw noise. Last thing I need is creatures getting into the archives."

Demi grinned and dropped a bit of pastry on the floor. The scrabbling noise grew louder until the floor shivered and the outline of a creature materialised, the body turning a dark, mossy green. The lizard was the size of a small cat but Demi wasted no time in stooping down and scooping it up.

"Sorry, this is Leo." She manhandled the lizard over her shoulder. "He tends to travel with me, even when I tell him not to. But he won't hurt your books. Milo even allows him in the library back home, and that's after he banned some of the Fae for being too noisy or too messy or too disrespectful to the books."

Tira snickered. If Milo trusted the lizard around his archives, then she would take that as a more than trustworthy reference. As Demi rubbed under Leo's chin and he started making soft grumbling noises, Tira inched forward.

"Is he friendly?" she asked.

Demi nodded and manhandled him down from her shoulder. He slumped over her arms with an unimpressed huff, but mashed his gums when Tira risked stroking the top of his head with a finger.

"I think Ace secretly reads to him when nobody's looking because he's got a bigger ego than Otto the otter," Demi joked.

Tira grinned. "Marinda would be horrified to hear that. Be careful or Leo will be her next inspiration."

"He'd love that. Although he's enough of a celebrity as

Arcanium's unofficial mascot as it is. I'm still wondering where Marinda gets all her ideas from, and I never see any of the twists coming."

Tira laughed and nabbed some of the premium lettuce from the windowsill. Leo chomped on it happily and a moment later he was crawling up her arm.

"She gets a lot of it from people watching and from old legends," she admitted. "Otto was actually inspired by the myth of a fire-otter spirit that could travel through the flames. It's old literature based on ancient artwork, but once she started writing the story she needed to change Otto's power to time-travelling for the sake of the plot."

"There's definitely a lot that legends can teach us," Demi agreed.

"My mother used to tell me many of them, and Marinda would listen and weave them into her stories."

Demi smiled at the subtle dip of sadness in her tone. Given the tales and rumours from the war, Demi had lost people too, Petra being one of them. She looked like she understood exactly what Tira was feeling.

"I haven't heard much of your mother," she prompted gently.

Tira sighed. "She could out-argue anyone. It wasn't even her ability to debate, just something about her manner. She never argued outright, never shouted. But she could sway legions with a few choice words and a smile. She was the one who told me that words had their merit but true meaning was best conveyed through art."

"You're an artist?"

"A bit." Tira thought of the paintbrushes she hadn't

touched since her mother's death. "She always said that words are overt but art can hide any number of things in plain sig-"

She froze as a memory crept to the front of her mind. Demi didn't rush her, but given the subtle narrowing of her eyes, she'd noticed the change in Tira's expression.

"My mother used to show me ancient paintings and make me tell them as stories to practice my oration." She grimaced at the memory. "She said stories don't count as lies if told right. But I remember now, one of the books had a painting in it that mentioned *atan* keys. She had me tell a story about…" she trailed off.

"About entry to another realm?" Demi urged, her tone tense.

She nodded. "I made up some nonsense at the time, but she insisted the keys weren't made of iron. They had to be elemental."

Demi's fingers fidgeted at her sides as she bit her lip, her eyes darting back and forth.

"Elemental, like earth, wind, fire?"

Tira grimaced. "I'm so sorry, I can't remember. I know she said the painting in the book was old though if that helps. I only remember the *atan* keys bit because of the inscription on the bottom and her telling me *atan* was the word for 'essence' in the old language."

Demi took a sudden step toward her and she flinched in alarm, almost dislodging Leo. He gave her a warning grumble but she still had half a handful of lettuce in front of his face so he let it slide.

"This might be what we needed," Demi insisted. "Is

there anything else you can remember? Anything at all."

Tira frowned, the rest of her memory playing dodge with her.

"Not much. My mother used to sing songs as well in the old language. I never understood any of them but she said it was important someone remember them. Ooh, there was one about the origins of our gifts and that had *atan* in it, but of course it was all in the old language."

Demi stood alert, eyes bright and her body almost vibrating with tension.

"Can you remember them?" she asked.

"Some maybe, but I don't know what they mean. I could write the words down though, phonetically at least?"

"Yeah, definitely. Not a word of this to anyone, I mean it. Not unless it's me or mine. Taz, Ace, Milo or the Eastwicks are fine."

Tira nodded. "Of course, I won't say a word. I'll go down to the archives now and get started. Do you have someone who can translate them then?"

"Milo's been working on it. I need to organise some things, come on."

Tira set off toward the door before realising Leo seemed determined to stay with her.

"Um, I don't mind him tagging along if he's going to be respectful to the archives," she hesitated. "He won't poop while he's on me or anything, will he?"

Demi shook her head. "No, he's very well behaved. He'll desert us the moment he sees Ace though because Ace spoils him almost as much as Taz does, and I think he's down in the archives with Milo. I can take him if you want?"

Tira hurried back to the windowsill and grabbed another handful of lettuce.

"If he wants to stay with me I don't mind. I'll take him down to Ace."

Demi opened the door to the hall and Tira walked through it, right into someone's waiting chest.

"Oof, be caref- oh." She stared at Marlon who was staring at Leo in horror. "Sorry, we're off to the archives but I have promises that he's extremely well behaved."

Marlon blinked. "I- right. If you say so. But the lord is demanding you go and see him. He's in his rooms."

"Oh, orbs."

Demi smiled and lifted Leo off Tira's shoulder. "I'll go see Milo, don't worry. You can join once you're done with your brother."

Unable to ignore a summons from him, especially when Demi wasn't overriding it, Tira sagged in defeat.

"Okay, hopefully won't be too long. Thanks, Marlon."

She handed the remaining lettuce to Demi and set off toward the main hall. The groups had all vanished and she walked through the silence with foreboding swirling in her gut.

Claus summoning her wasn't a good thing. He would be angry at her after the altercation with Marinda and her part in defusing it, but she'd forgotten about that what with her headache. She could handle his shouting and the incessant put-downs he flung her way, along with the half-hearted attempts to pretend he was doing what was best for her. But it wasted her time. She'd given up the title so he had what he wanted. Yet still he treated her no better.

Steeling herself as she walked along the corridor that led to his suite of rooms, she brushed her fingertips along the smooth wall of stone. The suite should have been hers, even though she loved her childhood bedroom that she still had now.

At least he hadn't bothered to make any decoration changes. The silver and blue curtains were still framing the wide windows on the right wall looking out over the snowy mountains, and the paintings of ancient and recent family hung as they should.

Tira stopped beside her mother's portrait hanging only a few metres from Claus' door. There was space for more lords and ladies to be hung on the wall, but each time a new one was titled, the other portraits got shunted a bit closer together to make everything even. Claus hadn't made any arrangements to have a portrait of himself painted yet, and Tira noted with grim satisfaction that none of the staff seemed in a hurry to sort it for him either.

She checked the flowers she'd left beneath her mother's portrait three days ago, delaying the inevitable, but they still had water.

A subtle hum of mumbling came from Claus' room. Tira glanced at the door and wondered if she should eavesdrop. Family loyalty over allegiance to royalty wasn't something she'd had to face until now.

She pulled her Fae connection strong around her and pushed her doubts down deep, sending her hearing gift out toward the door.

"...in place but it's not going to be enough," her brother

hissed.

"Don't be dramatic." A strident female voice answered him. "We have everything we need so join us at the prime point. Tell no-one and leave your group there to take care of the queen. We can't risk her following us. They might not be strong enough to take her out, but she's soft enough to stay and protect people. Do you have any idea what she knows exactly?"

Tira's blood ran cold. She recognised that voice, had heard it often as a child. Without seeing who was on the other side she couldn't be entirely certain, but she would have put money on it being Belladonna Elverhill.

"She's only been here two days and is chumming up to my brat of a sister. She barely entertains me."

Tira ignored the brat comment, focusing instead on the whine in his tone. Fury born from shame filled her insides, her skin burning hot as she realised yet again how much of a catastrophic mistake she'd made in giving up the court to him.

*I need to warn Demi.*

"Who cares?" Belladonna scoffed. "If all goes as planned, she won't be queen much longer. Meet at the prime point and remember, realm-skipping in won't work. You'll have to take the *human* route."

Disgust filled her tone and Tira waited for her brother to continue griping. He was surprisingly good at it when he didn't have to pretend to be charming.

"I have things to do also."

Tira froze when she heard Lorens speaking, but the absence of any female retort suggested Belladonna was gone. She couldn't imagine Belladonna taking the risk of realm-skipping into the actual court with Demi in residence; more likely she'd been talking to them through the orb-waves.

"Are you going to meet with her?" Claus asked.

Lorens scoffed. "I will eventually, but let her run around a while having her fun. She needs to wear herself out trying to enter the prime realm."

"But… if you have a contact on the other side already, surely-"

"Loth is secretive," Lorens snapped. "He is also not to be trusted, but his power in the prime realm is useful."

A moment of silence dropped and Tira strained her hearing gift despite the loud echo of her blood pounding in her ears.

"So you do know what these keys are everyone's been searching for?"

Lorens sighed. "If I knew how to get in, I would be there already. Still, Belladonna is convinced she knows where to go so let her try. That way any casualties will be her doing. Once the way through is obvious, I will be the first. But not a word of that to her, understand?"

"Of course not. Bella has her uses as you say, but she's far too torture-happy for negotiations, something we'll no doubt need to do in order to get access to the *metirin* iron."

Another silence swelled and Tira leaned closer to the door. Any moment now, she would have to retreat.

"How much has she told you?" Lorens asked, his tone dangerously intrigued.

"Not much, but that would be an astute guess for anyone

to make," Claus said.

Tira noted the bite in his voice, the panic there which told her that Lorens was the one in control, the one to be feared.

"Well, I'll leave you to your guesses, Lord. Don't underestimate the queen either, she may be fairy but she's smart. She'll be close behind."

Tira took a step back, knowing she had to go to Demi. Claus might punish her somehow for not seeing him immediately, and he'd definitely take his anger out on her if he found her betraying him, but she couldn't risk giving the enemy any kind of advantage by keeping quiet.

She took a step back, halfway through turning as the door swung open.

Claus strode out but stopped dead when he saw her. Fear leapt into her chest, her pulse thundering as understanding dawned in his eyes and he advanced toward her, his face filling with malice.

"How much of that did you hear?"

# CHAPTER ELEVEN
# MERYL

Meryl wasn't sure if she should trust the tiny strain of optimism she'd woken up with. Her room at the Word Court was the epitome of comfort and she wondered if anyone would care too much if she simply refused to leave. Then Beryl was banging on the door loud enough to disturb the entire court, and that made her mind up. But nobody said anything about her excusing herself to go to the kitchens to see the frost cats, so she escaped.

On finding Marlon, she asked about Tira and suddenly he was utterly a-flap with so much to do, she ended up agreeing to take Tira's morning tea to her.

The chaotic mess of Tira's room had been a huge amusement, so much that she was still smiling a little as she walked through the main hall afterwards.

"Meryl!"

She didn't recognise the male voice, but turned to find a familiar face approaching. Her insides squeezed tight and a wash of freezing anxiety cascaded over her. She'd prepared herself before coming that she might run into some of Petra's family here, but seeing the youngest brother was like seeing a ghost. His dark hair had the same messiness as Petra's, and his wide brown eyes looked identical.

Meryl clenched her fist and shrank into her sweatshirt. "Hi, Niko."

He smiled, the hesitation on his face mirroring hers.

"I thought I'd say hi. I know you and your sisters are here with the queen, but Hutch and Harvey have already stopped by to see how things are."

His rambling unknotted the tension in her shoulders slightly. Petra never rambled.

"I didn't know you were here," she said. "I mean I did, kind of, but…"

He chuckled. "I'm the chef here, or one of them. Lady Tira's doing, Faerie gift her."

Meryl gawped at him. She'd heard Marlon and Tira mention a Niko around the kitchens before, but never put the two together. Niko was only a year or so older than she was, but no doubt he'd been in training for a while if he was a chef already.

She forced a smile. "Tira does seem to be very dedicated to the court."

"Oh, she is. She doesn't miss a thing either. Our main chef is still here but she's not as spry as she used to be. Lady Tira comes into the kitchen a lot and she noticed how much I do, so she insisted I get promoted."

Meryl could well imagine that, Tira storming up to her mother and insisting Niko be recognised appropriately.

"Good job too," she admitted. "The food is amazing."

"Thanks, although if you think it's good already, wait until after dinner. I'm trying some new biscuits and they're something else entirely."

She nodded and his easy smile faltered.

"It's still difficult, isn't it?" he asked.

Meryl grimaced. It took a second to answer, the swoop

of grief so comfortingly familiar it was almost frightening.

"I've been struggling." She hesitated. "I can't balance the guilt of feeling sad with knowing I shouldn't be moping around. Or I laugh then I feel awful because it's not been long at all."

He nodded, one hand rubbing the back of his neck.

"I know. I feel awful carrying on like nothing's happened. She mentioned you a lot, you know."

Meryl wiped a hand over her face, not sure if knowing that made her feel better or worse.

"She talked about you as well," she said.

He smiled. "Offensively I bet. We loved her but we drove her mad. Not me so much, but the others were all older and they thought she needed protecting."

*She never needed protecting, but in the end it didn't matter.*

Niko's hand landed on her arm as her eyes burned. She flinched.

"She was the strongest, most savage fighter I've ever seen," he insisted. "Nobody could have saved her if she couldn't even do it. Don't blame yourself. Blame them."

The darkening rumble in his tone at the end echoed to something equally vengeful in Meryl's heart. She nodded. Petra wouldn't have wanted them to risk themselves for revenge, but justice? She'd always insisted on fighting for that. Easier to fight the battle on her behalf than crumble under the weight of the grief.

Niko patted her arm and stepped back.

"Come on, dry up. She'd be the first person to shout about how we're 'wasting time mourning over a pile of bones'."

Meryl couldn't stop the surprised snort of laughter as he mimicked Petra's voice so badly.

"That sounds like her," she admitted. "Were she and Tira ever friends?"

The question escaped before she could think it through. Niko frowned.

"They were nice enough to each other, but we were only here at the Word Court until she was eight, then mother moved everyone else to the Flora Court. Even back then Tira was often off at her lady lessons. Why?"

Meryl shrugged. "Just wondering."

"Oh. She's a good person if that's what you need to know. I guess the queen is poking about for all sorts of information, but Lady Tira is one of the best Fae around. I can't count the amount of black eyes and bloody noses we got from her stepbrothers when we stood up for her."

Meryl froze. "What?"

"Yeah. Clau- his lordship used to pick on her with his brother Lyle. Not a mark on her of course, not with her mother about, but they'd torment her in other ways."

Meryl's mind skipped back to Tira's butterflies and her insistence on keeping the gift secret from her brothers. Anger flared, hot and roiling, her blood beginning to thud.

"We stood up for her as often as we could and they had no issues lashing out at us." Niko shrugged. "But I'd do it again. A lot of the court are worried now though. Some of the people we've seen lurking since he became Lord aren't those we want to associate with. Traditional values, if you get my meaning."

Meryl inhaled a sharp, chilly breath and squared her shoulders.

"I really do." She nodded. "But I don't think the queen has any doubts about Tira's loyalty or reliability."

Niko smiled. "That's alright then. Oh, hello."

Meryl glanced over her shoulder to see Beryl, Harvey, Milo and Ace looming behind her.

"Hi, Niko," Beryl nodded. "Shouldn't you be working? It's almost lunchtime."

Niko didn't bother hiding his grin, and Beryl hissed when Harvey patted her on the head, mumbling something about thinking with her stomach.

"What? It's good food!" Beryl protested.

Meryl tried to think of a reason to slip away as her sister and Harvey started their arguing double act. She wanted to go and find out if Tira was up and feeling any better yet, just to be polite, but if she followed Niko to the kitchens Beryl was bound to tag along.

Neither of them noticed Demi ambling toward the group, but Milo did with hawk-like precision. Before she could reach them, he had his arms out, his hands bunched around reams of paperwork.

Demi eyed the papers and groaned.

"I will, I promise. I've literally just told Tira to go down to the archives once she's done with her brother."

Meryl tensed, but Niko spoke before she could query it.

"Oh, is she in trouble?" he asked. "Sorry, um, my queen."

He bobbed a low bow and Demi rolled her eyes.

"I don't think so, why?"

"Did he summon her?" Niko pressed. "I only ask because usually he doesn't, he just turns up wherever she is. I might um… yeah, I should just check where Marlon is maybe."

Meryl frowned. "I don't like the sound of that. How long ago?"

Demi seemed to be thinking the same, her arms folding across her chest.

"Maybe ten minutes ago?" She hesitated. "Milo, now might be the time to go and ask Claus for permission to remove the paintings. See what he says."

"You've already had the paintings removed," Milo reminded her, even though he vanished the paperwork with an anxious frown.

"I did, but he doesn't know that."

*Ten whole minutes.*

Meryl pulled her connection into her fingertips, her gifts tingling awake.

"I'll go with you," she said. "I need to ask Tira something anyway."

She didn't hear Niko murmuring excuses about getting back to the kitchens, and she ignored the suspicious look her sister sent her way.

With Milo hurrying along at her side, Meryl strode toward the door leading into the court chambers.

If Claus had done anything to Tira, anything at all, she wouldn't be losing any sleep about what would happen to him.

# CHAPTER TWELVE
## TIRA

Tira stared at Claus while taking hurried steps backwards as he approached her. There was no sign of his usual mocking smile on his face, or his charming mask either. His eyes narrowed, his mouth pressing thin.

"How much did you hear, Tira?"

She opened her mouth to find some kind of excuse but the words dried as Lorens loomed behind her brother, smirking at her over his shoulder.

"Don't let her go to the queen by any means necessary," Lorens said.

Claus nodded. "Remember your promises. She won't go anywhere after this."

Lorens chuckled, spitefulness shining in his eyes as they remained fixed on her.

"I'm so sorry to lose you," he said, his tone sickeningly sweet. "But little sneaks that listen at doors aren't a fit bride for someone with my future aspirations. You should have taken my deal when I promised it."

Tira wanted to spit in his face. She wanted to give some spirited comment at least, but her shaking limbs took over and her mouth wouldn't move. Lorens winked at her, laughed to himself and vanished, leaving her at the mercy of family.

Claus lunged and grabbed her wrist, spinning toward his room and hauling her behind him.

She struggled but his grip was like iron, his fingers biting into her skin. He shoved her in front of him through the doorway and slammed the door shut behind them.

Tira faced him, heart pounding until it was throbbing in her ears. She'd never seen him this angry before. Maybe once or twice with Lyle when they were children, but never since and not once had it ever been directed at her. In that moment, he towered over her every inch a fearsome Fae court lord.

"I heard you talking to someone," she said quickly. "Not much else. Something about your friends staying here."

She kept it vague, knowing anything else would drive him to panic. He might lock her in her room if he thought she would go to Demi with anything more incriminating. She rubbed at her smarting wrist and his eyes flicked to the movement.

"That's not all you heard, I'll bet. Are you working for the queen already? Has she made you fancy promises to get you to betray your family?"

Tira's cheeks burned with outrage, her fists clenching. "She hasn't promised or asked me for anything you wouldn't already give her. Access to the archives, information-"

"What kind of information?"

She took a step back, her mind racing. The hesitation drove him forward and she yelped in fright, dodging behind an armchair.

"Information about the archives, what else?"

A question wasn't a lie, but she already guessed he

wouldn't believe her now. Her only hope was to get out of the room and down the hall. She was fast when she needed to be but so was he. He hadn't forced her to swear allegiance to him or the court yet at least, so he couldn't force her to obey.

She twisted past him with her eyes fixed on the door, so focused that she never saw his foot swinging out in front of her.

Claus caught her ankle with the tip of his boot and knocked her onto her hands and knees. She rolled to get away but he had hold of her arm before she could get free. She found her feet the same moment he grabbed her shoulder with his other hand and threw her at his desk.

She hit the corner. Pain radiated through her stomach, her arms flailing as she toppled to the floor.

She curled her knees to her chest and held onto her legs with all her strength. If he thought she was beaten enough, he might give in. He'd lock her in her room or forbid any of the court from speaking to her, but anything was better than another round of being thrown across the room. The pain in her gut felt like the desk had sliced right through her.

Fingers closed around her throat, unyielding and cold. She scrambled her arms and legs against the floor as the pressure tightened, fear screaming in her head as she started gasping from shock and breathlessness.

The fingers slid away, a warning only, but she couldn't get her breath back.

*Did the table crush my chest as well?*

Either way, she could still get to Demi if she tried. She

sent her hearing gift out to sense where Claus was, wondering if he might be kicking her next or if he'd already left her there.

Raised voices punctured through her head and her hearing gift recoiled as she whimpered at the blast. She opened her eyes in time to see the back of Milo disappearing through the door, but he hadn't arrived alone.

A flash of blue crossed the room, stopping in the middle of the floor. Meryl and Ace stood facing Claus at a distance, but it wasn't out of fear of him.

Tira managed to get herself up on one elbow, watching as a full suit of armour that was usually kept on the wall thudded to the floor. Its ridged hand twisted around her brother's arm, the other clamping on the back of his neck to force his face and torso over the fully blazing fireplace.

"Touch her like that again and nobody will be able to recognise you," Meryl snarled.

Tira blinked away the haziness of shock, astonished to see Meryl's cheeks an angry pink and her eyes narrowed with fury. Ace opened his mouth, perhaps to intervene, but Meryl gave him a look and he stayed silent. With a sudden Fae-like smile, Meryl twitched her fingers and the suit of armour dipped Claus slightly lower as though they were in some kind of garish mimicry of a dance.

"You'll regret threatening a court lord," he spat out, his head lifted back at a painful angle to avoid the heat. "I have powerful friends."

Tira flinched as Ace dropped to one knee beside her, but if he was with Meryl she could trust him. He wrapped his arm around her and she clung onto him as he helped her to her feet. She wasn't sure if he was casting a warding over them but she didn't have any energy left to cast one of her own.

"Maybe you have powerful friends right now," Meryl said, her voice taut. "But the queen will likely remove your title when she finds out about this. They're not going to want to bother with you after that."

The flowing ribbon of choice wavered in front of Tira, offering her a second-chance strand to be strong. She took it without a second thought.

"I overheard him talking to someone, I'm pretty sure it was Belladonna Elverhill. She told him to meet them at the prime point and that his friends should stay behind to handle the queen. Lorens was here too, but I'm not sure what his connection with-"

"TRAITOR!" Claus roared.

The suit of armour pretended to drop him and he screamed, but Tira could feel the accusation branding its way through her. She was a traitor to her family by betraying him, and technically to her court because it was his.

"What's going on? I heard yelling."

Demi strolled in like she was out for a morning walk in the fresh air, her hands in her pockets and Milo hurrying behind her with his face bright red.

*He must have run like the wind to fetch her.*

"Tira's just confessing her brother's treachery," Meryl said.

"Ah. And that's why you're one step away from burning the lord of one of our courts?"

"Well, mostly because he was beating her up, but yeah sure, that too. He shouldn't be lord of one of our courts anyway."

Demi's eyes narrowed. She glanced to Tira for confirmation, and Tira forced herself to nod. Claus would cast her out from court now, she had no doubt of that, or he might keep her around to torment. She had a few friends in town at the bottom of the mountain but she couldn't imagine them being able to give her somewhere to stay long-term. Marinda might put in a good word for her somewhere, or let her come on her next book tour, but this was her home, her court.

"I don't hold with violence as a rule," Demi said, her voice silky with warning. "Not if the fight isn't between two people who are going in prepared and willing at least."

"He was talking to Belladonna, I'm sure it was her," Tira babbled. "She told him to meet her at the prime point, whatever that is, and that his friends should stay here to deal with you. She said they have everything they need now. Lorens was there too, talking to someone called Loth from the other realm everyone's trying to get into."

Demi fell still. Tira wanted to apologise for not being more helpful in time, but she didn't dare interrupt.

"Ace, run and get Taz. Bring him here. Milo, go and summon everyone we discussed and have them realm-skip here immediately, then gather everyone already here. Prep them for a long journey too."

Milo hurried off as Ace glanced down at Tira.

"You okay to stand?" he asked.

She nodded, then braced herself on the desk just in case.

"Meryl, you good?" Demi asked.

Meryl nodded. "More than. Can I punch him a little bit?"

"Tempting, but no." Demi ambled toward Claus, eying the sweat on his face with a wrinkle of her nose. "See, I agreed to titling you because I knew so little about you. No doubt you expected to charm me and have me none the wiser while you and the Forgotten were carrying on. You got cocky. Do you think I wouldn't recognise your friends when they got here? Or have someone here who would recognise them as Forgotten supporters at least?"

"Belladonna said you wouldn't get the right information in time, and she was right," he hissed.

Demi sighed. "She might have gotten there ahead of me by like a day. I can admit where I'm beaten. This is not one of those times but that's not your concern anymore. I officially rescind your appointment as court lord. You no longer have the right to call yourself lord, or have any say or sway over the Court of Words, so on and so on."

Tira flinched as Demi eyed her over Claus' head, but he saw the look and laughed breathlessly.

"She can't do it," he insisted. "She's sick. Ill."

Demi frowned. "So?"

"She won't cope. She's weak. You're damning the entire court by leaving them leaderless without me."

When Demi looked her way, Tira flushed with shame.

"I get really bad headaches. Gut issues as well sometimes. I can do everything, but I need to rest a lot in between."

Demi left Claus hanging over the fire with Meryl

merrily bouncing him on the end of the suit of armour. She walked over to Tira, folding her arms across her chest.

"Is the Court of Words particularly eventful then?" she asked. "Daily sledding runs, chasing people up and down mountains, that sort of thing?"

Tira let out a snort before she could claw it back. "No, but there's always things to manage. Although I've been doing most of it for a while now."

She glanced at Claus but he didn't see fit to say anything derogatory back for once. Perhaps because his legs were shaking an alarming amount from being hunched over the fire too long.

Demi sighed. "The Word Court is yours if you want it then. From what I hear it always should have been anyway. If you need support I can send you someone from my court to help. Probably not Milo though. We'd never get him out again."

Tira stared back at the queen. In all her anxiety about becoming lady, then all her shame about giving up the title, she'd never once considered that someone might offer her support.

"You being ill isn't a weakness," Demi added, strength lacing her tone. "If anything, it'll make you kinder to the people you have to lead. More mindful. I'd rather have someone leading kindly with more help around them than leading with absolutely no brain or humanity at all."

Tira opened her mouth to accept. Because it was the easiest decision in all of Faerie now, to take on the role she was always meant to have.

The door banging open stole any chance she had. Lord

Kainen of the Illusion Court burst in, his eyes rolling wide and his face pale.

"They took her. Reyan, they took her from the Fauna Court." He panted before forcing the remaining words out. "I'll kill them."

He snapped his fingers and Tira strangled a scream in her throat as an enormous and unnervingly familiar painting crashed into existence, taking out two pot plants.

Demi groaned. "What? Why? How do you know?"

Kainen lifted his arm. A wraith of shadow in the form of a snake curled possessively around his arm, thick enough to cover the whole length from hand to neck.

"Betty found me at home. I don't know how Reyan managed it, but Betty had a whisper of mind-speak stuck inside her that she passed to me. They're taking her to the prime point, which I'm guessing is the place we've all been getting worked up about. We have to go now."

Claus chuckled loudly and Kainen noticed him then. He stormed across the room, curls of glittering black smoke dancing from his hands as the snake moved around his shoulders like a huge shadowy scarf.

"If there's even one scratch on her…" Kainen swore.

Claus turned his head in Kainen's direction. "Your lady has what we need to cross over. If Belladonna has her, she's already as good as dead."

Kainen reached forward but the suit of armour lifted a foot to hold him back, balancing on one leg without a single wobble.

Tira eyed Meryl but she showed no signs of tiring with her gift, her eyes bright and her back straight. Kainen leaned over the leg and glowered inches from Claus' face.

"Where is she?"

"Don't need to know that," Demi said. "We'll go and get her back. But why do they think they need Reyan?"

Claus' face contorted and he struggled against the unyielding metal holding him for several moments before the words were torn from his lips.

"Because Belladonna thinks she has the answer."

"Why?"

"We didn't get told."

"How do they plan to open the veil?"

"I don't know."

Demi picked up the painting and eyed it for a long, silent moment. From her crouched over vantage point, Tira could see the same image of the underground hall of vaulted stone from the three paintings they already had. She squinted hard enough to make out the word 'life', and a mark on the final pillar.

Demi rubbed a hand over her face as Ace came in with the king consort and Meryl's sisters.

"Right, Taz, you escort Claus here to the forever mountains under charges of being part of the Forgotten and a violent thug who deserves to have his bits chopped off."

Taz raised his eyebrows. "Said like a true queen."

"Take Beryl and Cheryl with you." Demi stuck her tongue out at him. "Ace, take this painting back home with the others. I've got all we need now I think. Oh and Meryl, you can let the armour go now, I've got him."

There was absolutely no sign of Demi having any influence over Claus, not visibly, but when the suit of armour pulled him back from the fire and dropped him unceremoniously on the carpet he didn't make any attempt to get up or escape. Tira almost laughed, half-delirious as the armour leapt back onto its plinth and arranged itself neatly back into the usual position.

"He'll have a nice brotherly reunion to look forward to," Taz said, grabbing Claus by the leg. "Your brother will probably have more friends than you by now, Claus. Isn't that nice? We'll meet you back here, right Dem?"

Demi nodded and Taz, Cheryl and Beryl vanished with the last of Tira's stepbrothers.

"I'm sorry we don't have more time to discuss this, Tira," Demi added. "But if you want this court, the title, it's yours."

Tira gripped the table and forced a pained smile.

"I'd be honoured. I would bow but the table whacked me in the stomach pretty badly."

Demi shook her head. "No need, bowing wastes time. I hereby confer on you the title of Lady of Words, Lady of the Word Court, etcetera. Milo will send you something official at some point to confirm it. Someone remind me to remind him."

Tira had the inkling that she should find some show of gratitude but action wouldn't come, so bewildered by the sudden whirlwind the queen had whisked around her.

"What about Reyan? Where are they?" Kainen demanded, his hands shaking as he paced toward Demi. "Why aren't you *doing anything*?"

Demi glowered back at him, her shoulders stiff with tension, but for all her queenliness, Kainen didn't back down an inch, his fists clenched at his sides.

"I am doing something, but I need to do it right," Demi warned him before turning to Tira. "Right, I'm sorry to do this, Tira, considering you've only just been titled and all, but we're going to need you to come with us."

Tira blinked back at her. "Um, okay. Where?"

"I can't tell you until we get there."

*It's the Queen of Faerie, you can't exactly say 'no thanks, I need a quick lie down'.*

"I'll need to let Marlon know," she insisted. "I reckon Marinda can keep the clubs and debates running until I get back, if she doesn't mind."

Demi nodded. "I can speed that along if you like."

She pulled a glimmering white orb out of her pocket and held it between both palms, but when she lifted it aloft and started speaking, no face appeared to answer her.

"Citizens of the Word Court, hello. Um, this is your queen speaking. Hi. Due to issues with staffing, Claudius Auren has been outed as a traitor to the crowns and will not be returning. Tira Starhollow has been chosen as Lady of Words by my command. Anyone still in the court who is loyal to the old rule, get out. Now, or there will be consequences. Cheers."

Ace pressed his hands over his face with a groan. "That was the most unqueenly thing I've ever heard. Milo is going to have a fit."

"All part of the fun." Demi grinned. "Right, Tira go get a bag together, pack light but we might be gone a couple of days. Delegate where you need to and we'll meet in the entrance hall. I'll have some FDPs drafted in to help keep the court safe while you're away. Ace, grab a group quick and bring them here. We'll meet in the main hall straight after. Meryl, give Tira a hand, would you?"

Tira stood clinging to the table as Kainen stormed out, muttering under his breath. Demi and Ace exchanged a weary look as they left the room.

Tira's insides fluttered. Her room. The state rooms were hers now. As was the entire court.

*I'm officially Lady of the Word Court.*

Meryl approached with a smile, stopping right in front of her.

"We should get your things together. Demi's nice but she's not the most patient when stuff like this happens, Lady."

Her amused tone softened the title, but Tira shook her head, wincing as every part of her ached. Even as she tried to stand straight, her torso throbbed.

"Don't please, I'll have to get used to that first."

Meryl laughed. "As you wish. You've got a tiny cut on your forehead, here."

Tira froze as Meryl reached out and pressed a thumb to her temple. Her eyes were brown but up close there were tiny flecks of yellow and green.

Meryl seemed frozen too, lost in thought as they stared at each other. Even though Tira had the mad urge to move forward, Meryl still had sadness in her eyes. Something she would need to find peace with before anything new could potentially happen.

*Not that anything can happen, even potentially. She's an FDP with a job to do and I have a whole court to consider now.*

Tira fought the sinking disappointment as she let go of the table and took a couple of steps toward the door. Once she'd forced herself up straight she could move okay and left the room with Meryl.

Her room now. Her court.

"LADY!"

Marlon's joyful voice nearly shook the entire court down from the mountain as he bounded toward her.

"It's a miracle!" he exclaimed. "I knew the queen visiting would be a good thing. I *knew* it. We'll see that your things are moved to the state rooms immediately, and the new painting must be done. I'll have Niko prepare a celebratory feast-"

"I have to leave."

Marlon blinked at her. "Leave?!"

"Yeah, queen's orders. Not for long or anything, a couple of days. I need to pack a bag. Also if there's any healing stuff for bruises that'd be awesome because I might have crashed into a table."

"Your stepbrother threw you into a table," Meryl added. "Don't dull it down for his benefit."

Marlon's face crunched tight and froze for several seconds. Then he righted himself and clapped his hands together with startling determination brewing in his eyes.

"You'll have Marinda mind the place in your stead I take it?" he asked.

Tira nodded. "Yes, for the debates. And you will manage the court in my stead, won't you?"

"Of course, until you return. We won't let you down.

I'll sort the whole thing. Go see to the queen and I'll pack you a bag to take, and I'll speak to Marinda." He beamed and dipped his head. "Lady."

Tira stared in bemused defeat as he hurried off again. She knew Marinda would relish the opportunity to boss everyone around for a few days before getting irritated with all of them and fleeing into solitude for a month. Marlon would keep the court itself running as he had done for her mother, and anyone who misbehaved in the archives would get the short end of Simone's sharp tongue.

As they walked after Marlon at a much slower pace, Tira sighed.

"You haven't had any time to process this," Meryl said.

Tira shrugged. "Probably best. I might start regretting it considering how everything is unravelling."

Meryl grinned, a wicked liveliness that Tira hadn't expected sparking across her face.

"Everything is always unravelling as part of Demi's crew. And for FDPs. We're always in some kind of bother. I imagine courts are much the same except it's nobles spatting instead of things exploding."

"Our nobles don't spat, we debate, much more civilised." Tira laughed then winced from the pain of it. "My mother was great at conflict resolution. She could debate any point but then convince the other side that they were being ridiculous, even if they were completely right. Sometimes she would start out arguing one thing, then for fun she'd argue the exact opposite to convince everyone back the other way again."

Meryl nodded. "Petra was a bit like that. She could fight

against anyone but also talk them down. That's why…"

She trailed off and Tira stopped at the door to the main hall. Once she opened it and stepped through, she would be facing her court and the queen's entourage as a lady in her own right. She had standards to hold to now, responsibilities to keep in mind. But something about Meryl's tone convinced her to linger a moment, to try and secure some tiny ember of hope for herself rather than just her court.

"I heard the rumours about what happened to her," she said. "About what the enemy did. There's no debating with malice like that."

Meryl sighed. "No. I think everyone who knew us assumed we were together, you know, like 'that'."

"You weren't?"

Meryl shook her head. "I wanted to be but she wasn't interested in that. We understood each other and I accepted she didn't want more, not with anyone. It was enough that she chose me though for what she was comfortable with."

Tira had no idea what to say to that so she settled for patting Meryl's shoulder and smiling sympathetically. Meryl shrugged and pointed to the door.

"Ready to face your new future?" she asked.

Tira pulled a face. "No, and yes. Not sure what to expect."

"None of us ever are." Meryl laughed. "Come on, if you're brave I'll hold your hand."

Tira thought she was joking and rolled her eyes as she pushed the door open. As Meryl's warm fingers folded around her own and squeezed, she flinched.

*Does that mean anything? Should it?*

Meryl let go again as they walked into the entrance hall, but the memory of the contact continued tingling. Tira breathed in deeply and focused on the now less unnerving situation of facing her court.

Tira glanced around the main hall and relaxed to find her brothers friends seemed to have fled. It was hard to tell with what looked like the whole court assembled in clusters, all pretending not to be desperate for any gossip or drama, but there was a decidedly empty circle around the queen and her group.

Tira held her head high and her shoulders firm despite the pain as she moved through the crowd. So many people smiled and nodded at her, signs of respect with relief written over their faces.

"Congratulations, Lady!" Someone shouted, cheers following straight after.

Tira smiled. She was her mother's daughter in charge of the court she loved. Her home. She could do this.

"It's an honour!" She raised her voice to be heard throughout the hall. "I will do my best by you all. Unless we're in a debate, then all bets are off."

Laughter filled the air and she blushed with pride. When she approached the queen, a wholly natural crowd noise sprung up, clear signs of the court accepting the natural state of things and moving on just as quickly to whatever the next drama might be.

As she and Meryl joined the group, Demi gave Milo a nod. Tira eyed his clipboard warily.

"Right, not sure who knows who, so we'll make this

quick," he announced. "When I call your name, raise your hand."

"Are we seriously doing this right now?" Kainen stood with his fists clenched. "They have my- well, technically she's- they have the lady of my court. Anything could be happening!"

Milo gave him a look. "It'll be even quicker without interruptions. Kainen. You have to raise your hand." Kainen glared pure fury back and Milo huffed. "Oh why do I bother?"

Demi grinned. "Introductions over, get to know each other on your own time. We're realm-skipping to a safe-space then taking transport through the human world because where we're headed there is no Faerie. Pretty clever really, hide it somewhere far from the Fae's ability to manipul- right, sorry. Everyone ready?"

Tira didn't have her bag yet, but given the jittery anger on Kainen's face, she had doubts about speaking up about it.

"Here you are, Lady." Marlon popped up beside her with unerring timing. "A special bag, one fit for a lady of our court with lots to carry. It was your mother's but when *he* was titled I hid it. Now it's yours. Everything you could possibly need is inside, including some healing tonic for bruises and your mother's travelling orb which was also mysteriously 'misplaced' a while ago. Keep us updated."

Tira nodded, not sure whether to laugh at his underhandedness or burst into emotional tears at how lucky she was to have him looking out for her.

"I will," she promised. "Keep the court safe until I

return."

"Of course. Travel safe."

Tira slid the bag onto one shoulder and faced the group. She didn't recognise a couple of those assembled, a young man with red hair and mismatched eyes holding hands with a dark-haired girl with glasses, but clearly they had the trust of the queen. She managed a shy smile at Lady Leilania who she hadn't seen in years, and a dark-haired young man she vaguely recognised from the recently moved Revel Court.

"Where exactly are we going anyway?" Milo asked irritably. "I should have had a chance to do proper reconnaissance before we leave."

Demi shrugged. "No time. Doubt the archives or our library would have much on the human world anyway. Right, next step, storm Edinburgh Castle."

Tira eyed everyone to see if they recognised the place name, because she definitely didn't. Castles suggested guards and some kind of fortification, which might prove tricky.

Nobody else showed any sign of recognition either, which comforted her somewhat.

Everyone except Ace whose mouth dropped open.

"Er… we're going to *what*?"

# CHAPTER THIRTEEN
# MERYL

*I held her hand.*

Meryl stood with her fists clenched in the front pocket of her hooded sweatshirt as the rest of the group started arguing about some kind of castle and how they were going to get inside it.

*I just up and grabbed her hand.*

She couldn't focus on the chaos now erupting around her. They were headed for the human world and her sisters were taking full advantage of the mayhem by being as loud and as dramatic as possible, but all she could think about was the residual tingling on her skin where Tira's hand had briefly rested.

"But will our gifts still work in the human world?" Harvey asked.

Demi nodded. "They should do."

"Should?" Beryl frowned. "You don't sound very sure. I mean, we're trained in combat, most of us, but gifts are handy."

"That's why we're not going to use them when we get there," Taz said, his tone dry. "We're to pretend to be humans unless things go wrong."

"Things always go wrong though," Cheryl pointed out.

Hutch grinned. "Exactly."

Meryl did the only thing she could do. She looked at Tira who stood talking to Marlon in whispers. Against her better judgement, Meryl sidled as discreetly as she could away from her sisters and toward Tira.

"Make sure you leave instruction for the debates," Marlon insisted. "Marinda!"

Tira winced and Meryl caught the subtle clench of her eyelids, as though the sound had hurt her head.

"Are you going to be okay?" she asked.

Tira frowned. "I'm fine. I just need to sort out the court before we leave. I've not even had it five minutes yet officially."

Marlon snorted in disgust as she moved away to talk to Marinda.

"Not officially, but she's been running it since the late lady died," he muttered.

Meryl froze as he looked at her next, really looked at her, a frown of consideration on his face.

"Would you mind carrying a little something?" he asked. "She gets in such a determined flap about me trying to take care of her. I put some *Beast Lite* in her bag but she'll likely forget, and it helps with the nausea she gets with her headaches."

Meryl nodded. "I can do that. She clearly pushes herself too far too often."

Again came that slight narrowing of his eyes giving her the needling sensation that she was being scanned and assessed. Then he clicked his fingers to summon several cans which he happily bundled into her arms.

"I have a perception gift," he said. "I know I can trust you to keep an eye on our lady. You have a good heart."

Meryl summoned her rucksack from her room and slid

the cans inside with her cheeks burning. The words were scarily similar to something Petra had said to her. Her heart ached at the thought, but Petra would tell her to stop clinging to what was gone and done, and to focus forward because what other direction was there?

"I do hope once this is all over, you'll come back and visit us," Marlon added. "Lady has many friends, but a court can be a lonely place all the same."

He bustled off, sparing a moment to pat Tira gently on the arm as he passed her. Tira finished talking to Marinda and came directly to Meryl's side.

"Sorry if he said anything untoward," she said. "He means well, but I think he's taken on the job of parenting me and the court. I'm literally just a figurehead."

She said it with a smile, a soft pink hue touching her cheeks.

Meryl laughed, her gaze passing over the group assembled in time to see both her sisters plus Hutch and Harvey staring at her like she'd grown two heads.

*They probably haven't seen me properly laugh once in three months.*

Meryl tensed. Now that they had seen it, they were looking at Tira with identical gleaming smiles of determination.

"Oh orbs," she muttered.

Tira didn't see them approaching until it was too late.

"Your ladyship." Beryl bobbed a ridiculous half-bow. "We haven't had proper time to introduce ourselves."

"Probably best you don't," Meryl said.

Beryl ignored her but Tira hid any pains well behind a

wide smile.

"Beryl and Cheryl Eastwick," Tira announced, a touch of amused flirtation in her tone. "Formerly of the Flora Court, FDPs at Arcanium with fearsome reputations. I'm surprised you haven't signed up to our annual sledding race yet to be honest."

"The what?"

"The annual sledding race. We do it every year and anyone can enter. First to the top wins."

Cheryl's eyes glazed over. "I want to do it!"

"Me too!" Beryl grinned.

Harvey approached and slung his arm around Beryl's shoulders, ignoring her when she huffed at him.

"I'm going to win, I've decided," he said.

Tira laughed. "Good luck then, nobody ever beats me."

Meryl's insides crunched painfully. Standing there, watching Tira interact with the madness that was the Eastwick family, probably soon to be the Eastwick-Hutchinson family if things kept going the way they were, it all looked so... *right*. Memories swarmed but she pushed aside the usual stabs of grief and guilt. She had to believe that Petra of all people would have wanted her to be happy.

"None of this is getting us any closer!"

Kainen's voice vibrated through the court, startling several people gathered nearby.

In the sudden swirl of her reincarnating social life, Meryl had forgotten Reyan, but one look at Kainen's clenched fists vibrating at his sides and the flicker of shadow and smoke around his body reminded her. She and Tira exchanged a look as Demi raised a hand to silence the lot of them.

"We're going now," she said. "Hands up who can realm-skip."

Meryl watched Tira raise her hand, nerves beginning to flutter inside her gut. Demi's usual process was to charge in, do some damage and trust everyone else to manage themselves, but those gathered from courts weren't FDPs. Odella and Sannar from the Nether Court were barely even court-sworn, and while Kainen had FDP training, and Lolly had trained with Petra in younger years, Tira might not have much protection at all.

Demi flicked a look over everyone.

"Right, Beryl and Harvey, stick with Sannar and Odella please. Cheryl, you and Hutch are with Lolly and Tyren. Meryl, you and Tira try to keep some sense over the rest of them, and Kainen will obviously go straight for Reyan. The rest of us are fighting if it gets that far. Milo, if all fails, get back home with as many people as you can."

She moved through the group, pressing the tip of her thumb to the foreheads of those gathered from courts.

"Right, you should all have the location to skip to now. Skip and wait for everyone, then we'll have to walk to the train station."

"There aren't any skip-ways where we're going?" Kainen asked, glittering black smoke roiling over his body.

Demi shook her head. "No, but I'm getting us in close as I can. We're going to get her back whatever happens, I promise you that."

It didn't appear to calm his fury any but Meryl could understand why. Seeing him all tense and irate, obsessing over someone he clearly loved, she kind of got why nobody had wanted to sit near her in the canteen the past few months.

"Well then, ladies and lords, we're following you apparently," Beryl said.

As everyone grabbed shoulders or wrists or hands to realm-skip together, Tira held out her hand, palm up.

Meryl took as discreet a breath as she could manage and slid her hand over Tira's, entwining their fingers and holding on tight.

"Here goes," Tira muttered. "First time for everything."

Meryl froze. "Wait, you've never-"

Her words were swallowed up by a swirl of purple and grey, the trepidation quashed by an unnerving realisation that she might just be willing to follow this girl anywhere she decided to go.

# CHAPTER FOURTEEN
## REYAN

The moment the nether settled, a blast of freezing rain streamed onto Reyan's face. She gasped and blinked against the onslaught. Despite the shock, Blossom's hand clamped tight on her shoulder was a constant reminder of her situation.

"What a dump," Belladonna sneered.

Reyan looked around, assessing the landscape for any potential escape route. Square brown buildings towered above them with black railings surrounding dirty grey concrete underfoot. Some sort of large cart made of metal painted white with four wheels waited nearby. She'd heard fairies talk about the human world before, and she'd read some of their stories, but with realm-skipping the natural way to travel she hadn't ever seen human transport before.

The vehicle looked nothing like the carriages and carts that Reyan had seen in her childhood, and nothing at all like the ornate wooden rickshaws and carts that most Fae used for public or private realm-skipping.

"Get them all in the back and tie them to the chairs," Belladonna demanded. "No mistakes. If they escape, it'll be your head I'll be taking next."

Reyan didn't fight as Blossom jostled her toward the large rectangle of metal.

"It'll be so much easier for you if you do as you're told," Blossom warned.

Reyan scowled as she stepped into the metal vehicle.

"Easier for you, you mean."

Two rows of chairs with questionable looking seat cushions stood on either side of the vehicle, but Blossom pushed her right past them and forced her down onto the back row. A strange scent wafted up, a bit like damp, stale bread.

"If you like." Blossom settled herself down right beside Reyan, wrinkling her nose as she glanced around. "Most of these things are inevitable, so you'll just make it harder by fighting."

"No doubt you'll be after Kainen once I'm out of the way."

Blossom shrugged. "Kainen is a lost cause for anyone supporting the Forgotten. He's a traitor. By time he comes to find you, Bella will probably have what she wants."

Reyan ignored the clench of panic in her chest. Kainen had no idea where she was, and Betty might not be able to find him or communicate the message she'd sent. Even if he did understand, she'd all but rejected him without meaning to. He might not bother to come at all.

*No, he'll come.* She inhaled sharply and sat taller.

"He's a better person than you or your lot will ever be."

Blossom didn't deign to answer that, staring ahead with her jaw set and her gaze fixed on Belladonna.

Reyan eyed the rest of the group. Three others were sitting with their hands bound and tied to the rail of the seat in front of theirs, a young woman with her blonde head bowed, a young man in a smart shirt who was visibly shaking and an elderly lady with determination in the rigid set of her shoulders.

"Dare I ask what the unlucky four of us are here for?" Reyan muttered.

Blossom sighed, exasperated. "I'm sure Bella will tell you what you need to know when the time comes. She has a flair for the dramatic though, so she'll likely toy with you a bit first."

As Belladonna strode through the vehicle toward them, Reyan searched for any sense of her Fae connection inside her, any hint that she might be able to dissipate into shadow. Her body remained fully formed and she sagged, defeated. Whatever Belladonna made her drink had stripped or bound all essence of the magic inside her.

"What use are we without our gifts?" she asked. "Or is that a delight just for me?"

Belladonna hovered with irritation flitting across her face and Reyan prepared herself for some kind of strike, verbal or physical.

A loud rumbling sound rose around them and Belladonna froze. As the vehicle lurched forward, she slid onto the back seat beside Blossom with a decidedly un-Fae-like stumble.

"You'll get your gifts back just in time to help me get through to the Prime Realm," Belladonna said. "Won't that be nice?"

Reyan frowned. "And what do our gifts have to do with the Prime Realm? I doubt any of us have ever seen it. I think you've probably got the wrong person. That or you're insane."

Blossom's tension increased, her elbow knocking

Reyan's arm as she flinched. Reyan forced her face into a mask of indifference. Belladonna might hurt her, but if she provided some kind of irritable entertainment she might end up causing enough chaos to jiggle out something useful.

*Assuming I ever get out of this alive enough to tell anyone.*

She pushed the thought away. Somewhere out there, Betty was looking for Kainen. Even if he didn't forgive her for doubting him, he wouldn't risk allowing the sleight to his court. He would have sensed that the court had officially claimed her, but she had no idea how long ago that had happened.

"You're definitely the right person." Belladonna sighed, eying her perfectly manicured fingernails. "You're a shadow-weaver. A bit of luck for us really as you're quite rare. We did have a shadow-snake hatching and we were going to use that, but it slithered off somewhere in the Nether Court."

"That's why you think I'm useful?" Reyan skipped quickly past any mention of Betty. "I can only dissipate into shadow. If this Prime Realm place is blocked to realm-skipping, I doubt I'll be able to reach it."

"Of course you can't. We don't need your body or your effort, just your gift. Orbs alive, this vehicle is intolerable."

Belladonna snarled in annoyance as they bounced over something on the long strip of road.

"You said it wasn't far," Blossom said, her tone entirely placating.

"Thankfully not, but we'll have plenty of time either

way. That bloodless idiot calling herself queen is too dim to realise what the secret is."

Blossom laughed but it didn't sound authentic.

*She's as scared as I am,* Reyan realised.

Belladonna didn't notice. "I've half a mind to take some fun here before we go to the entrance. A few stolen children, a few burning buildings. Some deals in exchange for eternal servitude. How long has it been since Fae were allowed free roam of the human world?"

"A long time," Blossom agreed. "But we should focus on what we need to do. Then we will have eternity to torment *everyone*."

Belladonna laughed in delight. "It's on these very rare occasions that I remember you are actually related to me. Very well. After I make it to the Prime Realm, it'll be free reign for all of us. I am intrigued to see what Emil has been so secretive about."

"He fears your power," Blossom said.

"Which is ridiculous. He of all people in Faerie should be embracing me wholeheartedly. He won't share his contact there or even give me a name but I'll find them."

Belladonna's eyes turned bright with glee as the vehicle lurched to a stop. She leapt to her feet and charged toward the front, leaving Reyan fighting against a sudden swell of nausea, her fists clenching tight around the railing of the seat in front of her.

"What do you mean we're not there yet?" Belladonna's voice scraped her ears. "Why are we stopping then?"

Reyan winced as Belladonna's hand wrapped around the vehicle driver's throat.

"I don't care if there's *traffic lights*. Get us there or I will snap you in half."

A flash of silver flicked next to the driver's eye and Reyan slammed her hand against the side of the vehicle as it surged forward again. As Blossom looked at her, she waited for the inevitable mention of tying her hands but surprisingly none came.

*How harmful can I be without my gifts?* She frowned. *I need to remember all the combat training Kainen taught me.*

The mere thought of him made her insides ache, but she kept her focus on the driver as Belladonna stood over him with a dagger handy.

Reyan turned her gaze to the window and tried marking the strange landscape outside in her mind, but she didn't recognise anything. Other vehicles much like their one zoomed past them constantly, some larger and some tiny in comparison, but the flat grey and brown land dotted with occasional swathes of green rolled by like one long, unending carousel.

Reyan flinched as the vehicle jerked to a halt a while later, her heart sinking impossibly further as the vehicle's door clunked open.

"Right, everyone out," Belladonna sang.

Blossom stood and grabbed Reyan's wrist.

"There's no need to push me about," Reyan snapped.

Blossom only rolled her eyes and gripped tighter.

The rain seemed even colder as they tumbled out onto a strange street between towering brown and grey buildings. Reyan shivered and scanned their surroundings for anything useful. There were no signs of trees or nature aside from a steely sky above, the entire landscape a vista of mismatched buildings boxing them in.

The moment the last of their group was off the vehicle, it zoomed off with a lot of crunching and squealing.

"Right, do what you need to do," Belladonna snapped.

A burly man stood beside her and grabbed a large plate of metal embedded in the paved ground. With one swift tug, he tore it free and disappeared into it.

"Throw them down," he hollered up.

Reyan flinched as Blossom pushed her forward, but she wouldn't let anyone else see her fear. Before anyone could push her into the hole, she dropped to sit on the edge and launched herself down, using the freedom of her unbound hands to orientate her balance.

She pulled a face as her feet landed with a splash, her shoes soaked through in an instant. An unpleasant smell swarmed the air and she wished she had thought to put her boots on before leaving the court.

Murky lamps on the walls gave her enough light to see by, illuminating a long brick tunnel that ventured off in opposite directions. Before Reyan could figure out if there was anywhere to run to, the man lifted Blossom down with surprising care. Reyan eyed the far end of the tunnel as Blossom appeared beside her.

"Don't even think about it," Blossom muttered. "The last thing I need is Kainen vowing to kill me if anything lasting happens to you."

Surprised, Reyan folded her arms across her chest.

"We both know your sister's going to kill me the

moment she has what she wants."

Blossom glanced over her shoulder as the remaining three captives were bundled down with their hands still tied.

"If she gets what she wants, she won't be here to kill you. If she doesn't, Kainen will probably be her first target just to spite you."

Reyan opened her mouth to ask more, but Belladonna appeared beside them, her face alight with vicious joy.

"We should be in the right place," she said, pointing to the nearest wall. "Start there."

A slender woman strode forward and placed her fingertips on the brick. With a piercing whistle, she slammed her hands on the wall. It crumbled under her touch, solid matter becoming rubble and falling away to reveal a stone-walled tunnel beyond.

"Now that looks more like it."

Belladonna eased herself through the gap and Blossom pushed Reyan behind her. They started walking and hints of magic lit fires in brackets along the walls as they passed. The tunnel smelled like dust but at least the floor was dry, an improvement from the previous one despite the horrible company.

"The human world is protected by the queens," Belladonna called back. "But this is not the human world. We're walking through a sort of 'in-between', an antechamber to the Prime Realm itself. It was hidden ages ago, and I shall be the first to conquer it and cross through the skip-way it protects."

Reyan glanced back as they turned a corner. The other

three captives were being jostled along with their bound hands in front of them, the young man still shaking and the young woman crying silently. The older lady caught Reyan's eye, firm understanding passing between them.

Whatever glib assurances Blossom made and no matter how misguided her hope for Belladonna's success was, the likelihood that any of them would survive was slim.

"Look at that!" Belladonna's voice raised with excitement. "All this time, and nobody would have known it was here if not for Emil's contact. It's almost making me want to forgive him for trying to hide that communication mirror from me."

Belladonna came to a stop, framed underneath a tall stone archway, flinging her arms out in delight at the sight in front of her. Reyan's skin rippled with chills as she stared. She recognised the room in front of them, from the low vaulted ceiling and the pillars to the enormous painted wall at the back. It looked a lot like one of the barrel rooms at the Illusion Court where they kept the wine to mature, except here there were no barrels and the room had a remarkable resemblance to the painting she and Kainen had found at the Fauna Court.

Belladonna clapped her hands, apparently happiest listening to her own voice as she started issuing orders.

"This is the fun part. We'll have the young lady over on that far pillar there. The young man here on this one, and our *venerable* friend on that one. And for the Lady of the Illusion Court, a front row seat for my triumph."

Reyan tried to shove Blossom's hand off her wrist, even though she wouldn't get anywhere if she tried to run.

Blossom held on tighter, hauling her by the arm.

The moment they reached the pillar nearest the painted fresco scene on the back wall, Blossom fought to pin Reyan's hands above her head. Reyan kicked out on instinct. Her foot landed on Blossom's hip but despite the pained grunt, the cold grip of cuffs replaced the fingers around her wrists seconds later.

"There now, you're all contained with bindings that are warded," Belladonna said. "Open your mouths nice and wide and you'll get your gifts back. Aren't you lucky?"

Reyan froze. If she could get herself under control in time she could dissipate. She could fold into the shadow and go running to get Demi. It might not be enough time to save the others, but if she could get a message to Demi even, as queen Demi might be able to realm-skip in where others couldn't.

Blossom advanced with a vial full of shining black and Reyan opened her mouth obediently. Even if she didn't escape, she wanted her gifts back.

Blossom frowned, hesitating.

"She can't escape you idiot," Belladonna snapped. "The cuffs are *metirin* iron and have been crafted by the best of the best. They can't escape, gifts or no gifts."

*That cancels that plan then.*

Reyan prepared herself all the same. As the liquid bubbled and swelled on her tongue, the tingle of utter familiarity rippled through her limbs right to the bone. The shadows leapt and surged toward her, a sense of complete rightness swirling around her. She pulled every essence of her ability around herself.

"She's vanishing!" Someone shouted.

Reyan's body dissipated, her legs and chest and head fading into shadow. But as she tugged at the cuffs, her hands, wrists and forearms wouldn't fade.

Reyan reformed her face so that she could see rather than sense. The moment she did, she wished she hadn't, staring at the length of Belladonna's crossbow.

"Told you." Belladonna laughed, delighted and cruel. "What are her choices, find someone to cut off her hands?"

The gathered group laughed, but a couple of them were looking increasingly nervous, eying the exit and fidgeting behind their sycophantic grins.

"We won't dance around this because I'm getting bored," Belladonna announced. "If you dodge the arrows, I'll start shooting at other people. Now, open the skip-way."

Reyan's mouth fell open. "What? I can't! I don't even know how."

"Don't lie to me."

"How can I lie to you? I'm Fae. I don't know anything about any of this. It's not like we got taught it in shadow-weaver classes, not that anyone ever bothered to give me any."

Belladonna smirked at the attitude. "You were given transmutation. You can turn the painting into a skip-way as easy as breathing, then I can walk through it." She tilted her head. "If you do this, I'll give you pick of the courts *and* I'll ensure you get to keep your fiancé too. Unharmed."

Blossom's soft gasp of indignation suggested that offers

and bargains didn't come often from Belladonna. The mere thought roiled like acid in Reyan's gut.

*And why are the others here? No, she's toying with me for some reason.*

"I doubt that," she said, playing for time. "You'll change the situation any time you choose. No boundaries, no guarantees. Why do you want the Prime Realm so badly anyway? Resources to fight the queen with?"

Belladonna sighed. "Partly. But I also need to know what Emil is hiding. He won't tell me what is so important about the Prime Realm or who he's been whispering to in that infernal mirror, so I'm determined to find out."

"He doesn't know you're here doing this?"

Belladonna stiffened, her eyes flashing with irritation.

"He doesn't have to know. He's not going to be king of Faerie when this is all over. I am."

Reyan tensed for the inevitable lash that would come next.

"You're going to be a king?" She forced a laugh. "Cool. Not sure your brother would be happy about that though. Sorry, half-brother. I forget he's the one with the purer Faerie blood."

Belladonna snarled and stalked toward her, gripping her chin in tight fingertips. Reyan winced, fear pounding through her insides as Belladonna's nails gouged into her skin. She resisted the urge to antagonise Belladonna even further by dissipating her face out of harm's reach.

Blossom huffed loud enough to draw both their attention.

"Enough of this," she said. "We have a back-up plan

anyway, right?"

Belladonna smiled, wickedly dark. "How true. And so much more *fun*."

Reyan sagged as Belladonna whirled away from her, taking a stance in front of the fresco.

"And what would plan two be?" Reyan muttered. "Ritual sacrifice?"

Blossom nodded. "Exactly. These pillars represent your gifts. You have shadow, those three have light, death and life."

"Oh great idea, tell her all the secrets," Belladonna snapped.

Blossom stepped away and Reyan prepared to become shadow or flesh, whichever made things harder for them.

*Reyan, answer me.*

A blissfully familiar voice blasted into her mind.

*If you're there for the love of Faerie Reyan, answer me!*

She almost cried out loud.

*I'm here!* She sent her frantic answer back with as much power behind it as she could. *Can you hear me? Where are you? Are you close? They took my gifts away and only just gave them back, they're going to sacrifice us to open a skip-way to the Prime Realm.*

She waited, hoping the message had transferred back to him. A second later, she heard the feral snarl echo in her mind and almost burst into tears.

*Stall her if you can,* he insisted. *We're close, really close. How many does she have with her?*

She counted quickly. *Eleven Forgotten, her and Blossom, then four of us as captives tied to pillars.*

Her entire existence narrowed down to that blessedly familiar voice in her head, her heart pounding with a sickening amount of hope.

Kainen had told her to stall them but she lifted her head in time to see Belladonna raise her arms and shout an incantation.

For several seconds, Reyan felt nothing. Even as she realised she should be warding herself, although against Belladonna's bountiful power it would likely be pointless, a blast of vivid white light exploded from Belladonna's fingers and Reyan's scream tore the breath from her lungs.

# CHAPTER FIFTEEN
## TIRA

The train was the weirdest thing Tira had ever encountered, a heaving mass of humans all fighting to get on and claim one of the many seats. She was used to horses, carts and sleds, and she knew there were trains throughout Faerie, but those were trundling things powered by natural resources, not the growling, rattling metal monster in front of them.

Demi and Ace seemed perfectly comfortable going through the door to enter the monstrous contraption, Ace insisting he had tickets, but everyone else hesitated. Even the apparently fearless Eastwicks weren't entirely convinced. Tira almost laughed at the way Cheryl was prodding the edge of the doorway with a suspicious frown and Beryl was muttering that it didn't seem natural. Then her mind spasmed away from fear of the human world as Meryl's knuckles brushed against the back of her hand.

The train jolted and shook the moment it started moving, but she quickly got used to the rumbling sway of it and took to eying strangers, all humans. They wore a similar variation of casual clothing to Fae but didn't seem overly keen on catching anyone else's eye, all more absorbed in strange little rectangles of varying colours.

Ace pulled out a rectangle of his own and explained it was basically a human orb reader, mindful to keep his voice low. Milo instantly turned his nose up at it, until Ace introduced him to something called the *inta-net*, which was apparently similar to orb-waves. Milo was lost for the rest of the journey.

"We should have realm-skipped straight in," Kainen muttered, his fist clenching and unfurling on his thigh.

Demi grimaced. "We skipped in as close as we could and we're almost there. We will find her."

His expression didn't brighten at that as he turned his face to the window and glowered at the strange mix of green and grey-brown flying past.

"If anything happens to her," he added. "I'll never forgive myself."

"It wasn't your doing," Taz said.

Kainen pressed his hand to the window as if he could reach through and summon Reyan with it.

"I shouldn't have left her. One stupid argument and she's gone. I was barely gone a minute, then I couldn't get back in. What if they've already hurt her, or…"

Taz glanced at Ace, wordlessly moving his knees so Ace could sit next to Kainen.

"She'll know you're moving the world to find her," Ace said.

Kainen groaned. "What if she doesn't though? We argued. She probably thinks I'm still sulking somewhere."

"What did you fight about?" Demi asked.

Kainen shot her a hostile look but it softened immediately into remorse.

"About our situation. I wanted to stop pretending."

Ace frowned. "Pretending what?"

Kainen slammed his hands to his head, fingers

threading through his brown hair as he folded over with his elbows on his knees.

"The whole thing was a fake," he admitted. "The engagement, all of it."

Tira managed to hide a gasp, and she did it much better than Beryl and the others who were outraged. Hutch and Harvey started muttering about not even having any bets down on it.

"You turned up suggesting I should consider getting engaged to Blossom," Kainen added. "I panicked. Pulled Reyan out of the crowd and made her pretend. She agreed and I made sure she had her freedom from the court out of it, the one thing she wanted. Then she wanted to stay at court, to keep pretending for a while. At that point I didn't even ask why, I just leapt at the chance to keep her a while longer."

Ace whistled softly. "I never would have guessed, even right at the beginning. But it became real? Also, forcing her to pretend, even in any way…"

"I know, trust me, I know." Kainen lifted his head, eyes bloodshot. "She made me suffer for it though, and I would have figured something out if she really hated it."

Tira wiped a hand over her face. She hadn't seen Kainen for a long time until he arrived at her court a couple of days before, but even in those brief moments he and Reyan seemed the most natural couple together.

Kainen sighed. "But then it all unravelled. I've been hoping it's become real for her as well, but she's worried about me getting bored and her going back to having nothing. Orbs, I'd give her the whole court if she wanted it but instead of saying that, I left. Even the court's annoyed with me. When I tried to grab my jacket from my wardrobe it kept throwing hers at me instead. Now that bunch of orb-munchers have her and it's my fault."

"It's their fault," Taz insisted, his tone rising strong enough that Kainen's eyes widened. "You can't be around her permanently. Trust me, it doesn't work."

Demi huffed at that. "And it's exhausting when you try. Besides, Reyan isn't stupid. She'll know you well enough to know you'll be tearing the realms and worlds apart to get her back."

"I think we're almost there anyway now," Ace soothed. "Let's focus on what we have to do when we get there, be prepared."

Out of place, Tira fiddled with the flap of her bag. Her fingers brushed something smooth on the underside and she pulled out a folded piece of paper. She read it, amused to find Marlon had given her an itemised list of everything he'd packed for her, including some bottles of *Beast,* sixteen sandwiches and her orb reader, as though she was off for a jolly day out. Then again if anything in there was able to help get Reyan back to Kainen, no matter how necessary, she'd sacrifice it. They'd all seen too much loss recently.

She glanced at Meryl quickly then away even faster as Meryl's head turned in her direction, as though she'd sensed the look.

Demi sat up straighter and glanced over her shoulder to check they were far enough away from any humans.

"This whole place will be protected," she said. "I don't

know the histories as well as I should, but it was warded long ago to stop random realm-skipping from Faerie."

"The nether seems to keep it clear of the human world also," Sannar said with a frown. "They call it 'matter' and 'anti-matter' here according to some old scribblings I found."

He sat beside his girlfriend, Odella, who was too busy cleaning her glasses on the corner of her cardigan to look up. Neither of them were a lord or lady but Sannar was well known for managing most of the Nether Court despite his lack of title. From what little Tira could make out by the rapid introductions earlier, neither of them were from any noble family, but Demi would no doubt have a reason for bringing them along.

Lord Tyren had entered the odd discussion readily enough but Lady Leilania of the Revel Court, and soon to be Lady of the Flora court also, was absorbed in a notebook. Every now and then she'd glance out of the window, frown at something outside then start scribbling things down.

*These are my equals,* Tira realised. *They'll hopefully be friends too.*

The thought didn't do anything productive toward getting Reyan back or defeating the Forgotten, but she couldn't help the wave of pride all the same.

"Right, we're there pretty much." Demi stood up with a bunch of tiny cards in one hand. "I'm going to give you each one of these. When we go through the ticket barriers, you feed the ticket into the little slot on the machine and the machine will eat it, okay? The little shutter door things will open and you walk through. Ace and I will go first and you copy us."

"Feed the machine, got it," Beryl sniffed. "I'm sure we can manage that."

Tira took the ticket Demi passed to her and clutched it with both hands as the train slowed down. It had stopped at several stations on the way, each time adding to Kainen's irritation, but now everyone was getting up and heading toward the doors.

She stuck right behind Demi and Ace as she hopped over the yawning gap between the train and the station. People streamed past them, humans who knew exactly how everything around them worked. Humans who could lie, a baffling reality to any of the Fae.

Tira flinched when something snared around her hand, but when she looked down she found Meryl's fingers laced through hers. Meryl didn't send a single look her way but the pressure was there all the same, firm, warm and reassuring. Tira clung on.

Demi looked back to check they were all together and followed the chaos of the surging crowd toward a mid-height wall of metal.

"Ticket in and walk through," she said.

Tira stared hard enough to strain her eyes as Demi fed the tiny card into a slot in the front of the machine. Any noise was lost in the crowd but the machine gobbled the ticket and a small door slid open in the barrier.

Demi walked through and Tira stepped up next as Meryl's hand slithered away from hers. She fed her ticket into the slot and darted through the barrier, huffing a relieved breath when Demi gave her a satisfied nod.

"It won't take it." Beryl's indignant screech echoed through the air. "It won't eat my card. Why won't it eat my card? Stupid human machine!"

Several humans turned to stare at her, a mixture of horror and unease on their faces. Ace, who seemed to be waiting to go through last, reached over to twist the card and feed it through. Beryl's cheeks turned red as Cheryl cackled at her, but Tira made sure Meryl was through before turning to look at the stream of humans moving away from the barriers at speed.

"Come on, hurry up," Kainen hissed.

He was at least trying to rein in his gifts, but little fizzles of sparking black smoke kept puffing from his fingertips.

"If anyone asks, you vape," Ace muttered.

Kainen glared at him. "Excuse me?"

"Come on, this way." Demi pushed past both of them, Taz hurrying beside her.

Kainen stormed after them and it was only then that Tira realised Kainen hadn't been given anyone as part of Demi's buddy system. She eyed the long stride and the fists clenched at his sides.

*Probably safest to let him be on his own.*

Tira made sure Meryl was beside her and followed the others outside onto a lane, shrinking into her coat as the cold air snapped around her.

Her mouth dropped open. It wasn't a lane they were on, but several lanes, with many metal carts whizzing by like something out of a garish sledding race going horizontally.

"Whoa." Even Meryl stared, wide-eyed.

Demi didn't seem to be bothered in the slightest as she strode along, keeping to the edge of the light brown building towering over them. Kainen didn't seem to notice as long as they kept moving, but even Taz was staring up and around with wide eyes.

*The human world is absolute chaos.*

Tira scrunched herself ever so slightly smaller, feeling less like a lady of her own court that she ever had done when she wasn't one.

They came to a section where one huge lane full of lanes crossed over another, the metal carts making an awful racket as they shot back and forth. Demi made them stop, pointing out a black pillar with a crude outline of man on it in red.

"So where exactly are we going?" Meryl asked, ignoring her sisters shoving each other beside her in a silent squabble.

"Edinburgh castle is very old," Milo announced. "Originally built on a hill to-"

"Which way?" Kainen snapped.

He stood twisting back and forth as though he could divine Reyan's location by feel alone.

"Follow me, and try not to interact with anyone," Demi said with a doubtful look in Beryl and Cheryl's direction.

The red man became a green man and the pillar started emitting a determined series of loud beeps.

Without warning any of them, Demi set off right across the enormous lane. Metal beasts were still roaring in both directions but none seemed to be coming straight for them. Tira sped her pace up all the same, glad she had Meryl striding beside her looking equally alarmed.

"Hey! Watch it."

Cheryl glared at the retreating back of a bicycle, made from metal and slimmer than the ones Tira recognised from court, but the same basic design.

"Avoid the bikes," Ace suggested gently. "You're walking right in a cycle lane."

The entire place was buzzing with people, none of whom seemed to be bothered about the noise or the mayhem unfolding around them.

"What's the term for a group of humans?" Tira asked Milo, more for something to do than actual interest.

"A crowd." He frowned down at Ace's little rectangle. "This phone thing is actually really quite well organised."

"It should be a chaos of humans," she said nervously.

At least Meryl laughed, although it sounded more out of politeness than actual amusement.

As they rounded a corner, the tall buildings fell away and a large swathe of green appeared in front of them with even more humans charging back and forth.

"There it is!" Milo hissed, pointing wildly. "That's the castle, look."

Everyone looked, heads turning dutifully to stare past the greenery and upward to a building high up on a hill, outlined by the stormy grey sky.

"Now that looks more like Fae architecture," Cheryl said.

Beryl huffed. "What do you orbing know about Fae architecture?"

Tira smothered a smile as they bickered, while Milo

shoved the phone under Taz's nose because he was closest. Taz nodded, his expression twisting with doubt.

"Will we be able to get in?" he asked.

Demi nodded. "Yeah, I checked ahead. This way."

She led them on a merry dance through the crowds, twisting this way and that until the enormous sprawl of the castle disappeared and they were swallowed by more towering brown and grey buildings.

They passed countless doorways and windows, many with brightly glowing signs above their doors, but no sign of an entrance suitable for the castle. Tira eyed the signs above the doors with a frown, wondering why they advertised themselves as shops if they had no produce out front to entice customers.

They walked on until fragrant smells of food filled the air and Taz slowed down, his eyes lighting up.

"There's doughnuts somewhere near here," he insisted.

Demi checked a phone of her own with a frown, then nodded to herself.

"Probably, but we don't have time right now. We're here."

She started toward one that promised to sell 'artisan baguettes'.

"Um… are you sure this is it?" Even Ace sounded unsure.

"Yep." Demi raised her hand to tap a grey square of numbers beside a random glass door. "What, did you think the entrance to a hidden prime realm location would be inside the castle itself? There would be too many scholars poking about over the years and unearthing things that way. No, we need to get underneath it, not inside it."

She tapped a complicated sequence of numbers on the panel until a sharp buzzing noise filled the air. The door opened when she pulled the long handle and Tira sucked in a determined breath. Further away from her court than she'd ever imagined being in her life, she at least had the strongest Fae in all of Faerie around her.

*Even if we aren't actually in Faerie. Do our gifts even work here in the human world? Demi said they should but she didn't sound sure.*

The thought hit her and she pulled her hearing gift to the fore. Distorted sounds from random passers-by sharpened, the clarity coming to her loud and clear, if a little echoier than normal.

*Phew.*

She shuffled through the doorway and took in the blank white walls, grey floor and three sturdy white doors on their left, with one at the far end.

Demi made sure everyone was inside before heading to the door at the far end and tapping another number panel.

"At least there's a use for that memory of yours," Taz said cheerfully.

Demi shrugged and pushed the door open. "Cheryl, you get those?"

"Yep." Cheryl nodded. "If anything happens, I'm the escape plan."

"Why do you get to be the escape plan?" Beryl demanded.

"Because I'm the one with the memory gift. You'd have to bust a hole in half of whatever this place was called.

Doubt the humans would appreciate that."

"It's called Edinburgh," Milo piped up. "It's actually one of the-"

Demi pointed at the doorway before Kainen could start throttling him.

"Everyone inside. Taz, Kainen and I will go first. Tira and Meryl next. Lolly and Tyren, then Sannar and Odella. Beryl and Cheryl, Hutch and Harvey, then Ace and Milo at the back. Let's go."

She didn't wait to see if everyone obeyed, striding through the doorway with Taz and Kainen right behind her.

"Wardings up obviously," she called back.

Tira entered the corridor on the other side and shivered as they moved into a hallway of ancient stone walls. With Meryl beside her and not much room to keep space between them, Tira raised a protection warding and matched her breathing to the shuffling rhythm of everyone's footfalls.

So absorbed in trying not to panic about what might be ahead, she almost squeaked out loud as Meryl's warding brushed against hers, a subtle tingle of energy that set her pulse pounding even harder.

"We can merge our wardings for strength," Meryl suggested.

Tira nodded. Her mother had trained her to do that from a young age, determined the future lady of the court would be able to protect herself if injured or against a larger group. It made sense also because she was still getting twinges and aches in her gut from where Claus had thrown her.

As she let her warding soften, she could sense the subtle press of Meryl's alongside it and focused on hers absorbing that pressure, welcoming it.

There was something almost intimate about the gesture, even though it was purely for added strength. She sucked in a startled breath as warm fingers snared around her own. Meryl's gaze was focused ahead, but there was a rigidity to it that suggested she was trying not to look down at their hands now joined.

*Focus on what's ahead. You have a court to represent now, and then a court to run when you get back home. Romance needs to take a backseat.*

And it would always need to take a backseat now, at least until she could run her court competently and find someone who would put up with all the caveats the role entailed. But she clung to Meryl's hand all the same, letting her mind fill with every unlikely but delightful maybe as the corridors twisted and turned, leading them deeper into danger.

"Oh thank Faerie."

Kainen's voice echoed through the corridor. Everyone came to a halt.

"You back in touch again?" Demi asked.

He nodded and started walking again, his pace even faster than before. Nothing more was said for a couple of minutes as they trotted along, Demi indicating left or right with her hand as he powered ahead.

"That'll be Reyan he's talking to with mind-speak," Meryl murmured. "That means we must be close now if their connection's re-established."

Tira nodded, gulping against the catch in her throat. She wasn't used to sparring, although her mother had insisted she train in both gift and physical combat in younger years. She also wasn't sure what Demi wanted her here for exactly, or what use she could be, but she owed Demi for both her title and the absence of her stepbrother.

"Um, do we know what to expect?" Milo asked, his voice wavering. "It's not like we had time to get blueprints or anything, so what if we're going in the wrong direction? How do we know where we're going exactly?"

Demi didn't even glance back. "Queen."

A loud huff echoed up from the back, Milo clearly not happy with the reply. He didn't say anymore though, either because he knew he wouldn't get an answer or because Kainen had stopped, one arm flung out an arm to block Demi going any further.

Taz's wings flared on instinct, the burnished orange feathers flaming bright and sending shadows dancing across the wall.

"There are thirteen enemy Fae down there," Kainen said. "Plus Reyan and three others in trouble. She says Belladonna is furious that her gift isn't opening the skip-way to the prime realm."

A strident voice rang out from the far end of the hall, the words indistinguishable but the derisive inflection in the tone clear enough.

"Any chance of normies or innocents this far down?" Taz asked, rolling up the sleeves of his hoodie.

Demi shook her head. "Next to none. Wardings firm and we go in calm. Stay in your pairs and don't engage until I say so. Kainen, if she's conscious, give her this. Healing tonic."

She handed a vial of dark purple liquid to Kainen and set off along the hall. Tira forced her legs to follow them, her nerves pounding in her ears.

"Can I ask what gifts you have?" Meryl squeezed her hand tighter, flipping the hold so that their fingers were interlaced. "You told me about the hearing one, but any others?"

Tira nodded. "A charm gift and a small fire gift. The fire doesn't do much but it's enough to light a match in the dark."

"Sometimes that small spark is all we need," Meryl insisted. "Stay with me for protection, follow my lead if you'll permit it, and we'll give them all we've got."

Tira squared her shoulders, reminding herself over and over that she was lady of a court now. If this were her court she'd be expected to fight for it, and these were her stepbrother's friends she was about to go up against.

The hall ended and opened into a vaulted room of brown stone and ancient brick. Even among the arched pillars towering throughout the space, it was the huge pastoral fresco on the far wall that drew everyone's attention.

A flash of light seared across the room accompanied by a chorus of blood-chilling screams.

Demi strode forward, inhaling a breath as the enemy rotated to face them.

"Get your orb-munching hands away from my fiancée!"

Demi froze, her mouth stuck open as Kainen ran past

her with an almighty roar, glittering black smoke roiling out of his body until he was a charging mass of sparkling darkness.

"So much for don't engage until I say so." Demi sighed. "Here goes nothing then."

With a flick of her hand she sent a wave of crackling ice-blue power radiating out, knocking the enemy down like skittle-pins. They tumbled and bashed into each other with startled yells as Kainen's darkness was puffed sideways.

Tira eyed the four people tied to pillars and her insides curdled with nausea. Two of them were already unconscious, or worse. Nearest the painting, Reyan managed to lift her head as Demi strode into the open space with a wide grin.

"Wow, thanks for holding the fun until we got here."

# CHAPTER SIXTEEN
## REYAN

*"Get your orb-munching hands away from my fiancée!"*

Kainen's voice blasted in Reyan's ears through the shattering pain and her heart lifted. Struggling against the cuffs holding her wrists, she winced as the metal dug into her bare skin.

"Are you okay?"

He sounded right beside her as the sizzle and clash of gifts filled the air. A flare of heat flashed past them closely followed by a loud crash. Reyan opened her eyes with great effort, the hazy vision of Kainen's face all she could see. For a moment she thought her vision was failing, but he leaned back and the whole scene focused.

"She tried to open the skip-way, but it didn't work." Her voice shook as Kainen started trying to tear at the cuffs binding her. "They were going to sacrifice us."

He snarled something she didn't catch and turned around. Reyan recognised Meryl as she raced up to press her fingers and thumbs around the cuffs. Reyan stared in confusion until the metal began to warm against her skin.

"Is it working?" she asked. "She said the cuffs were immune to gifts."

Meryl grimaced. "*Metirin* iron, but they skimped because it's only on the inside to create an unbroken circle, so I can warp the rest of it. Give me a second."

She pulled something out of her sleeve with her mouth,

most of the cuff melted to the sides like the parting of a sea, but the rest she picked at with a long pin.

"There we go." Meryl stepped back as the cuffs fell away.

She was off across the room again with Tira Starhollow speeding behind her before Reyan could thank her.

A flash of something lit the air and sparks rained toward them, doming a few feet from hitting them. Sinking into Kainen's arms, Reyan tried to summon a protection warding but Kainen shook his head, one arm anchored around her waist and his free hand pressing against her cheek to sweep her hair back.

"I've got us, relax. You're safe now. Are you hurt?"

She pulled a face. "Nothing lasting I don't think. Few bumps and bruises. It's the painting though, it's all real. To open it they need shadow, light, death and life. It's our gifts."

"I know, sweetheart. Don't worry about that now." He held out an open flask filled with something ominously dark purple. "Drink this, Demi swears by it."

Reyan grabbed the flask and downed the contents without a second thought. The liquid burned her throat but she trusted Kainen completely.

*Unless he's glamouring...*

"Are you really you?" she asked, panic scraping her already raw throat.

Realisation flashed in his eyes.

"I am definitely Kainen Hemlock, Lord of the Illusion Court, I should have said that first, sorry."

Even with him mind-speaking to her before, she needed

that reassurance, needed to know it was definitely him. But some of the physical pain seemed to be receding, her skin shaking off the burns from the rope and her aching limbs loosening.

"I feel better," she said. "Not great, but mostly normal."

He snorted and hauled her downwards as something zipped over their heads.

"It's a healing tonic. Stick with me now and we'll fight with Demi and Taz, okay? Are you fit enough to fight?"

She nodded. "After whatever that drink was, I feel fit enough to take on an entire court, or use transmutation against them at least."

She pressed against him and followed through the melee toward the fresco where Demi and Taz were sending out their gifts to keep the Forgotten at bay. Lolly and Tyren were moving fast to keep the enemy fractured while Odella, Sannar and Beryl had the rock around them dancing through the air like arrows. Meryl and Tira stood together near the exit, fighting with combat against the enemy.

"Did Betty find you?" she had to ask, had to know.

Kainen nodded and dredged up a cloud of sparkling black smoke, sending it out toward someone charging at them. The woman crumpled to the floor, her hands clutching her head.

"She gave me your message and I went straight to Demi. I will never forgive myself for leaving you. Never."

She pulled her transmutation power to the fore and sent it out, turning the floor underfoot to dust. Two men flailed as the ground shifted beneath them like sand, but before they could topple over she felt another force separate from her own gift tugging at the earth, hardening it around their ankles.

"Easier to keep them pinned than let them get up again," Taz shouted with a grin as he dashed past.

Reyan nodded and aimed for Belladonna next, who stood with sparks flying from her fingers, snapping out and exploding on wardings with no sign of any aim or chosen victims. Even with the ground yielding to Reyan's gift and turning to liquid, Belladonna's warding kept all attacks outside the boundary.

Reyan yelped as Kainen shoved himself in front of her to ward off someone charging toward them with a large whip. The crack hit their warding and Reyan recognised the smirk on the face before she recognised the person it belonged to. Fighting alongside the enemy, Lorens was someone she had no qualms about attacking.

She turned the end of the whip to a gloopy mess, the leather turning pulpy and flopping to the floor with a sad splat that got lost in the carnage.

"I still can't manage water," she muttered.

Kainen rolled his eyes. "You're doing great, stop griping. Do you forgive me at least? For leaving you I mean?"

"Yeah. Don't do it again though."

He smiled even though his eyes were still full of guilt and sorrow.

"Missed me, did you?"

She grinned. "You wish."

He reached out through their warding and grabbed the

arm of a random man passing, clamping a hand to his head. The man shuddered and dashed toward the exit, ignoring Belladonna's shouts for him to come back.

"I do want you to miss me," he admitted. "More than you can ever imagine. But more than that I want you safe. When we get home I'm never letting you out of my sight again."

Reyan snorted loudly and practiced relaxing the earth under the enemy's feet and solidifying it around them. Their panic at being contained in one place seemed to be fracturing their efforts much more successfully than knocking them over did.

"Never mind that. I'll need a break once this is all over, assuming we make it out alive."

Kainen held his hand out, the black smoke curling through the crowd without his attention on it.

"Don't worry, I can't let anything happen to my future wife. Think of the scandal."

"Fake future wife, you mean."

He winked at her. "Only if you say so, sweetheart. I've put Meri in charge until we return, and officially named you lady in my stead if I don't survive and you do. Demi's endorsed it too, or she will when I tell her to."

Despite the battle raging around them, Reyan stopped focusing outside their warding. She knew something he didn't, or at least she had to assume he didn't know the court had claimed her by itself.

She took a deep breath. It would be the only test she would put his way, and she would honour his answer in whatever way it came.

"But how will you reverse it if the worst happens?" she asked.

Kainen frowned. "Reverse what?"

"The whole me pretending to be lady thing."

"Why would I want to reverse it?"

"Kainen, if something happened to you, and if I was only a pretend lady, you'd need the real next in line to take over at some point. This whole thing was a fake, our engagement, my title, all of it."

He grinned. "Is it? Everyone in Faerie believes you're mine, even those who know the engagement is technically pretend. You've been lady of our court ever since you agreed to fake marry me. The multiway door opens to you. The court accommodates your needs without you asking. Meri accepts you and even reports to you, something she never condescends to do for me. Not without grumbling about it anyway. Even Demi recognises you as my successor. The court has claimed you, sweetheart, with or without me."

An almighty explosion shook the foundations of the chamber, dust and rock shuddering down around them.

Reyan took a step back, aware that this wasn't the time for debates, but Kainen reached out for her and pulled her back to him.

"You *are* Lady of the Illusion Court, no fakes or pretences. The only question is, are you only the lady of our court or are you also mine? Because it turns out that I'm hopelessly in love with you and have been for months."

Taz dashed in front of them with his wings outstretched,

his hand waving random patterns in front of him.

"This is not really the time you two!" he yelled, his voice whipped up in the chaotic sizzle of gifts flying all over the place.

Reyan clung to Kainen's arms to right herself and drew on the strength of the shadows around her.

"We'll discuss this later," he conceded, grimacing at the mayhem.

Reyan took a deep breath and shook her head, a wicked smile breaking across her face as she sent her transmutation gift flying into a pillar, turning it to a dust cloud for the shadows to obscure the enemy with.

"No point discussing it," she said, decision made. "I should have told you before at the Fauna Court but doubt got the best of me. No more doubting. If you want me I'm yours, court or no court."

The kiss that followed had no delicacy and months of pent-up frustration poured into it. Reyan's insides exploded with fizzles of utter delight and she wrapped her arms tight around his neck as his anchored around her waist. The touch of his mouth on hers chased away all thoughts, all noise and even the shove and crash of the fight on their warding faded into insignificance as his fingers wove into her hair, pulling her closer.

When he finally released her uncountable moments later, Reyan faced the fight with a ridiculously dopey grin on her face.

# CHAPTER SEVENTEEN
## MERYL

"Heads up!"

Meryl ducked as Beryl burst past her with trailing bits of rock falling behind her. Seconds later, Harvey chased after her with a bright pink umbrella to avoid the worst of the debris.

Tira gasped as someone sent a wave of hot air toward them, but Harvey swished the umbrella down and used it to swipe the onslaught aside.

"Stick close to me," Meryl called out.

Tira nodded then dodged off to the side, her hand held out with fire dancing on her palm. Charging after her, Meryl stumbled to a halt as Tira flicked her fingertips through the flames and pulled back like she was aiming a tiny archer's bow. Bolts of flame shot out from her fingertips like arrows, searing against wardings and setting one man's clothing on fire.

"Whoa." Meryl couldn't keep the amazement in. "You said it was just a small fire! Can you warm metal?"

Tira shrugged, a pleased smirk on her tired face.

"Probably, if it stays in the flame. I have to be careful not to get confused and end up summoning any nearby butterflies and accidentally sling-shotting them instead though."

A laugh bubbled up and Meryl let it out, a strange elation tearing through her with distant familiarity. She reinforced her warding strong as a woman stumbling away from a swarm of needles almost crashed into them. Not thinking, Meryl reached out and wrapped an arm around Tira's waist, pulling her out of the way. She closed her eyes as a subtle brush of her nose against Tira's hair had all kinds of unhelpful thoughts filling her head.

"Thanks," Tira muttered.

Meryl smiled to see her cheeks going bright pink, clinging on for a second longer than she had to before letting go. It didn't stop her boldly reaching forward and grabbing Tira's hand either, lady or not.

"I've got an idea," she explained.

Tira followed her without a single protest through the chaos, ducking and dodging whenever someone came at them. Someone crashed to the floor in front of them and Tira squeaked as she had to hop over them.

Meryl couldn't seem to shake her smile, even though the fight was evenly matched on both sides with no sign of ending. Tira sounded so ladylike but she had that inner strength plastered over her face, fire dancing on her palm as they stopped in front of the captive tied to the first pillar.

"I'm going to melt the cuffs," she said, pointing upward. "Can you burn the ropes around his middle?"

Tira nodded. "On it."

The young man pinned to the pillar with his hands over his head was unconscious but the subtle rasp of breathing kept them working together to break the bonds.

Meryl steadied his lolling body until Tira finished burning through the ropes and they helped him down.

"Cheryl!"

Meryl hollered until her sister and Hutch appeared beside them.

"Get him out, we'll do the others."

Hutch heaved the man into his arms bridal style and charged off, Cheryl right behind him with a warding raised.

The next pillar held an elderly lady, and Meryl seethed as she worked on the restraints. The wave of hatred increased when Belladonna appeared in the corner of her vision, fighting Demi and Taz with wave after wave of vindictive power.

With the old woman released, also unconscious, Beryl and Harvey arrived to spirit them to safety. Meryl had no idea where they would take the captives if realm-skipping was a problem, but she turned to the young woman tied to the pillar opposite Reyan's and nearest the large forest painting on the back wall.

Sorrow sank in her heart as she realised the young woman wouldn't be seeing the outside world again.

"Whoa!"

Tira dodged as something lashed into the space she'd been standing in. Meryl wrapped a protective arm around her waist, the movement instinctive as she pulled Tira close and hemmed the protection tighter around them.

The length of whip retracted and Meryl followed the line of it right back to hands attached to a familiar body.

Lorens, the one Demi was so worried about, gave them an indolent smile.

*Not us. Her.*

"You should have accepted my proposition, Tira," he

said. "Although, I hear you've taken your brother's place at court now. You have more spirit perhaps than I gave you credit for."

Fury danced in Meryl's head. He'd been there when Petra had died. He'd been roaming around, causing trouble. She eyed the metal studs in his whip, sending her power out with a sharp jab of her hand. The metal softened, wielding to her touch. To make the whip unholdable was the humane thing to do.

One glance at Tira's stubborn scowl hiding so much weariness and fear though, and Meryl was beyond humane.

The metal morphed into spikes under her command, piercing through Loren's fist. He winced and looked down as she twisted those sturdy points, curving them into his flesh until they scraped bone.

He yelped and tried to shake it off but the metal spiralled and spiked. His trousers sagged as the metal from his belt conceded to her will and rivulets of it dribbled up his body, arcing through the air and forcing small plates around the entry points, reinforcing their hold.

"Hey, let it go."

Tira's voice echoed through the maelstrom of fury and grief powering her. Meryl blinked, her lashes clogged with tears.

She didn't fight when Tira took her hand, the thumb rubbing soothing circles over her knuckles.

"Let's get this lady out," Tira insisted. "Her family would want that."

Meryl nodded. Staring at the young woman's body, the corpse of someone she didn't know, made her think of people she did know. Had known. Had loved even.

"Okay, we've got her." Hutch rested a hand on Meryl's shoulder and she flinched, almost about to start fighting him. "Just undo those cuffs. Demi's got contacts here now so they'll do what needs to be done."

Meryl fumbled with her gift, sluggish after using such a splurge of power. She glanced at Lorens still trying to ease the spikes out of his hand. She couldn't regret hurting him.

"Well, this is nice," Beryl said, frowning when everyone stared at her. "Not *nice*, but it's good to do things as a family."

Even Harvey, ever doting, pressed a hand to his face in torment.

"We don't usually have company for it is what I mean," Beryl added, nodding at Tira. "Especially not nobility."

"It's not the first excursion I would have chosen as a court lady," Tira replied. "But it'll do."

Beryl smiled wide. "Well, when you get round to meeting the fam- *why are you kicking me?!*"

Meryl stopped kicking her sister, but she couldn't do anything about the bright red burn that was no doubt covering her entire face.

"Ignore her," she muttered.

Tira helped Hutch cover the woman's body in a blanket someone had summoned and watched as he jogged away with her, Cheryl alongside him. Meryl eyed the fight, tense and ready to protect, but she caught Beryl frowning at her.

"You don't need to be so tetchy," she grumbled.

Meryl sighed. "You can't go round inviting ladies of courts round to meet the family."

"Why not?"

Tira raised her brow, amused. "Yeah, why not?"

"Because-" She had no answer. "It's not done."

"Are you saying you don't want me to meet your family?" Tira asked, openly grinning now.

"No, but-"

"We could even get a selection of guest towels specifically for nobility," Beryl joined in merrily. "Our mum's absolutely bonkers about having the right type of towel. She's probably dying for an excuse to get a set of hers and hers- *Seriously with the kicking!*"

Meryl stopped kicking and gave her sister a shove instead, pointing into the crowd.

"We're supposed to be fighting the enemy," she growled. "Go talk at them if you have to annoy someone."

Beryl gave her a wicked grin and launched back into the fight, joining Harvey as he turned to face an entire group of grown men and women. Before Tira could start teasing her, because it looked like she was about to, Meryl grabbed the first change of topic she could think of.

"We're still no closer to figuring out this skip-way to the Prime Realm situation," she said.

Tira nodded, turning to face the fight. The Forgotten were grouping together in the far corner furthest from the exit to fight out as one unit, but the fringes of their protection wardings were pinning Demi, Taz, Kainen and Reyan against the painted wall. Meryl clung to Tira's hand like a lifeline and dragged her toward Hutch and Cheryl running back in.

"We're not going to get it figured out, are we?" she said.

"We should retreat and try to figure it out before anyone else gets hurt."

The others sent her sympathetic looks, but her attention snagged on Tira's distracted frown.

"Why did they have captives tied?" she asked. "Why one on each pillar? And why were there different markings on each painting, one on each pillar?"

She was off before Meryl could stop her, fingers slithering free and the warding parting around her.

Meryl swore and darted after her, pushing her protection warding forward and stretching it so it formed a shield between Tira and the Forgotten still sending out attacks in all directions. A thud hit her shield, reverberating hard enough to rattle right to the bone as a shower of bright red sparks exploded against it. Meryl winced and kept running until Tira stumbled to a halt in front of Demi and Reyan.

"We're outnumbered," Demi said, her voice tense.

"The paintings," Tira insisted. "They had a symbol on one pillar each, and titles. Reyan, what did they want from you?"

Reyan shook her head. "Belladonna wouldn't say, then she attacked. It felt like my soul was being flayed open. She kept going on about my shadow before though, telling me to transmutate the painting to a skip-way and use the shadows to send her through. Then Blossom was going on about sacrifices, I think."

Meryl eyed those around them as realisation dawned.

"Light, shadow, life and death." She stared at Tira's fingers devoid of flame while the others stared at her.

"*Atan* was essence in the old language, but what if by essence it meant magic? Could it… Could it be referring to gifts?"

# CHAPTER EIGHTEEN
# REYAN

Reyan overheard Meryl's suggestion about gifts being the key to opening the skip-way to the Prime Realm, but even if she was right, whatever Belladonna had tried using her and the other three captives for hadn't worked. If it was a case of using gifts to open a skip-way to the Prime Realm, either they were in the wrong place or they were using the wrong gifts.

*Or the process didn't have enough time to work.*

A crowd of Forgotten surged at them, men and women, young and old. Some still wore expressions of excitement about being part of the carnage, until Demi sent out a wave of crackling energy to hold them back. Even with all her bountiful power, there was a noticeable pinch at the edge of Demi's eyes. She was exhausted, as worn as Reyan felt deep down to her bones despite the tonic. Meanwhile Belladonna seemed to have fighters streaming in as quickly as they were incapacitated or knocked down.

Tyren had an arm around Lolly's waist as she tried to reach Belladonna, her face red and her lips torn in a feral snarl that got lost in the commotion.

The Eastwicks and Hutchinsons had taken care of the other captives and now stood clustered with Sannar, Odella, Lolly and Tyren, all sending out attacks wherever they could. Their efforts landed savage blows but the Forgotten were spreading out as a wall now, cutting them off. Reyan eyed those beside her, Meryl and Tira together, Taz and Demi exchanging doubtful looks. And Kainen pushed right against her, his arm tight around her waist.

"I'm taking her," Taz muttered.

He shot forward with the flash of a glimmering sword appearing in his hand, his flaming wings stretching wide as he lifted off the floor.

Demi screamed after him but he was out of the warding and above Belladonna before she could react, his sword slashing a hole in the top of her protection.

"That sword is *metirin* iron," Kainen said, his tone awed. "Is that the one that killed the Old King?"

Demi nodded, her face tense with panic. Taz bore forward, hacking at Belladonna's protection like a vengeful fallen angel. Beryl and the others turned their attention to defending him, their rock and fire attacks battering at Belladonna's now partially unprotected back. She staggered, the movement ungraceful, and Reyan faced the wall of Forgotten pressing in on them.

"This is a straight fight," Kainen shouted. "You don't have to listen to the ravings of an outcast drunk on power. You don't have your sacrifices either to get anywhere, so leave while you still have your lives!"

Reyan felt the wave of compulsion ripple over the crowd. How he was targeting the Forgotten without somehow snaring their own group in the command she had no idea, but it seemed to be working.

A couple of the Forgotten faltered in their attacks. Kainen's black smoke plumed, covering them in a black haze of doubt that Reyan could sense even through the warding. Sending out her shadows, she bid them carry the smoke if they could to ease his efforts.

Blossom pushed through the crowd, her eyes wide and her mouth moving over words Reyan couldn't make out. One thing she did know was that Blossom had threatened Kainen's life, told her that he'd be next if she didn't cooperate. She wasn't having that.

"Keep it going," she shouted.

Dodging out of their warding and throwing up her own while Kainen was too occupied to stop her, she ignored him roaring her name and sent her transmutation gift flying out toward Blossom and the ground beneath her. Zipping into her shadow form, she darted around Blossom in an arc, carving a pit. The urge to scare her enemy rose and a surge of power thrummed through her shadow-form. The ground beneath them became a swamp, the earth turning to mud, then dirty water that Blossom sank into with a startled scream.

Digging it deep and wide, Reyan re-formed her body to flesh and bone, clamping her warding tight around her.

"Threaten him again, or so much as look at him, and I'll turn your eyeballs to shadow," she seethed.

Blossom opened her mouth to answer, to protest maybe, but she seemed to be flailing and sinking under.

*Sinking.*

Reyan saw the substance around Blossom clearer now, the quicksand sucking her down.

*Crud. I can't actually let her die.*

She looked around for something to throw out, or something she could turn solid at least, but saw nothing.

"Betty!" she shouted.

If the snake was lurking close by, she would come. She saw Lorens nearby too, his whip attacks now focused on the rest of their group. As he glanced her way, she opened her mouth to call out. Blossom was on his side; he would help her.

Lorens grinned and turned back to his fight.

*He doesn't even care.*

Determined not to be the same, Reyan huffed in relief as a solid darkness slithered through the shadows toward her.

"We need to get her out!" Reyan pointed at Blossom.

Betty gave her a look, the shadowy lids narrowed as if to say 'really?' but the outline of her head sharpened and her body began to glimmer. The faint hint of scales became solid, wholly real, as real as Reyan's skin and bone body, the shining black mass of her extending right to her mouth and the wickedly lethal beige fangs hanging from her open jaws.

Blossom screamed and sank underneath the surface as Betty's mouth snapped after her, the scaled nose submerging until Reyan was sure she'd lose them both. With an almighty jerk of her body that almost knocked out some of the Forgotten fighting behind her, Betty lifted her head and reappeared with Blossom's legs flailing over the edge of her mouth.

*I could eat her. Tasty fish.*

"No! Spit her out." Reyan held up both hands in alarm. "You don't know where she's been!"

Betty hesitated, then daintily spat Blossom's grimy

body onto the floor. Reyan solidified the quicksand as best she could and dodged back beneath her protection warding. Even as she firmed it around her, she felt it knitting with Kainen's, which had no doubt been over her the whole time.

Blossom scrambled to her feet like a sand-monster and snapped her fingers.

"Betty, out of here, now," Reyan shouted.

Betty lashed out with her tail but somehow Blossom managed to dodge it and took aim at Betty's head with an outstretched hand. A crossbow materialised, its dark iron arrow glinting the firelight.

Screaming at the top of her voice, Reyan charged at Blossom and barrelled her to the floor. The crossbow twanged right beside her ear, the arrow whistling past her head. She shoved her hands against Blossom's wriggling shoulders made slippery by the quicksand and twisted to see it embedded in the wall.

Betty was nowhere to be seen, which was better than hurt. Whether she'd gone for help or just decided it wasn't worth the fight, Reyan wasn't sure, but she clambered to her feet and inched away.

If Blossom could summon unlimited iron crossbows, they were at a huge disadvantage.

A shout rose up and Reyan turned on instinct, twisting her body to try and keep Blossom in sight, although Blossom was staring past her, the crossbow tilting in her hand. Demi stood by the fresco, unnervingly still as she stared at it.

Reyan flinched as Lolly and Tyren reached her.

"I can feel it," Lolly said, her tone uncertain. "And you, I can feel some kind of pull toward you. What is this?"

Tyren nodded. "Me too. I can feel death in the painting, beyond it somehow. It's not just dull rock now but actual absence of life, the non-existence."

"The void of absence," Reyan echoed. "I feel the shadow in it as well."

She looked for Belladonna but she was still fighting Taz. A flicker of movement caught in the corner of her eye. Blossom had the crossbow raised and Reyan didn't need to look behind her to recognise the arrow's line to its intended target.

With a feral yell she shot forward and shoved her hands against Blossom's chest. Her fingers pressed against Blossom's warding, the resistance of it bowing against her touch but holding firm enough to keep her back.

*TWANG.*

The arrow whistled right past her ear and she turned on her heel, stumbling over her feet in a mad attempt to dash toward the fresco.

She screamed as the arrow hit Kainen's warding. It pierced through easily and scraped into the side of his arm, bouncing off the blank stretch of wall to the side of him. He dropped to his knees, his head lifting and his expression frozen. Demi caught Reyan's eye as she bent over, already summoning a wad of cloth to bandage him with.

*He'll be okay. Demi will get him to a healer, or she'll heal him, or stop the blood at least. He has to be okay.*

Rage caught her in a burning grip and she shoved against Blossom's warding with all her strength. She didn't need to get through it; her target was right behind them. Pushing and kicking and shunting everything she had, Blossom had no option but to step back, and back. And back, right into the path of Taz's twirling sword.

Blossom's eyes widened as the blade swiped a hole in her protection. Reyan kept pushing. She would push Blossom right into the path of that sword until she paid for what she did to Kainen. What she'd intended to do. She didn't care that Taz was Blossom's brother, or that she was essentially attacking a princess of Faerie. She might incur the Oak Queen's wrath in retribution but it didn't matter. The Oak Queen wasn't here.

"Summon us some more help, idiot!" Belladonna yelled. "A new gift, some weapons, anything that will give us time to get the skip-way open."

Blossom met Reyan's furious gaze, the sheer resigned quirk of her mouth stilling the rage momentarily. As Blossom closed her eyes and inhaled deep, Reyan lifted her hands to keep attacking any way she could.

"What the-"

Belladonna's shout was lost as an alarming ripple shuddered the foundations around them. Everyone left fighting froze, gifts sizzling to nothing. Reyan took a step back, ready to grab Kainen and run if she had to. They only needed to get out of the danger zone and she would be able to skip them home.

Reyan froze as a savage punch hit between her ribs, the force so sudden she wondered if Blossom had somehow shot an arrow right through her. A bright flash wiped away any hope of sight and a brush of hot air roared over her body before she landed against something solid with a resounding thud. Her skin burned with prickles and tiny stinging stabs, the sensation of something not right radiating through her entire being.

But she could still feel the shadows too and gathered them to her, sliding partially into them and using them to dull the sparkling in her vision. She lifted her head, even now searching for him. Across the slew of bodies, several trying to get to their feet and others not moving at all, she found him.

Demi had a hand on Kainen's good shoulder but he was ignoring her, his eyes fixed on Reyan. She wriggled, trying to get on her hands and knees as his eyes widened and his entire body froze. Beside him, Demi jerked like a puppet, her mouth forming silent words.

The painting behind them was moving, a flicker of wind waving the painted trees as any hint of actual rock from the wall dribbled away from sight and existence.

"No!" Reyan screamed, fighting her uncoordinated limbs to reach them.

Something flashed past her, not another explosion but Taz flying fast, his hands outstretched as Demi and Kainen began to shrink. Still scrambling forward, Reyan caught Kainen's gaze as he grew smaller and the rock began to re-materialise beneath the fresco, closing in around them.

Kainen's last lingering look was for her, his lips mouthing something so meaningful it crushed her ability to breathe. She opened her mouth, huffing in a breath to mouth the same words back, the attempt dying on her lips as he and Demi vanished.

Reyan's insides crunched but she couldn't move. Her gaze was still fixed to the place where Kainen had disappeared as Taz crashed into the wall beside it. Numbness spread throughout her body, separating her from the awful prickling still needling her to the bone. She had no idea if she was becoming shadow or if losing Kainen had rendered her immobile.

As the paint of the fresco began to bleed from the wall in faded dribbles, the image of it now a garbled mess of dripping colours, Taz's scream echoed the same unimaginable pain that radiated through to her soul.

# CHAPTER NINETEEN
## TIRA

Tira stared in horror as Demi and Kainen vanished into the painting. The skip-way had swallowed them before disappearing, the rock of the actual wall still solid as the fresco began to drip to the floor. Taz banged his fists against the rock, screaming and shouting intelligible noises, calling for Demi.

Nobody answered him.

"Come on, up, quickly."

Tira realised she was still lying on her side from the explosion of light and looked up at Meryl standing over her. She took Meryl's hand and clambered to her feet, looking around at the wreckage.

"Did they skip?" Tira asked, hoping but not believing.

Meryl winced. "I don't know. Mind-speak is the first thing they'll try and if Taz can't reach her through that then something's gone seriously wrong."

Which left them in a room with the enemy minus a queen. Pillars were missing half their stone and any more damage might bring the roof down on top of everyone. Several people were nursing injuries and Belladonna stood with Blossom, both hands on her shoulders as she shook her viciously.

"You can't do anything right!" Belladonna screamed. "How could you muck up transferring my gifts into someone else? They're *all gone*, all of them! Who has them? Who stole my gifts? I'll slaughter the lot of you!"

"We're still vulnerable in the human world," Cheryl shouted. "Ace, Milo, get Taz. Beryl, help them. Everyone else, follow me."

Tira didn't fancy Ace and Milo's job. The queen was gone, disappeared to Faerie knew where. Taz was still pounding his fists bloody on the wall, his front and head covered in splatters of paint. Tira grimaced as she saw Reyan still down.

"Help me get her up." She tugged Meryl's hand still in hers and started across.

Meryl dropped the contact and passed her hand over Reyan's shoulder.

"Come with us, Lady," she said softly. "Quickly."

Some kind of realisation dawned on Reyan's face, widening her eyes although she didn't drag them away from the wall.

"Wait!" Tira called out as Reyan broke free.

Taz didn't notice Reyan appearing beside him, but seconds later she dissipated into shadow and reappeared. She repeated the same thing before slamming her hands against the rock.

"I've tried that," Taz shouted. "It won't work. Demi! For the love of Faerie, answer me!"

Reyan slid to her knees, the telltale sign of sobs in her shaking shoulders.

Ace and Milo weaved past and managed to clamp hold of Taz, one on either side of him, murmuring things as he fought against them.

When Meryl reached down to help Reyan up, she

accepted the hand, so Tira offered her an arm on the other side. Reyan's feet slithered when she tried to stand so they supported her to where the others were waiting. Ace and Milo had Taz in some kind of body clamp, even though he was struggling and clawing at them to escape.

"Yeah I know, mate," Ace soothed. "But she's not on the other side of the wall and that skip-way isn't opening again. We go back to the ogle, we get everyone at home working on it. We'll find her but we can't do that here."

Taz slumped between them and Tira helped Meryl hurry Reyan along the corridor. She had a feeling Cheryl wanted them out quickly before Belladonna decided to charge after them and destroy half of the human world in the process.

"You okay?" Meryl asked.

Tira nodded, her jaw tight. She wasn't, not in the slightest. Her stomach was churning and the flash of light that knocked everyone down had done a number on her headaches. She wanted to be sick, the queasiness making her dizzy, but she kept putting one foot after the other, pacing it out with the constant thought revolving that Taz and Reyan had it way worse than she did right now.

"Don't let them get away!" Belladonna screeched.

Tira flinched as Lorens appeared, racing toward them with a hand outstretched. A tight sensation wound around her like invisible ropes choking the air from her body. Meryl's hand tightened around her fingers and panic flared.

She fought to push her connection that little bit further, to throw some kind of shield between Lorens and Meryl, her vision blurring as she saw the backs of the others disappearing into the tunnel.

Beryl lifted one hand behind her and made a swiping motion, glancing over her shoulder and stumbling to a halt. Tira didn't hear what she shouted, the roaring in her ears overtaking everything else as dull pain radiated through her knees.

The world around them shuddered and she rasped out a soundless scream as Lorens froze in front of them. He tilted his chin back, his head tipping up. With a gasp, he heaved sideways but the chunk of rock tumbling from the ceiling caught his legs.

Tira choked in stale air as the attack faded, her throat burning and her chest not easing on the pressure. Meryl struggled closer, both of them checking each other with watery eyes and uncoordinated hands.

As Tira's vision cleared, the others returned. Cheryl helped her to her feet and Meryl managed to get up on her own, the three of them clustering together as Cheryl wove protection around them all.

"I call it in," Lorens panted.

Tira frowned but it was Odella from the Nether Court who stepped forward, her face hard like stone.

"You call in our debt for this?" she asked.

Lorens nodded, his eyes roving frantically over the chaos around them. Belladonna was still screaming demands and obscenities at Blossom and those still unfortunate enough to be both conscious and still nearby, but she would attack again.

"There will be no debt left between us," Odella

demanded. "You'll adhere to leaving the Nether Court, the town and our realm alone. You'll never return and you'll ensure your friends do the same."

Lorens grimaced but after a few moments, he nodded. "I accept."

Odella doubled over beside him, her hands reaching out for the rock. Tira stared in amazement as the rock began to mould to Odella's touch, the surface parting for her hands like water. She scraped and huffed, working fast, until Lorens could lift his legs. Even as she finished, Sannar had his arms around her, hauling her to her feet and pulling her back as the others set off for the exit.

"We're done," Odella spat. "But I'm not."

Tira stumbled past her and into the tunnel with Meryl's hand tight around hers and Cheryl's arm through hers, but she had enough support to glance back as Sannar's groan vibrated through the tunnel.

"Stop her!"

Belladonna's screech tore through Tira's fragile head as Odella fought to seal part of the wall around the tunnel over the doorway.

Leaving Odella to finish her handiwork, Tira stumbled and almost fell, but she forced herself to move faster and match Meryl's pace. Each step made her head spin but she kept going, trusting those around her to know the way.

"It won't hold them long, but it'll thin them down a bit," Odella panted behind them.

Tira focused on moving forward, trying to breathe against the urge to throw up. She almost cried in relief as they burst through to the front hall, the daylight spiking into her eyes. She winced and closed them momentarily, the dazzles turning to colours against a dancing world of reddish purple behind her eyelids.

"There, I've locked them in at least," Cheryl said.

A loud bang rattled the door from the other side and everyone exchanged panicked glances.

"Won't hold them for long by the sound of it," Beryl insisted. "She's still got people with gifts down there to blast them all out. Come on, once we're on that train thing they won't be able to chase us."

The daylight burned as they hurried outside and down the street. Tira kept her head down but she noticed the odd looks random humans were giving them. Perhaps it was odd for them to see a group of people in a hurry, or perhaps it was the sight of both Taz and Reyan almost catatonic and being hoisted along.

*It's only a short way home. Almost there. You can do a couple more hours. You can rest for days when you get home. Just don't faint. Don't pass out.*

She dug her nails into her palm, hoping the bite would keep her mind from dropping out completely. It happened so rarely now that she passed out from her headaches, but knowing her luck it would happen in the middle of the human world when she was supposed to be helping not making things worse.

"Here we are," Cheryl announced, sounding extremely relieved and out of breath. "Orbs alive, I almost forgot. Ace do you have those card things?"

Ace handed out cards to everyone and Tira clutched hers, letting the bite of the sharp corner dig into her thumb.

"Everyone through, quickly," he insisted.

Milo went through first and supervised the card usage. Even Beryl managed to get hers eaten by the machine without a fuss, and Tira stumbled through with her head pounding.

"Okay, everyone onto the platform, this way." Ace stood making wide arm movements. "Oh Faerie save us, hurry up!"

Tira didn't dare glance back to see what he was huffing about. Beryl and Cheryl had Reyan between them now so she didn't even have a duty to focus on. She blinked in pain as Meryl appeared beside her.

"You're hurting, aren't you?"

Tira grimaced. "I'm fine."

"Here, take this. Marlon gave me a bunch of them before we left."

Tira took the bottle of *Beast Lite* with so much gratitude. Mad thoughts of vowing to kiss her for it swilled in her beleaguered head, but she only popped off the cap and drained several mouthfuls.

"Thank you."

Meryl busied herself handing the rest of bottles out. The crowd noise on the train platform scratched against Tira's sensitive ears, but none of them could have avoided the familiar sound echoing after them, and probably travelling halfway through the human world too. Tira had no idea how big the human world actually was, but Belladonna's incensed screaming probably carried all the way to Faerie and the Prime Realm beyond, skip-way or no skip-way.

"Get away from me you filthy human! I don't care

about tickets! Don't you know who I am? Let go of me! Blossom! Blossom stop them! Summon Lorens! Anyone! *Blossom!*"

Tira lifted her head and blinked hard, forcing her blurry gaze to focus in time to see Belladonna being pinned to the floor by four humans in matching black and green outfits. With her gifts she would have been unstoppable, but even without them she was giving the quartet an almighty fight, struggling and hissing and biting.

"Oh, the police have her." Ace grimaced. "I don't know if that's bad for her or for them."

"At least she seems to have exhausted her gift, or she would have used it already," Milo added. "She should still have her ability to ward a protection, but maybe she's too arrogant to remember such a simple thing."

Tira shuddered. "She lost her gifts. Said something about Blossom transferring them to someone else."

Reyan's head lifted. Her cheeks were drenched with tears, but her eyes were focused and she was standing unaided as the train screeched up in front of them.

"Blossom accidentally transferred Belladonna's gifts into me somehow. Or one of them, I think. That's what caused the big bang. Or maybe it was the bang that made the skip-way."

The train doors opened and people streamed out.

"Oh. Well, that's something," Beryl said quietly. "Everybody in."

Meryl slid her arm under Tira's as she stepped up onto the train, wordlessly supporting her. Tira dropped into one of the seats nearest the window and pressed her hand over her eyes. The darkness helped a little although the pounding in her head wouldn't go away now without sleep, but at least she could settle. Tilting her head back against the seat, she flinched as the train started moving and a wave of nausea washed up her throat.

"Nope." She tilted forward, pressing her head against the seat in front instead.

A hand appeared as a gentle pressure between her shoulder blades steadily moving back and forth.

"Is that any better?" Meryl asked.

Tira nodded. "A bit, thanks. I'm just a bit flushed."

She didn't even twitch when Meryl reached around her and moved something weighted on her lap.

"Clever," she said.

Tira grimaced. "Hmm?"

"Marlon's given you an inventory on your bag. Here, put some of this on your neck, apparently it's cooling."

Tira sat obediently as Meryl grabbed her hand and slathered something that tingled and chilled over her fingers. Even when her hand was pressed to the opening of her shirt without any effort from her, she let Meryl take control.

She could hear the heartbreaking sounds of Taz sniffing and muttering under his breath and Milo's quiet attempts to reassure him, but she didn't dare lift her head to look.

"I've warded this carriage as best I can." Ace's voice filled the quiet air. "We have to keep going. Belladonna might be incapacitated a short while but the others are still out there with other minions. They won't take this as a failure now they know there's definitely somewhere to get into."

"We'll go back to our court and keep researching," Lolly offered.

"And us too," Sannar said. "It'll take us a while to get through our lot, but if there's anything else to be found, we'll find it."

Tira lifted her head groggily. "I'll do whatever I can. Just let me know what you need."

"I'll send you the official deed of your title as Lady of Words," Milo said as she dropped her head back down. "Everyone back to their courts for now and we'll keep in touch. Reyan, are you going to be able to cope?"

"Cope?"

Reyan sounded so frail. Tira wanted to reach across the train and hug her, to reassure her somehow, but with the train moving it was all she could do not to start being sick on people. She gulped a couple of times and pressed the *Beast Lite* bottle against her forehead to cool another part of her burning skin down.

"You're Lady of the Illusion Court," Milo insisted. "Both Kainen and Demi recognised it."

"It was a fake. The whole thing. He was meant to marry Blo- that- *her*. He got me to pretend to be his bride so he didn't have to. I mean, the court claimed me anyway, but he… I can't…"

Tira huffed quietly to keep the sickness at bay. Reyan didn't know Kainen had already confessed as much.

A loud bang punctured the quiet and even Tira forced herself upright in time to see Taz's fist bouncing back from the now cracked window.

"He's in love with you." Taz growled, his voice even more broken than Reyan's. "Even if that part wasn't real to you, it was to him, the whole time. You're Lady of the Illusion Court by his command and by the court's choice. Don't throw it away now."

Silence descended. Nobody, not even Reyan, dared say another word about it. Tira made a mental note to orb Reyan in a couple of days, to make sure the lines of communication were open if Reyan ever needed help or advice.

*Running a court on your own is scary but I've been trained to run mine. I know the folk and they like me well enough. She's going to find it so tough with hers.*

Sleep tugged at her but each lurch or stop of the train woke her again. By the time Meryl shook her shoulder gently, she was feeling half feverish with exhaustion.

"Come on, it's a short walk to the skip-way to Faerie," she said.

Tira stumbled off the train and let Meryl link arms with her. She wasn't making a great impression as a person, let alone as the lady of a Faerie court, but getting home was all she was capable of. Worrying would have to come later.

They walked the two roads from the station to the nondescript residential lane they needed in silence, but Meryl kept a firm, guiding pressure on her arm the whole way. When a soft brush of air finally stroked her face, she looked up to see the small cottage they'd realm-skipped into on the way there.

"I expect everyone to be working on finding her," Taz said, a subtle threat dwelling in his voice. "There is no other business until we get them back, got it?"

Ace and Milo exchanged a look behind his back but he vanished without waiting for anyone to agree or reassure him. Beryl sagged with a tumbling sigh.

"He's going to be insufferable, isn't he?" she muttered.

Milo frowned. "Wouldn't you be? I'll skip you and Cheryl home then come back for Ace and Meryl. Oh, no, Sannar, Odella, I'll take you back to the Nether Court first."

He grasped their wrists and they vanished before even having a chance to say goodbye. Tira made another note in her mind to reach out to them too. The courts would need to stand strong together now if they had any hope of holding back the Forgotten and those who supported the old ways.

"Tira, if you need any help, or if you want to discuss trade or anything, let us know," Lolly said.

She managed a weary smile before taking Tyren's hand and vanishing with him as Milo reappeared alone. He grabbed Beryl and Cheryl next, disappearing again and leaving Tira with Ace and Meryl.

"Are you okay realm-skipping back to your court?" Ace asked. "Can you?"

Tira nodded and winced as her head swam. "I know how to well enough. Not done it this sick before but it should be fine."

"If not, wait for Milo and he'll take you." He sighed. "Well, this is yet another monumental cock-up that we're going to have to solve. Go home, rest and see to your court. We'll be in touch."

It was a dismissal, even though Tira guessed he was probably further down the Faerie hierarchy than she was. Perhaps he wanted some time alone or had things he needed to discuss with Meryl.

"The Word Court will continue supporting the king consort until the queen returns," she insisted. "We're there any time you need us."

With a last look at Meryl, who seemed to be watching her just as furtively, Tira focused all her attention and intent on home. The nether wisped around her and she dropped to her knees as a familiar sight wavered into view.

"Lady!"

Marlon rushed forward, panic in his voice.

"I'm alright," she muttered. "Head's bad though."

She had no strength to protest as he leaned down and hauled her up, supporting her with an arm around her waist.

"There's a matter, lady," he muttered. "I tried to get rid of him, but he refused."

She froze, lifting her gaze until she found Lorens standing a few metres in front of them. He took a limping step toward her, and he'd not bothered to glamour away the scuffs and tears on his clothes from the fight. A bloody bandage poked out from beneath the tattered leg of his trousers and one entire hand, the one Meryl had maimed, was swathed in thick fabric. Even his normally cocky smile was pinched. To him she was a necessity he had to take care of, but she had no intention of giving in, sick or not.

"Don't leave me," she muttered to Marlon, before lifting her voice and forcing verbal steel into it. "You're not welcome in my court, Lorens."

She couldn't push her health aside but she had enough experience pretending it wasn't there. It would cost her more in terms of recovery but she was Lady of the Word Court now, and she would defend it from scum like him to her last breath if she had to.

He had no sign of contrition about him as his shoulders relaxed, hands in his pockets and the cocky smirk she recognised reappearing on his face.

"Perhaps I was a bit rash, Lady," he said. "I was to be a member of this court under your brother's leadership. Surely you wouldn't outcast a willing member of your court if they show penitence?"

Tira laughed. She'd learned young that courts tended to develop themselves, not sentient exactly but able to wind themselves around their mistresses and masters like parts of a soul. She took strength from her court now, allowing the quiet of it to fill her heart, the cold wind sharpening her tongue as she let her gaze fix on his.

"You're not penitent. You're not a member of *my* court either. You've not sworn to it or to me. My brother is a traitor to the queen and so are you. Especially after what just happened. You're banished from the Word Court, effective immediately. Leave now or I'll have you removed."

"Oh dear." He laughed, malice in every rolling note. "You'll regret that. I'll tear you and your puny court to rubble when I get my rightful due."

Fear stabbed her insides, tearing panic through every part of her. She warded herself and Marlon, pushing herself away from him to stand strong on her own. The wind whirled through an open window and rattled the banners above them.

"You can try." She shrugged. "Your rightful due is a one-way ticket to the Forever mountains and don't worry, we'll ensure you get that. Now get your orb-munching state of a self out of my court."

He winked at her and she held firm as the subtle prickle of his gift crept over her warding, testing the edges. She could feel Marlon adding his own strength to hers but he didn't move to support her any more physically than he already was, letting her hold her own with dignity.

Lorens vanished and Tira let her warding drop, tearing over her newfound bond with the court until she could be sure Lorens wasn't anywhere inside it still.

Marlon tutted loudly as her knees buckled, her gift sinking deep inside her and her head exploding with unforgiving pain.

She mumbled a timid apology as Marlon bent down swept her up into his arms like a child.

"Luckily it's late," he fussed. "We'll get you to bed, but Marinda is determined to have a word with you first. Nothing urgent, she assures me, but you know how she is."

"I heard that." Marinda appeared beside them, striding merrily along. "Is your room still a tip?"

Tira managed a weak smile. "Yes."

"Oh, not to the state rooms then?" Marlon asked, sounding dejected.

"I want my own bed right now. Consider it my first demand as a proper lady. I can move to the state rooms bit by bit over the next few days or so."

She closed her eyes and they said nothing until she was properly settled in bed, Marinda hovering with a tiny light so as not to aggravate Tira's head.

"I'm happy to inform you that the Word Court is at peace now that you're the lady of it," Marinda began. "Marlon is already interviewing court painters and the debates have been a success. Actually, when I say 'interviewing', he's convinced that three of them are faking their credentials and has asked all of them to do samples in different styles."

Tira groaned. Now that she was home, she could rebuild her strength. Adventures wouldn't come all the time and she could make running the court manageable. Demi had promised her support too. A swell of sadness rolled through her when she thought of Demi and Kainen, hopefully out there somewhere and still together rather than alone.

"I'm almost done with the ending to my book as well," Marinda added. "Not that anyone's bothered to ask. I swear, this place doesn't appreciate my star status, but I will stick around for a while to get a proper rest."

"You love it and hate it. That's why you move around so much."

"True. Oh, your orb is flashing."

Tira lifted her head and groaned to see the surface of her mother's travelling orb that she'd placed on the bedside table glowing sky-blue. She reached for it, peered at the surface, and almost dropped it when she recognised the face inside.

"Not seen you smile like that before." Marinda chortled. "I'll make myself scarce."

Tira wiped a hand over her hair as Marinda crossed the room, not to the door to leave but to sit on the chair in the corner, clearly intending to eavesdrop with absolutely no shame whatsoever.

With a deep breath and mad thoughts about not having checked her hair filling her mind, Tira forced a smile onto her face and answered the call.

# CHAPTER TWENTY
## MERYL

Meryl paced back and forth in front of the main desk of the Arcanium library. The towering wooden stacks were quiet, the lamps dimmed and the rest of the FDPs and staff probably all in bed.

"Will you sit down?" Beryl grumbled. "You're making me dizzy."

Meryl sighed. How to explain that she was restless and grouchy because the moment they'd returned to Arcanium with all the familiarity of home, it felt too small, too chaotic.

She'd had all of a couple of nights in solitude at the Word Court and now the thought of going back to sharing a room, to constantly fighting over space in the communal bathroom and wandering around as fifth wheel to her sisters and their boyfriends, it all made her frantic.

"I can't explain it. I love Arcanium but now it feels like it's closing in around me," she admitted.

She ignored the wary look Beryl and Cheryl gave each other.

"Probably need a bit of a break," Harvey suggested.

Hutch nodded. "Touch of fresh air maybe, do you good."

That was the problem, the one she didn't want to admit. The only fresh air she wanted was at the top of a mountain in a far-flung part of the Word Court's realm. Which was ridiculous because she barely knew Tira, *Lady* Tira now. She stopped pacing as Milo hurried up with Ace behind him.

"Sorry, it took us a while to find Taz something to do," Milo muttered.

Ace patted his arm and hoisted himself up to sit on the desk.

"We've got a bit of a task for all of you," he said. "But Milo can explain."

Milo threw him a weary look. "Right. In my official capacity as the queen's aide, and with the king consort currently sort of indisposed, I'm worried about the courts."

He stopped when Beryl held up a hand, a wry grimace flicking over her face.

"Sedated him?" she asked.

Ace nodded. "Yup. He's going to be insufferable when he wakes. Sorry, Milo, carry on."

Milo sniffed. "Thank you. I've considered bringing the Oak Queen into play-"

He broke off as a woman popped into existence beside him. Tall and slender with black hair and a deep purple dress of clinging velvet, Queenie looked supremely unconcerned about the current events. As Director of Arcanium, she commanded respect, but everyone knew it would be Milo managing things in Demi's absence. Even Queenie.

"No point going to my sister," she said. "She won't do much to help. Taz is my nephew so I'll manage his inevitable volatility, don't worry."

She sighed at the thought then gave Milo an expectant

look.

"The only option I have to cover the courts is to send FDPs in," Milo continued. "Above all, we need to ensure the lines of communication are kept open. I've asked someone from the quarantine floor to play go-between for the Fauna Court already, and Sannar and Odella have obviously pledged for the Nether Court."

Meryl sat up like a meerkat as Milo ticked courts off on his fingers.

"I've already agreed to go to the Illusion Court," Ace said. "I can support Reyan and I've been there enough before to know the layout."

"That'll leave us five to go to the Flora and Revel Courts then," Beryl insisted.

Milo nodded, but he caught Meryl's eye.

"Four of you, yes."

Beryl scowled. "What do you mean, four? There's five of us and we always go together."

"The Word Court is still without an FDP," Milo reminded her.

Beryl opened her mouth but Cheryl wisely clapped a hand over it. Meryl leaned forward, anticipation beginning to race mad jolts of adrenaline through her system.

"I'll go to the Word Court." She almost shouted it at him. "I could do with the peace."

Beryl's muffled indignation sounded weak at best, which meant she already knew and understood why. With any luck, Meryl would be able to avoid her sister harping on about it before she left.

Milo smiled. "I hoped you might. Everyone keep your

orbs handy and report in daily, or we'll be sending someone in after you. Any sign of mischief, report back to me. In the meantime, Arcanium will be working to retrieve our queen."

Before her sisters could pounce on her, Meryl hurried away. She dipped further into the depths of the library until she stood on one of the wide walkways that arced over the enormous pit that dropped through the central core of the entire library. With a sigh, she glanced up at the statue of the Oak Queen holding the Book of Faerie. Milo had a point about not bringing the Oak Queen in. While she was Taz's mother, she was also Blossom's and Belladonna's. She wasn't exactly known for impartiality either.

But none of that did anything about the mad flutters bursting like butterflies through Meryl's insides when she thought about what she was about to do. A few deep breaths later, she held her orb up in front of her face.

"Tira Sta- Lady Tira Starhollow."

She waited with anxiety jittering through her limbs, tapping her foot and shifting her weight.

Then Tira's face bloomed into pearlescent grey clarity in front of her and she couldn't stop the smile spreading over her face.

Tira looked tired and her hair was loosely dishevelled. No doubt she was still suffering from her headaches but Meryl would make it brief. The quicker they discussed it, the quicker she could pack and be back at the Word Court.

"Hi, Meryl," Tira said.

Meryl tried to push down the flare of excitement inside her chest as Tira smoothed a hand over her hair.

"Wow, you're all shadowy." Meryl laughed, the nerves swelling at how ridiculous she sounded. "Not that orb calls aren't always grey but you look particularly veiled. Are you okay to talk? I know it's barely been any time since you've been home and you need to rest, but it's… a bit time sensitive."

"I'm okay, what's going down?"

*What's going down, is she nervous too?*

Tira grimaced a second later and Meryl fought the urge to grin.

"Can you talk freely?" she asked.

"Yeah, I'm fine to talk."

Meryl nodded. "Okay, good. Milo's now insisting on each court having a queen's aide with them until the whole thing is sorted. It'll be an FDP in secret for the lord or lady's protection, but also to keep lines of communication clear. Ace is going to support Reyan, and there are people going to Nether, Revels, Flora and Fauna, but I wondered if you would consider letting me be the aide to the Word Court for a while?"

Tira didn't say a word for several moments. Meryl's insides gave an almighty lurch and she wasn't sure in that moment if she was going to swoon or be sick. Then Tira pressed a hand to her forehead.

"You want to come and stay here?" she clarified.

Not the reaction Meryl had been hoping for, so she went for the personal touch.

"Look, I love my sisters dearly but they're mad. We share a room here and it's absolute mayhem. Plus, they're going to various courts with their boyfriends anyway. I need to find some independence for myself and… well, I kind of hoped that maybe there was something between us that might have a spark for the future in it? Not that I'm assuming anything. You're a lady now and- well, anyway."

She hated sounding so hesitant, but then she heard the tell-tale hiss of people whispering somewhere just out of range of the orb, possibly Marlon or Marinda having opinions if she was going to use her instincts. And one thing she had learned from Petra was to use her instincts when all else failed, even if it involved excruciatingly babbling her feelings to someone way above her own social status.

The hushed whispering continued in the background, but nothing from Tira who looked completely stunned.

She grimaced. "Tira? Um, I mean, Lady?"

"Oh!" Tira nodded vigorously with one hand clamped to her head. "Yes, absolutely. The Word Court has plenty of space and quiet, but we have fun stuff too, and I've already said I'll help the queen however I can, so absolutely, yes, absolutely."

*Definitely nervous, that's probably a good sign.*

Meryl cleared her throat. "Great, I'll let you rest tonight and arrive in the morning. Try to get some sleep though, okay?"

Tira smiled, the ghostly grey projection of her lighting up.

"Yep, see you tomorrow. Bye."

Her face disappeared.

"I knew it would all turn out right in the end," Beryl

said, appearing with half a pastry hanging from her mouth. "A good story never leaves the readers wanting."

Cheryl joined her with a frown. "Things aren't settled. The queen is missing, taken into another realm, one we can't get to easily. Oh, and Kainen I guess. There's the enemy still out there too. The Forgotten will want revenge on all of us after what happened."

Beryl's expression soured. "So the story isn't done yet but it will be one day, one way or the other. Your girlfriend was right though, got to take the good in case the bad gets you."

"She's not my girlfriend!"

"Oh please." Even Cheryl chuckled at that. "The two of you making gooey eyes at each other was almost enough to make Marinda Silverfern's pen itchy. Don't think I didn't notice her eying you two talking together and muttering things. You'll be the stars of the next *Carrie's Castle* book."

Meryl looked for something to throw at her sister, but apart from the Book of Faerie, the throwing of which would earn worse than a death sentence from Milo, she had nothing. Almost nothing.

Beryl shrieked in outrage as the remaining half a pastry was snatched from her mouth and lobbed after their sister.

Instead of attacking the thrower, Beryl hurried after the pastry and Cheryl. Meryl didn't follow.

She would have to get used to not relying on their company now, and she'd have time to say goodbyes tomorrow morning. For now, she had some space to think.

The situation out in Faerie would be on them sooner

rather than later, and she felt awful for Demi and Kainen out there somewhere, and for Reyan and Taz panicking about them.

*But there's nothing I can do until they need our help. I need to put my efforts into my FDP duties and supporting Tira.*

She tried to focus on what they might need to do in the coming days, but her mind kept wandering back to thoughts of the Word Court.

*Not that we'll be making gooey eyes at each other or anything, whatever Cheryl thinks.*

With that thought filling her mind full of less gloomy things than of late, Meryl took out the small orb-print she kept in her pocket. Petra's disapproving face stared back at her and she smiled sadly.

"We didn't have enough time," she murmured. "But I'm happy that we had a little bit all the same. You'd be shouting at me for wasting life grieving. I'll miss you always."

She put the photo back into her pocket, but perhaps it was finally time to leave the past in her memory box and walk forward instead of holding back.

# CHAPTER TWENTY ONE
## REYAN

Reyan stood in the middle of Kainen's court with her insides roiling. She'd arrived back to whispers, which likely meant there were still Forgotten friends or sympathisers among the courtiers.

But whatever the situation, she was alone and Kainen had named her lady of the court in his stead. She wouldn't let him down, but she wished her entire body would stop trembling at the mere idea of it.

"Attention!" She shouted it, expecting it to get lost in the hubbub of the crowd.

Her voice blasted through the air, the court responding to her intention as the command cut conversations short and stilled tongues between lips.

Several scandalised faces focused on her again. This time, the silence was deafening.

"Our lord is going to be away from court for a while," she announced. "He's left me in charge."

Several strident voices protested at that, although she couldn't work out who they were. Shame threatened to force her into fleeing but she took strength from the court and pressed her hand to the cool stone banister.

She made them wait, ascending each step with slow purpose.

*Breathe. Just keep breathing. Address them, dismiss them and go to your room. Worst case they all leave and you won't have to worry about them anyway.*

She reached the top of the stairs and glowered out over the main hall, as much a safety measure as to stand above them.

"Lord Kainen has named me lady of the court in his stead," she announced. "The queen has agreed it and the queen's court has made it official."

When more mutterings surfaced, she forced herself to stand strong. She should have had time to prepare for this, to work out how best to attack the situation and get them all onside.

"What happens now?" Someone shouted. "Isn't Diana Hemlock next in line?"

"She's an FDP. We don't want queen's court people ruling us!" someone else complained.

Frantic, Reyan eyed the baying crowd.

"I will be leading the court while he's away," she repeated. "He will be returning, but until then he and the queen's court has named me its lady. Until he returns, you answer to me."

Furious buzzing grew louder, drowning out the end of her sentence. The Fae of the Illusion Court were there because they didn't want the restrictions of the queen's court, or the specific one-track-mindedness of the other courts. They were the dark corners, the more debauched revels and the Fae that liked to trick rather than trade.

*Kainen never ruled them as himself. He had his court lord mask to convince them he wasn't to be messed with, so I need to create the same.*

She drew the shadows around her but flinched as Betty

slithered over the stairs toward her. She almost exclaimed out loud, but apparently it was a day for surprises that she couldn't voice out loud.

Betty's shadow form had morphed into a fully solid body of shining black scales, the one she thought she might have imagined in the chaos of the fight earlier. Not only had Betty taken on a flesh and bone form, but she'd chosen a size for herself, and that size was massive. Her tail curled around Reyan's body and the width of her head was the same size as an overly stuffed armchair.

The crowd noise swelled but with Betty beside her, Reyan could be brave. To keep Kainen's court running for him until she found a way to claw him back, she could be the lady he needed her to be.

"SILENCE."

She let her voice blast over the chaos, no doubt or hesitation.

The entire hall fell silent, their desire for drama overtaking their innate need to be a part of it.

"Kainen and I will still be married," she said, sending that out into the nether in the hope it would ring true enough to bring him back for it. "Any sleight against me is an insult to him, and he will not take it lightly."

The mutterings started again but she let Betty coil around her legs, a warning hiss slithering from the wide-open jaws.

She forced a wicked smile. "But don't let me mislead you into thinking I'll be standing behind his reputation while he's not here. I won't tolerate any insult or attack against us either and I'm not as forgiving as he is. Go play, and remember I warned you what will happen if you cross me."

She turned and slid into the adjoining hall that led to his bedroom as the court exploded in a cacophony of noise. As Betty dissipated into a smaller puff of shadow and wound her way up Reyan's body, Reyan slumped against the wall, quietly panicking.

"Well done." Meri strode up toward her. "That took serious guts. He's not *gone* gone, is he?"

Reyan shook her head. "No. At least, I hope not. It's a long story and one I will trust you with, but not here. Not now. I can't…"

Meri raised her hand to interrupt. "I understand. We'll keep the court running until he returns. For what it's worth, you have my loyalty and my full support. As I swore loyalty and service to this court under his rule, I'll swear to it under yours also."

Touched, Reyan nodded and managed a weak smile.

"Also, there's someone here to see you," Meri added.

She nodded to the other end of the hall and Reyan's hope leapt. Even as Ace walked toward them, he shook his head with a grave frown.

"Nothing yet." He folded her into a tight hug. "But Milo's insisted on each court having an emotional support FDP, and I'm yours."

Reyan blinked in surprise. "You're staying here?"

"Yep. All yours until this is over, or until Milo changes his mind and demands me back. Dunno how he'll cope without me but-"

"Excuse me, Lady." Meri glanced over her shoulder to

the noisy main hall. "Might I recommend you continue this in your rooms? Privacy and all that. I'll bring you some drinks and some snacks."

Reyan nodded. "Good thinking, thanks."

She led Ace into Kainen's room and stood staring at his bed. The covers were rucked and she wondered if they still smelled of him.

"You can take my room," she decided. "It'll be safer and I can reach you easily that way. It'll also likely be more private."

"You're staying in here?" Ace asked.

"I think so, yes. I spent so long being unsure of how he felt, of what was real. Now I know exactly what's real and he's not here to do anything about it."

She huffed over a laugh even as the tears sprang to her eyes. She pressed her fingers to them to soak up any tears and sat down in her armchair. The balcony overlooked the main hall but she had no desire to see or hear what might be going on in there. She'd seen Ciel lurking in the crowd while she addressed them, not someone she wanted to have around but she knew Kainen had kept him there for a reason, so she would do the same.

*Last thing I need is him trying to get his claws in again now Kainen's not here.*

She might not be able to do much about the courtiers and their distaste for her, but she was lady of the court now and could wield the fabric of it to her will. Flicking out a hand and wishing for silence, the sound from outside the room vanished.

"How are you holding up?" Ace asked.

She shrugged. "I've hardly had time to process. I don't even know where to start. How do we go about searching for them? Do we try to get through that way again, or do we look for another route in? Is there a super summoning gift that could bring them back, or should I be trying to wake the void to get more information from the visions it gave me last time? Taz must be going mad."

Ace nodded and with the silence around them, now that she'd started she found she couldn't stop.

"Most of the courtiers hate me for being low-born, and I have no idea how to run a court. I don't know if I need to reinforce old debts or issues because it was Kainen who had sway over them or if they still reside with the court while he's not here. I have no idea where he is or how easily we'll get them back. He was shot in the shoulder by that horrid bitch. If I ever see her again, I'll end her, I swear. If anything happens to him…"

She exploded off the chair and stalked across the room, pacing with vengeful fury.

"And this gift! Whatever moved from Belladonna into me is constant, it's like a permanent needle all over my skin and right through the muscles. It feels like a raw and dark power to be holding, volatile, like a single tap or temper will make something explode. I haven't made anything happen with it yet, but what if I do? I mean, I think Tira said Belladonna mentioned gifts, plural. Does that mean there are others inside me dormant, or have other people accidentally caught some of them? And the one person I probably could ask for advice is wherever Kainen is. I've been frantically trying to send mind-speak to him but I'm getting nothing back."

She didn't pause her pacing as Meri materialised in the room with a large tray. It was overflowing with a plate of her favourite pastries, a decanter of court wine and a wobbling pile of *Beast* bottles.

"I would have gone for the *Lite* but I reckon you could do with sleeping a while," Meri said. "Nobody will disturb you, I'll make sure of it."

Reyan huffed. "You have full permission to banish them on my behalf if they do. Unless it's someone from the queen's court, or one of the other courts. Or about him."

Meri nodded and vanished. Reyan grabbed a pastry and set off back and forth across the room again.

"You must keep your true social circle small," Ace said eventually. "Trusted confidences only. We're not sure how much sense we'll get out of Taz, but he's tried mind-speaking to her too and getting nothing. We've got the whole of Arcanium working on opening contact with the Prime Realm and sourcing any information we can about how to get in there."

Reyan nodded. "If there's anything we can do, we'll do it. Anything. I've sent word to his court realm-skipper already to try and see if she can get to him, I've tried orbing." She pointed to the bathroom door. "I've even tried asking the multiway door to take me to him, but nothing."

Ace poured himself a cup of wine and indicated to the tray. She shook her head and grabbed a bottle of *Beast*. Meri was right; she would have to sleep and attack the situation with a fresh mind. If Kainen could get himself stuck in the Prime Realm or wherever he was, then someone else could manage it too, or better yet somehow manage it in reverse. She also had to explore Belladonna's assumption that she could get through via the shadows. If there was anything in that, she had to consider it.

"All the courts are combing their libraries and archives now," Ace added. "Whatever there is out there, we'll find it."

Reyan sipped her drink before collapsing back onto her armchair.

"Well, we have free reign of our library here of course." She sighed. "The only thing I've got left other than that is my last resort."

"What's that?"

Reyan sent her mind through the shadows and sank back against the armchair. She noted the uneasiness in Ace's eyes as he looked past her toward the door. She could sense the shadows spilling underneath, roiling into shape as Betty took her solid form and slid her thick body toward them.

*Go into the shadows, into the nether and the void beyond if you can,* Reyan told her. *Don't do anything to endanger yourself, but if you can find the enemy, please let me know if they know anything that might help us find him. Or if there's a way in somehow, or a way out for him.*

She watched as Betty faded into shadow and fractured, dissipating out of sight. Leaving the court wasn't an option for her, not now she had to hold it strong and face the adversaries inside its walls. Kainen needed a court to come back to, because he was coming back. He had to.

She graciously ignored Ace's subtle shudder, guessing he wasn't a fan of snakes, but she accepted the strong hug he got up to give her.

"Wherever he is, he'll be fighting with everything he has to get back to you," he promised.

She frowned. "What makes you so sure?"

"I've known Kainen a long while now." He chuckled. "Seen him at his worst for most of it. But he never looked at anyone else the way he looks at you. Not even Demi. It's like you made the world new for him and something in him switches off when you're not in it."

Reyan let that thought soothe her. She was tired and heartsick. She was frightened. She had no idea how to run a court, and she knew that most of the courtiers and nobles were already against her, only civil because she was Kainen's chosen favourite. She would need to send an orb message to Tira and ask for some advice, or Lolly even. Both had been trained for leadership where she hadn't. She wasn't trained or raised to run a court, but she would learn.

Even though she knew it was pointless, she sent the mind-speak out anyway.

*Wherever you are, come back to me. The court needs you. I need you. Please.*

Then, because Fae couldn't lie, she added a final concession.

*You win. I'm yours. Just come home.*

# ACKNOWLEDGEMENTS

Huge thank you to every reader who has joined Demi and Taz and friends on their journey! To those who've shared on social media, done ARC reads or just given me compliments about the book to keep me going.

To my family and also my writing family as always, your support means everything to me – Anna Britton, Debbie Roxburgh, Sally Doherty, Marisa Noelle, Emma Finlayson-Palmer, Katina Wright, Aerin Apeltun, Estelle Tudor, Maria Palmer, the amazing ARC readers (who have caught so many printing blips it's not even funny…) writing Twitter, everyone who joins #ukteenchat, the WriteMentor crew, libraries and schools who took a chance on this series, shops that are still stocking these books and giving this indie author a chance to reach more readers, and to the readers who will find these books in the future:

THANK YOU!

# ABOUT THE AUTHOR

While always convinced that there has to be something out there beyond the everyday, Emma focuses on weaving magic realms with words (the real world can wait a while). The idea of other worlds fascinates her and she's determined to find her own entrance to an alternate realm one day.

Raised in London, she now lives on the UK south coast with her husband and a very lazy black Labrador who occasionally condescends to take her out for a walk.

Aside from creative writing studies, an addiction to cake and spending far too much time procrastinating on social media, Emma is still waiting for the arrival of her unicorn. Or a tank, she's not fussy.

For the latest news and updates, check the website or come say hi on social media:

www.emmaebradley.com
@EmmaEBradley

www.ingramcontent.com/pod-product-compliance
Lightning Source LLC
Chambersburg PA
CBHW061525210726
48287CB00006B/1828